10/20

F Johnson
Johnson, W. Bolingbroke.
The widening stain

OTTO PENZLER PRESENTS
AMERICAN MYSTERY CLASSICS

THE WIDENING STAIN

W. BOLINGBROKE JOHNSON was the pseudonym of Morris Bishop (1893-1973), an American scholar, historian, essayist, translator, and versifier. While best known for his writings on the Middle Ages and his work with light verse, he was an authority on many subjects, including the history of Cornell University, where he taught and served as the university historian. *The Widening Stain* is his only work of fiction.

NICHOLAS A. BASBANES is the author of nine works of cultural history, with a particular emphasis on various aspects of books, book history, and book culture. In addition to his books, Basbanes has written for numerous newspapers, magazines, and journals, including the *New York Times*, *Los Angeles Times*, and *Washington Post*, and lectures widely on a variety of cultural subjects. Among his most well-known titles are *A Gentle Madness: Bibliophiles, Bibliomanes, and the Eternal Passion for Books* and *On Paper: The Everything of Its Two Thousand Year History*.

THE WIDENING STAIN

W. BOLINGBROKE JOHNSON

Introduction by
NICHOLAS A. BASBANES

AMERICAN MYSTERY CLASSICS

Penzler Publishers
New York

Published in 2020 by Penzler Publishers
58 Warren Street, New York, NY 10007
penzlerpublishers.com

Distributed by W. W. Norton

Cover image: Andy Ross
Cover design: Mauricio Diaz

Paperback ISBN 978-1-61316-171-5
Hardcover ISBN 978-1-61316-169-2
eBook ISBN 978-1-61316-170-8

Library of Congress Control Number: 2020907573

Printed in the United States of America

9 8 7 6 5 4 3 2 1

THE WIDENING
STAIN

INTRODUCTION

ACADEMICS AT venerable institutions of higher learning throughout the United States must have had great fun back in the 1940s wondering who, exactly, among their lofty ranks had taken pen to paper and written a delightfully irreverent biblio-mystery that took gentle aim at the foibles and passions of their profession, while ostensibly considering the untimely deaths of two scholars who had been working with rare books and manuscripts in the University Library.

As a work of fiction, *The Widening Stain* was a one-off performance for the mysterious author drolly identified on the original dustjacket by the publisher Alfred A. Knopf as being one W. Bolingbroke Johnson, "a native of Rabbit Hash, Kentucky" and former librarian for the American Dairy Goat Association and Okmulgee Agricultural and Mechanical Institute—an unsophisticated rube from the hinterlands, in other words, whose previously published works (or "so he says") included modest contributions to the *Boot and Shoe Recorder* and the *American Musselman*—none of which, of course, could have been further from the truth.

In reality, W. Bolingbroke Johnson was the nom de plume of Morris Gilbert Bishop (1893-1973), a greatly admired educator and scholar whose reputation as a widely published biographer, historian, and authority on Romance Languages would be responsible for wooing Vladimir Nabokov to join the Cornell University faculty as a professor and lecturer of Russian Literature in 1948, and become his closest friend during his eleven years on the Ithaca, New York, campus.

Bishop's body of professional work was formidable—a "polymath in his field," according to Alden Whitman's three-column obituary in *The New York Times*—with fluency in German, French, Spanish, and Swedish among the feathers in his linguistic cap, along with an ability to "sight-read" Latin. His corpus embraced a broad spectrum, some four hundred published works over half-a-century, four dozen of them books he either wrote or edited, including respected biographies of Petrarch, Pascal, La Rouchefoucauld, Ronsard, Samuel de Champlain, Saint Francis of Assisi, and the Spanish explorer Álvar Núñez Cabeza de Vaca. To that was a two-volume *Survey of French Literature* that went through multiple printings, a critically-acclaimed history of the Middle Ages, translations into English of Molière's dramatic works, and an institutional history of Cornell, where he spent sixty productive years as student, instructor, professor, official historian, and provost of the university, his time there interrupted only by a brief stint in advertising and military service in Europe during World War II.

Quite apart from Bishop's scholarship—which was unfailingly praised for its accessibility and clarity of expression—was a more whimsical side that found rich expression in light verse and casual prose, and a genius for composing limericks—the latter a skill that is brought to bear in *The Widening Stain* by one of the faculty members at the heart of the murder mystery. From 1927—a year after receiving his Ph.D. from Cornell—to 1960, a span of thirty-three years, Bishop wrote, on average, fifteen poems and prose pieces a year for *The New Yorker*. Of his 1929 collection of verse, *Paramount Poems*, William J. Strunk Jr., author of the legendary *Elements of Style*, wondered if William Wordsworth was "ever more simple and direct than Bishop when he begins a lyrical ballad with the words, 'The modern boys were bold and bad, / The modern girls were worse?'"

Bishop's attitude on the role poetry had to play in contemporary society is relevant to the laid-back tone and self-effacing approach he had employed in his mystery novel. "Our serious poets, writing deliberately for an elite and despising the average reader, have ruined poetry in the mind of the general intelligent public," he wrote in the introduction to his 1954 collection, *A Bowl of Bishop*. It was the light versifiers, Bishop maintained, who were "helping to keep alive in the general mind a consciousness of poetic form and thought. They are holding poetry's little forts amid the desert sands of the commonplace, awaiting the relief that shall come when the Poet arises, to fill our world with his overwhelming music."

What prompted Bishop, in his mid-forties, to set a tongue-in-cheek murder mystery on a college campus much like his own—the fictional library he describes with painstaking detail is a dead-ringer for Uris Library at Cornell—he never said publicly. With the exception of a few confidantes, he pretty much kept the work-in-progress to himself during the ominous days of 1941, with world conflict looming on the horizon. "I am writing a mystery story," he informed one friend that June, six months before the Japanese attack on Pearl Harbor. "The mystery itself would not deceive an intelligent chimpanzee, but I think I can make it more obscure on second writing. The background may carry it. Most of it is laid in our University Library, a kind of Notre-Dame de Paris. I have written half the book in three weeks, so there will be no great loss if no one wants to publish it and, in the meantime, it serves as a most admirable retreat. Come to think of it, 'The Corpse in the Ivory Tower' wouldn't be a bad title."

As things turned out, there was not one corpse lying amid a "widening stain" of blood in the Ivory Tower, but two, the first victim an instructor in the Romance Languages Department named Lucie Coindreau, a "black-eyed, black-haired French-woman in her early thirties," good-looking "in the smoldering southern incipient-hairy way," with an accent, according to some of her countrymen, that "took on a flavor of garlic" when she got excited. Lucie's death one night after a cocktail reception in the home of the university president is thought at first to have been nothing more than a horrible accident during an after-hours vis-it to the rare books wing of the library, a head-first fall from an upper gallery where the young scholar was believed to have been retrieving a difficult-to-reach volume—a high-heel, possi-bly, getting stuck in her long evening gown triggering the fatal plunge.

Not everyone is convinced, however, least of all Gilda Gor-ham, a summa cum laude graduate of the university whose day job is Chief Cataloguer of the library—"the brain of the Li-brary's sluggish body"—unmarried, also in her thirties, with an alert and inquisitive mind.* "She was bright and pleasant," every-

---

* Editor's Note: According to Bishop's granddaughter, Margaretta Jolly, the Gor-ham character seems to be modelled on his wife, the artist Alison Mason Kingsbury, whom he met while she was painting the mural in Cornell's Willard Straight Hall.

one agreed, "and knew what people were talking about," qualities that earned her invitations to all the faculty parties.

The obvious suspect, in Gilda's view, is Angelo Casti, a tenure-tracked assistant professor like Lucie vying for promotion to associate professor, with whom she had at one time been romantically involved. The previous spring, Gilda is told, the two had "spent a lot of time in the Phonetics Laboratory, prolonging their research late into the night, and it is suspected that the time was not devoted exclusively to recording each other's vowels and consonants."

Casti's "pseudo science" scholarship, as some call it, involves studying the pronunciation of the vowel sounds in the combinations of "uff" and "ugg," according to the medievalist Professor Hyett. "He has determined, I believe, that the average subject pronounces the 'uh' of 'uff' in 169 thousandths of a second, while they take 176 thousandths of a second to pronounce the 'uh' of 'ugg,'" raising an eminently logical question: "But what good does that do?" Professor Hyett explains: "We seek pure learning, knowledge for its own sake. That knowledge may well be of some practical use to someone some time, but we don't care whether it is or not. We just seek the fact. It's the essential difference between pure and applied science. Wouldn't you rather be pure than applied?"

That the first death was most assuredly not an accident becomes evident with the discovery, in an inner sanctum known as the "locked press" where the rarest books and manuscripts are stored, of Professor Hyett, strangled where he sat before a reading desk, and a twelfth-century manuscript of rhymed verse in Latin gone missing. How does it all fit? Who among Gilda's list of suspects could be responsible? It gives nothing away to say that the epiphany for her comes during a concert she attends with Francis Parry, composer of the clever limericks that enliven the pages of this smart and witty book. At novel's end, there is the hint of romance in Gilda's future, which leaves the reader to wonder if there may have been some thought to her becoming a continuing character—a female amateur detective, perhaps a research librarian who solves crimes in her spare time.

Appearing in print during the early days of World War II, *The Widening Stain* proved to be something of a distraction for an anxious nation, going back to press several more times, appearing in English and French editions, generating a degree of curiosity as to the actual identity of the author, which Bishop never confirmed publicly. "We do not know who W. Bolingbroke Johnson is," a reviewer for *The New York Times* wrote, "but he writes a good story with an academic atmosphere that is not so rarefied as we have been led to believe it should be in university circles." The closest Bishop came to outright acknowledgement is to be found in a limerick he composed and inserted in a volume of the novel, now housed in the Cornell University Library:

> *A cabin in northern Wisconsin*
> *Is what I would be for the nonce in,*
> *To be rid of the pain*
> *of* The Widening Stain
> *and W. Bolingbroke Johnson.*

—NICHOLAS A. BASBANES

THE WIDENING
STAIN

Chapter I

IN THE women's rest room of the University Library, Miss Gilda Gorham, Chief Cataloguer, looked at her face. It would do, she thought. Not the sort of face to launch a thousand ships, unless you wanted to bounce it off the bow like a champagne bottle. But not exactly revolting, either. Showing a certain wear and tear to the acute observer, she decided; not so juicy as it was once. The lips pursed too tightly, in the habit of disapproval. She wiggled her lips briskly. Pity she had to do so much disapproving, in the way of business. Well, everyone couldn't be beautiful, and probably a good thing. What was that pretty bit from the *Bab Ballads*:

> *Skin-deep, and valued at a pin,*
> *Is beauty such as Venus owns—*
> *Her beauty is beneath her skin,*
> *And lies in layers on her bones.*

That wasn't her trouble, anyway. She was rather on the thin-spinsterish side. That is, if she was actually a spinster. When does one become a spinster, exactly? Thirty-two? Thirty-three? Alarming thought!

Miss Gorham walked into the catalogue room, and took her seat at the high desk as the Library clock boomed nine unhappy strokes. Only three of the girls were present at the great circular desk with the reference works on an enormous revolving wheel in the center. The Library admitted nothing low like a time-clock, and trusted to the staff's sense of duty, with the result that the staff was likely to arrive from five to fifteen minutes late. When Miss Gorham had pointed out this fact to Dr. Sandys, the new Librarian, Dr. Sandys had replied that the moral sense of the staff was the best time-clock; it would keep them at work after five o'clock, until their duties should be done. But in fact most of the staff left ten minutes early, and took an hour and a half off for lunch.

As the girls entered, Miss Gorham greeted them, combining a smile, a frown, and a glance at the clock. You couldn't really blame them for sneaking a few minutes. They were nice girls, and fearfully underpaid. The Library paid its minor employees on about the same scale as the five-and-ten, and got away with it because it is so respectable and elevating to work among great books. Miss Gorham cast an eye at the shelf on which the books paused on their way from Accessions to Classification. *Eyak Indians of the Copper River Delta; Variations and Diseases of the Teeth of Animals; Colloquial Japanese; Anglican Humanitarianism in Colonial New York; Rural Waste Disposal.* So inspiring to work with the great productions of scholarship. Yeah.

"Oh, Miss Gorham, just a moment, please. . . ."

It was Dr. William Sandys, the Librarian, large and imposing, with an educator's goatee and a somewhat conscious air of executive decision.

"Miss Gorham, there is just a little question of routine procedure. About that Latin miracle-play manuscript in the safe, you know—"

"Manuscript B 58."

"Yes. Well, Mr. Casti of the Romance Language Department wants to take it out in order to make some investigations with it in his Phonetics Laboratory. Now, is that in accord with your custom?"

"Absolutely not. No manuscript may leave the Library building. And anyway B 58 is one of our most precious possessions. It is unique and unpublished, and some of the illuminations are very remarkable, the ones showing the staging of thirteenth-century plays. Mr. Wilmerding paid twelve thousand dollars for it in 1885, and probably it would bring ten times that today."

"Ah, just as I thought. But Mr. Casti seemed to think—"

"He has a microfilm of it. What more does he want?"

"I see. Quite so. I simply wanted to make sure about your procedure. I don't want to make any egregious errors at the start. I want to know the ropes, as the boys say. You see?"

"Oh yes, of course, Dr. Sandys."

"Well—huh—I guess that's all, Miss Gorham."

Miss Gorham, watching him go, commented inwardly that the Librarian had made himself an imposing façade, but from the rear he was less convincing.

She glowered at one of the girls who was snickering into the telephone. Obviously a personal call, and obviously too long a one. She made a note to speak to Miss Loring. Badinage was all very well, but not on University time.

Professor Belknap of History, tall, dour, and sour, was making his way toward her desk. He was carrying an old discolored vellum-bound volume under his arm. All the girls looked at Professor Belknap; two put their heads together and made what were apparently cute remarks. Professor Belknap looked at none of them; he walked in an oblivious cloud of scholarship. He wore his invariable suit of steel gray; a great golden Phi Beta Kappa key hung on his stomach from a gold watch-chain. "The scholar's crucifix!" murmured Miss Gorham, rather pleased with the conceit.

"Good morning, Miss Gorham." Professor Belknap was not one to waste time in frivolities. "Miss Gorham, you know that manuscript, the *Filius Getronis* of Hilarius?"

"B 58."

"Yes. You know that I am planning to publish it, with the co-operation of Mr. Hyett of the Classics Department and Mr. Parry of Dramatics? Well, I am not sure if you have heard that Mr. Casti of Romance Languages is interested in it from a linguistic point of view. He thinks that he may find in it influences of the presumably Angevin dialect of the author. Some of those involuntary influences, you know, of the linguistic habit of the vernacular on the written Latin. Mr. Casti has asked to examine the manuscript in his laboratory. He thought that I might persuade you to persuade Dr. Sandys to let him take it out. I consented to convey his request to you."

"I'm afraid not, Mr. Belknap. You know as well as I do that in principle no manuscripts may leave the Library building. Of course, if you are all agreed that a laboratory examination is necessary, it might be arranged."

"I should hardly go so far. I myself thought the request a strange one, and curiously devious. But Mr. Casti asked me to speak to you. He seemed to think that I might exert an influence which he lacks." He smiled. One could almost see his will hauling at rusty muscles, lifting the mouth's corners.

He laid the vellum-bound volume on Miss Gorham's desk.

"And by the way," he said, "here is something for the Library."

"Why!" gasped Miss Gorham. "It's the *Hammer of Witches*! The *Malleus Maleficarum*! And the edition of 1489! That must be the first edition, isn't it?"

Professor Belknap's smile was warmed with real delight. "Yes. It is a shameful thing that the Library has no copy of this epoch-making book. When I saw this offered in Thorp's catalogue, I tried to get the Library Council to buy it. The Council refused, with characteristic stupidity. But I felt that we had to have it. The great classic on the detection of witches and the methods of torture to extort confessions!"

"This is wonderful of you, Mr. Belknap! Dr. Sandys will write you a letter of thanks."

"No, no, no! None of that nonsense. It's just a book that the Library needed. Well—"

He glanced about, evidently looking for an excuse for escaping from gratitude. Conveniently, he perceived Professor Parry of the Department of Dramatics heading toward Miss Gorham's desk.

"Good morning, Parry. I yield my place to you."

He bowed formally to Miss Gorham. The smile dimmed on his face. He turned, clasped his hands behind his back, and stalked away, his eyes fastened on the ground. One of the girls at the catalogue desk said something that made two others snort and strangle with laughter. Miss Gorham rapped on her desk with a pencil. Those girls, acting as if they were working in a model bakery on visitors' day!

Professor Parry, tall, blond, handsome, and forty, whose greatest grief was his thinning hair, watched the Professor of Medieval History out of the room. He turned to Miss Gorham with the irresistible boyish smile which had captured the audiences of innumerable college plays and of Faculty Dramatic Club performances.

"Good old Belknap!" he said. "Buried up to the neck in scholarship!"

"And why not, indeed? Scholarship is his business."

"No reason why not. It just amused me to watch him. All the girls were staring at him, and he was staring at the floor. Pretended he didn't know they were looking, but he knew, he knew. He makes me think of one of the saints I ran across in this medieval work we're doing. Saint Ambrose of Milan I think it was. He never raised his eyes from the ground for fear he would be polluted by seeing a woman. The result was he was run over by a chariot or something. And when he came to he was in bed in the hospital of a nunnery. A frightful shock."

"If Mr. Belknap gets run over, my fellow nuns and I will be glad to take care of him."

"I'll be run over first. Will you bring me my breakfast in bed?"

"Mr. Parry!"

"Just an idea that came to me."

"Mr. Belknap is after all a very eminent scholar. And I rather admire his devotion to learning. So wholehearted. Look what he's just given us—a first edition of the *Malleus Maleficarum*!"

"What's that?"

"The *Hammer of Witches*. He paid somewhere around three hundred dollars for it. I remember the item in the Thorp catalogue."

"*Hammer of Witches*! Not a bad job for Belknap! I'll bet you that a lot of those old inquisitors were taking it out on the witches just because they were shy and awkward themselves."

"Kind of tough on the witches. I must say most of my sympathy goes to them. Maybe they were shy too. Probably most of them were just middle-aged spinsters going a little sour. Mr. Parry!"

"Yes?"

"What is a spinster?"

"Haven't you got a dictionary in this Library?"

"I mean, when does one become a spinster?"

"Well, offhand I should say when you get your first set of false teeth. Why?"

"I was just wondering."

"Wondering about when you are going to become a spinster? Oh, my dear Miss Gorham! Never!"

"Well, after all, time is passing."

A slow smile spread over Professor Parry's face. "Did you ever hear the one about the morbid young miss of Westminster?"

"No, and I don't want to—"

> "A morbid young miss of Westminster
> Was in terror of being a spinster;
>   But they say that you can't
>   Make a spinster enceinte,
> And that is what really convinced her."

"Mr. Parry!"

"How lovely you are when you turn that sort of tearose color! You aren't the spinster type!"

"You know, I could listen to you all day, Mr. Parry, but the Librarian has a theory that I work here, and I suppose I ought to humor him."

"No doubt. In fact, here he comes now. Probably trying to find out what has happened to his theory."

Dr. Sandys approached, carrying in his left hand, according to his custom, a sheaf of letters and documents, ready for instant reference. He seldom had any occasion to reveal what these apparently urgent papers were; it was the opinion of the catalogue room that he carried them only as a symbol of the busy man, and as a hint to all others to be busy too.

"Hello, Sandys!" called Professor Parry genially. "Come over here and sit down! We were just telling each other some snappy limericks!"

"Hello, Parry. I'm afraid I'm pretty busy this morning. Quite a rush of work in the Library." His look at Miss Gorham was charged with meaning.

"Miss Gorham was telling me some beauties. Did she ever tell you the one about the rapid young lady of Erie?"

"Mr. Parry!" cried Gilda. "Dr. Sandys! Mr. Parry! I never—"

> *"To a rapid young lady of Erie*
> *Her mother is stuffy and dreary,*
> > *Saying: 'Young ingenues*
> > *Should never confuse*
> *"To date" and "to fecundate," deary.'*

That's right, isn't it, Miss Gorham?"

Miss Gorham and Dr. Sandys uttered noises compounded of a giggle and a snort, but in unequal proportions. In Miss Gorham's case the giggle predominated over the snort, while Dr. Sandys's response was considerably more snort than giggle. Both blushed to a uniform pink. The girls at the great round catalogue desk suspended all their work to watch and to strain their ears.

"Dr. Sandys!" said Miss Gorham. "You certainly won't believe that I told any such limerick?"

"Oh no. I know Mr. Parry's reputation. In fact, I know Mr. Parry. He is the mysterious figure that the world has been hunting for for years—the man who makes up the limericks."

"Oh, not all of them, my dear fellow."

"Maybe not all of them. There was one I heard in California—I'll tell you some time."

"Not now?"

"Certainly not now. We all have our work to do."

"I haven't any work to do. But don't worry, I'll go away in a minute. I only have a little more business to discuss with Miss Gorham."

"Oh, well, I'm afraid I must be going."

Dr. Sandys looked earnestly at the papers in his left hand and went his way.

"Curiously enough, I do have some business to discuss with you, Miss Gorham. Two items. One, Casti asked me to use my influence with you, which he regards as compelling, to permit him to consult that medieval manuscript in his laboratory. I said: 'Why, of course, my dear fellow; anything to oblige.' I therefore exert my compelling influence upon you, in behalf of Professor Casti."

Professor Parry made a horrible Svengali face at Miss Gorham.

"Nonsense. He knows it's against all the rules."

"Something seems to have gone wrong with my influence. But you are quite right. Don't let that manuscript get away from you, and don't break any rules, especially with Assistant Professor Casti. Now I'm going to try my influence again, and for myself this time. Are you going to the President's reception tonight?"

"Why, what day is this?"

"Monday, September 29. Formal reception for the opening of the term. President Temple and Mrs. Temple invite the staff to have ice cream and cookies in the Presidential Mansion."

"Why, I think I ought to go. Part of my job, I suppose."

"And you will go with me?"

"Well—"

"Save a taxi fare, anyhow. I'll stop for you at eight thirty."

"Thanks."

"Fine. Well, I must be up and away, so that the Librarian and the rest of the Library can get back to work. Good-by, Gilda."

"Good-by, Francis."

Professor Parry strolled out, pausing for a word with the cataloguing girls, in their fairy ring. He waved a benevolent farewell to the group. Gilda returned to her work.

"Oh, Miss Gorham!" It was Dr. Sandys.

"Miss Gorham, are you going to the President's reception this evening?"

"Why, yes, I suppose so."

"I might—ah—stop and get you, perhaps?"

"Oh, I'm so sorry! Mr. Parry just offered to pick me up, and I told him I'd go with him."

"Oh yes, of course, yes. I just thought I might save you the bother. But of course, yes."

Dr. Sandys seemed quite annoyed.

Chapter II

THE UNIVERSITY Library was first erected in the fifties of the last century, as a replica of the Baptistry of Pisa. In the seventies a considerable addition was built, in half-hearted imitation of King's College Chapel at Cambridge. In the nineties, as the University and the Library continued to grow, the building was enlarged and revised in the Boston Romanesque manner. In the twenties, when the need for space again became acute, two new wings were added, rectangular solids of steel and concrete. Sensitive visitors staggered drunkenly at their first glimpse of the structure. Professor Halsey, of the College of Architecture, referred to it in his lectures as "our architectural emetic." But there were some who found a naive and endearing charm in its pathetic effort at ostentation, in its record of the architectural ideals of successive generations. For a really inexcusable monster, they said, go to New Haven.

It was not well adapted to library purposes, certainly. The arrangement was inconvenient, the lighting bad, the shelving of the books capricious. All these disadvantages were compensated, however, in the eyes of some, by the magnificence of the stonework, the richness of the wood-carving, and the endless novelties that greeted the explorer. The men's washroom had been the

Librarian's office in the original Baptistry of Pisa Library. It contained a fireplace with a monumental mantel, reproduced from the Château of Blois. Since in the Library any flame was banned as from a straw-filled barn, no one had ever thought of lighting a fire in the fireplace. This was a good thing, as it had no chimney.

The books were housed in endless book-stacks, thrusting out in every direction, climbing to the tower and burrowing to the crypt. The books dwelt in darkness; messengers and researchers were trained to snap on lights to guide them to their goal, and to snap them off on returning. These interminable shelves of books, waiting pitifully in the dark for a reader to come, worked strongly on some imaginations and filled them with eerie fancies.

The wanderer in the stacks kept meeting delightful, or annoying, surprises. Broad purposeful corridors ended suddenly in solid walls. A glassed sentry-box, or bartizan, thrust out from a bastion over a dry moat. A graduate student's desk was established here; the student was alternately blistered by the sun and frozen by icy drafts. To get from Volume XLI of the *Edinburgh Review* to Volume XLII one had to climb two spiral stairways, cross a musicians' gallery above the periodical room, and descend two more spiral stairways. Here and there, in areas of waste space, study cubicles had been constructed. Looking in, one would perceive a graduate student, asleep.

A constant, distant rumble sounded in the solitudes, from the great fan of the ventilating system. Installed, with much pride, in the rebuilding of the nineties, the ventilation system penetrated the Library as the lymphatic system does the human body. Modern engineers looked on the ventilation apparatus with scorn. It neither cooled nor humidified the air, but only annoyed it, blow-ing forth lifeless blasts from concealed vents, and causing a great deal of coughing.

The catalogue room was situated on the ground floor, between the main reading-room and the wing containing the Wilmerding Library. The catalogue room was the brain of the Library's sluggish body. It was also a small library in itself, for in its alcoves were shelved the catalogues of the world's great libraries, the files of *Book Prices Current,* and all the aids, in many languages, to which the bibliographer must refer. It was also the room in which Miss Gilda Gorham had spent half her waking hours since her graduation from the University, *summa cum laude.*

On this September morning Miss Gorham kept glancing at a vacant chair at the enormous circular desk in the middle of the room. When her visitors left her a moment's respite she strolled to the desk.

"Where's Miss Loring?" she inquired of a girl next to the vacant chair.

"Why, she went up to the Architectural Collection to check on the description of a book. She should be back by this time."

"She's been gone half an hour."

"Here she comes now, Miss Gorham."

"I'll speak to her at my desk."

Miss Loring, with bright blue eyes, bright golden hair, and bright pink cheeks, reported at Miss Gorham's desk. Her cheeks were even pinker than usual, and she was panting.

"What's the matter?" said Miss Gorham. "Have you been running?"

"Yes, Miss Gorham. I—I got scared."

"Who scared you?"

"Nobody. Just the Library."

"Nonsense!"

"Well, it did! I went up to the Architectural Collection in the tower, and I took along the key to the reserved section and let myself in and left the key in the door. I found the book all right. But there was a gargoyle there, right over the shelf where I was working. And it was all sort of queer and lonesome. It made me nervous. So I kind of rushed for the door, and it has a sort of snap lock on it you have to press underneath in a certain place. I couldn't find the place, and I got scared. I was locked in! And I screamed, and finally that janitor came and let me out—you know, Cameron. And I started to run back here and I got lost, and I went on running in and out and up and down for miles and miles, and not a soul around anywhere. My! I thought I could be murdered there and nobody would find me for weeks! All those great big books and all so dark! And finally I landed somehow in Anthropology and I knew where I was. I don't think people ought to go into those stacks alone."

"Nonsense! There's nothing on earth to be scared of. You go back to your work."

"Yes, Miss Gorham."

Miss Loring turned and started for the catalogue desk.

"Miss Loring! Come back here a moment."

"Yes, Miss Gorham?"

"Don't wiggle so when you walk. There's no sense in wiggling so when you walk."

"Why, Miss Gorham, I just walk. That's the way I always walk."

"It isn't the way you walked last week. I suppose you've seen somebody in the movies. Somebody with a fascinating undulating walk. Well, don't undulate around here."

"No, Miss Gorham."

"Maybe you expect to be sent to Atlantic City as Miss University Library?"

"Oh, no, Miss Gorham."

Miss Loring undulated to her desk and whispered gleefully to the girls at her left and right.

"Miss Gorham, please?"

"Yes, Miss Cornwell?"

"Professor Zabel has just brought in two hundred more offprints of his article on the *Effects of Malnutrition on the Grasping Power of the Octopus*. We already have a hundred of them. What do I do about these? Return them?"

"Heavens, no! Never refuse anything. Put them down in the crypt with the stereopticon slides and the Wilmerding Collection of Railroad Time-tables. You never can tell; maybe he'll come around some day and want them back. And have Miss Worcester write a gift letter for Dr. Sandys to sign."

"Yes, Miss Gorham. And another thing. I have a thesis called 'Retroactive Inhibition as Function of the Length of the Interpolated Lists.' I've been trying to read it, but it doesn't seem to make any sense at all. I don't know where in the world to classify it."

"Put it under Education and you can't go wrong." Miss Gorham smiled to herself. That was the sort of little joke she enjoyed. The best little jokes are plain statements of fact.

"My!" said Miss Cornwell. "This is our busy day! Here's Old Harmless! Going into the sale-catalogue alcove."

"You don't mean Professor Hyett? Why is he Old Harmless?"

"Don't you know? The girls in the dorms have a kind of faculty blacklist. Useful if they are called in for conferences or if they are advisees. I believe there are two of the profs who are marked DANGER, in red. The girls are cautioned to leave the door open when they go in. Probably all tommyrot, of course. The girls love to imagine things. Well, Hyett isn't dangerous, but he's a friendly patter. All very kindly and fatherly, of course, but some of the girls get mad. He doesn't seem quite like their own fathers. And there is said to be some relation between the friendly pats and the marks in course. You know how the girls talk; I'm just telling you what they say. But anyhow, they call him Harmless Hyett, or just Old Harmless."

"That makes me think of Mr. Parry's limerick which he says he dedicated to Mr. Hyett."

"Oh, what's that?"

> *"Said a nasty old man of Freehold:*
> *'The young of today, I am told,*
> *   Are so used to the nude*
> *   That it doesn't seem lewd—*
> *Oh gee, but it's great to be old!'"*

The two ladies snickered together.

"He's heading our way!" said Miss Cornwell. "Good morning, old—er—Professor Hyett."

Professor Hyett made a curious double impression on one who saw him for the first time. His face was that of an old Roman, firm, handsome, cleanly modeled. But floating wisps of white hair, misting the ample baldness of his skull, confused the effect of manly force. His body was an evident misfit to his face. Gangling and loose-jointed, he minced as he walked. His voice, deep and resonant, was likely to break into a boyish falsetto. He was perhaps sixty.

"Good morning, Miss Cornwell. And how are you this beautiful morning? I hope you are as well as you look. And, my dear Miss Gorham, how are you? Blooming, assuredly?"

"I'm all right, thank you."

"One glance should have told me that. But I come on business. It never seems right to talk business to you, my dear Miss Gorham. One doesn't talk business to a rose."

"One doesn't talk roses to a business woman, my dear Mr. Hyett."

"Oh, doesn't one? I'll send you a dozen American Beauties tomorrow. Remind me if I should happen to forget, will you?"

"Certainly not."

Professor Hyett laughed. "And quite right too, my dear. I find that it is the promise that gives pleasure, not the fulfillment. However, that is by the way. Has Casti been in about that manuscript?"

"No, but Mr. Belknap and Mr. Parry both asked to let him take it over to his laboratory."

"If you really want my opinion, don't let him take it out. Leave it in the safe, where it belongs. He can do anything he is likely to do with the microfilm. Just between us three, or I should say among us three, he is no classicist. He's excellent on phonetics, no doubt, but he's never had any proper cultural background."

Professor Hyett glanced around and lowered his voice.

"You know who Casti is, don't you? His father is an Italian barber in Detroit! And he worked his way through college by barbering in the College Shop!"

"Well, after all," said Miss Gorham, "barbering is an ancient and respectable trade."

"Assuredly. But the barber-shop background is hardly ideal

for the future interpreter of civilizations and cultures. Casti is one of these bright young Italian-Americans—I don't deny he is bright—who pick up languages quickly and think that linguistic facility qualifies them to be professors of literature. The Romance Language Department is full of them. An amusing young rascal in one of my classes alleges that he went into the Romance instructors' room and said loudly: 'Haircut?' And every instructor sprang to his feet and stood beside his chair!"

"Tell me," said Miss Cornwell, "just what does Mr. Casti do in his Phonetics Laboratory?"

Professor Hyett smiled with pleasure at the opportunity.

"He has a magnificent lot of machinery there, recording machines with smoked cylinders, artificial larynxes that gobble as if they were human, and things like that. And he carries on long investigations experimentally. For instance, he is now studying the pronunciation of the vowel sounds in the combinations 'uff' and 'ugg.' He has determined, I believe, that the average subject pronounces the 'uh' of 'uff' in 169 thousandths of a second, while they take 176 thousandths of a second to pronounce the 'uh' of 'ugg.'"

"But what good does that do?"

Professor Hyett laughed delightedly.

"My dear Miss Cornwell, that is a question you must never ask on a university campus. What good, indeed! We seek pure learning, knowledge for its own sake. That knowledge may well be of some practical use to someone some time, but we don't care whether it is or not. We just seek the fact. It's the essential difference between pure and applied science. Wouldn't you rather be pure than applied? And you can't deny that Casti has got a fact there, about 'uff' and 'ugg,' that no one has ever known before.

Remember the fine aphorism of Dr. Johnson: 'All knowledge is of some value. There is nothing so minute or inconsiderable that I would not rather know it than not.'"

"Yes," said Miss Gorham. "And there is nothing so minute or inconsiderable that it doesn't need to be catalogued. And if everything didn't need to be catalogued, what would all the cataloguers be doing?"

"Housework," suggested Miss Cornwell.

"Sh-h-h!" said Professor Hyett, with great glee. "Don't let any of the profane overhear us. We on the faculty spend our lives delving in the kitchen-middens of space and time, and everything we dig up we want ticketed with our name, whether it's a nugget of pure gold or a rusty tin can. And your job is to label everything, the tin cans with the gold. Some of my colleagues don't seem to be able to tell them apart. In the Classics, our field contains a large share of gold—the great thoughts that are still valid after two thousand years. But some of my colleagues' fields, I fear, are rich in nothing but tin cans."

"Question of point of view," said Miss Gorham diplomatically.

"A question of method, also. Today people have a blind faith in the machine. So everyone must have a laboratory. All the appropriations go to the departments that have a laboratory full of machines. I didn't realize that in time. Now, my own little hobby, of reconstructing Greek vases from fragments—I have some very beautiful ones, and some that are very comical. I don't know if I would dare to show them to you—"

"I have seen them," said Miss Gorham.

"To be sure. And you looked at them, I remember, with the cool, detached eye of the student of civilization. Well, I was going to say that if I had called my little workshop a laboratory, and if I had demanded a lot of expensive machines, the trustees would have given them to me like a flash, instead of grudging me even a little working space in the Liberal Arts basement. Every year they turn down our request for an extra instructor; but I'll wager they would give me ten thousand dollars to construct an irregular-verb machine that would give the student an electric shock every time he pressed the button for a wrong ending."

"That's quite an idea," laughed Miss Gorham.

"It *is* quite an idea. It is a wonderful idea. It is even more— it is pedagogical. There are millions in it. I think I will make a small model—in my laboratory."

"In the meantime," said Miss Cornwell, "I must be doing a little work myself."

"It might work like one of these slot machines that you see in clubs, where a lot of concentric cylinders spin to make a poker hand. It is really quite an idea."

"Don't let us interfere with its construction, Mr. Hyett," said Miss Gorham.

"Oh, good-by, my dear Miss Gorham. By the way, who is that pretty little thing at the cataloguers' desk? The one with the long yellow hair. She's new, isn't she?"

"That's Miss Loring. Yes, she is new."

"A sweet child. She has an attractive little way of walking. You know, that is really quite an idea."

Miss Gorham returned to her work with a sigh. She picked up an order slip from the History Department. This was the fourth time they had ordered a copy of Walpole's *Historic Doubts on the Life and Reign of King Richard the Third,* of which a sound copy was already shelved. She dropped the slip in the waste-basket.

Frowning, she watched Mademoiselle Coindreau approach her desk.

Mademoiselle Coindreau, Assistant Professor of French, was a black-eyed, black-haired Frenchwoman in her early thirties. She was good-looking, in the smoldering southern incipient-hairy way. She had come to America as a *boursière* from the University of Montpellier, had taken a very creditable Ph.D. in French literature from the University of Chicago, and had attained her assistant professorship early. Some Frenchmen criticized her accent, saying that when she got excited it took on a flavor of garlic. Americans criticized her temperament; she would fall into month-long fits of sulkiness, obviously hating America and her own misfortune at being cast in the dull routine of elementary teaching. "She reads too much French," said Professor Parry. But she would emerge from the dumps, to be gay and amusing, to throw herself actively into the organization of French debates, language picnics, and productions of *L'Anglais tel qu'on le parle.*

"Good morning, Miss Gorham."

"Good morning, Mademoiselle Coindreau."

"Tell me, how do you say *radiesthésie* in English? I do not find it in the card catalogue."

"Radiesthésie? If you wait a minute, I'll look it up."

"But I do not find it in the dictionary either."

"Then I'm afraid— What is it, anyway?"

"It is something very important, and perfectly veritable. It has had a great vogue in France in recent years. One has a little ball on a string. But here, I will show you."

Mademoiselle Coindreau drew from her bag a small paste-board box, from which she took a silvered leaden ball, about half an inch in diameter, pierced by a fine string, some eighteen inches long and terminating in a tight-drawn knot. Mademoiselle Coindreau held up the contrivance by the knot.

"Scientists in France have done wonderful things with radi-esthésie. It serves to discover water, or gold, or any hidden thing. It indicates many diseases, such as cancer. The little ball is in-fluenced by the vibrations emanating from all the earth's sub-stances. It swings so many times to the right, so many times to the left, according to a scale worked out by scientists. I know a man in Paris who discovered by this means stores of concealed stupefying drugs. For the police. The little ball is very sensitive, very delicate. It can determine sex. For a woman, it swings four times to the right, three to the left. For a man, it is the opposite. Only look—"

Mademoiselle Coindreau held the knot aloft. The leaden ball hung motionless. Slowly it began to swing, pendulum-wise. Left, right, left, right, left, right, left. Again it was still.

"Perhaps I remembered it wrongly," said Mademoiselle Coin-dreau, doubtfully. "I will look it up in my little book. It remains, however, a remarkable scientific invention. It is strange that in America, which prides itself on science, there are no books on radiesthésie."

"You might look under Divining. Or under the general head-ing of Occult Sciences. See what there is in that big *Handwör-terbuch des Aberglaubens,* by Hoffmann and Krayer. Try looking under *Wünschelrute.* You know where the Occulta books are shelved, don't you?"

"Oh yes. On the top gallery of the Wilmerding Library. You

have there some very curious books, very curious. I have been interested in the prophecies of Nostradamus, which are very astonishing, in the light of actual events. And there are books, so bizarre, on medieval torture. That Mr. Wilmerding, he must have been a droll one."

"A great collector," said Miss Gorham primly.

"Yes. Certainly. And since we speak of the Occulta section, it is my duty to tell you something I observed from there only yesterday. Something that was going on in one of the graduate students' cubicles. There was a young man and a young woman in that graduate students' cubicle, where there is hardly place for one. Yes. There was a young man there. And a young woman." Mademoiselle Coindreau's eyes flashed, and her well-furnished bosom heaved.

Miss Gorham sprang up in alarm. "Don't tell me—that they were smoking?"

Mademoiselle Coindreau sneered. "No; they weren't *smoking.*"

"Oh. Thank God. For a moment I thought you meant they were smoking."

"Hah!" snorted Mademoiselle Coindreau. A shrug of the left shoulder said: *"Ces Américaines!"* Aloud she said: "I will go and look for those books of which you tell me. It would be strange that this great library should contain nothing on radiesthésie!"

Miss Gorham returned to her work. She was, after all, used to interruption. Her tickler noted that Young's *Analytic Concordance to the Holy Scriptures* had now been missing for six months from the open shelves of the reference room. The thief, apparently, was not going to return it in a fit of remorse. Better pick up a second-hand copy, she decided, unless there happened to be one among the duplicates in the crypt.

"Good morning, Miss Gorham."

"Why, good morning, Mr. Casti."

Assistant Professor Casti was dark and tense, with drawn, sallow skin. Without invitation, he sat down in the chair by Miss Gorham's desk. He drew from his bulging brief-case a slim pamphlet.

"I have brought you a present—an off-print of my latest article, from the *Phonetic Review*. It is on the Displacement of the Point of Articulation of *i* under the influence of certain plosives and fricatives. It is not for the Library; it is for you personally. You see, I have inscribed it to you." He pointed to the words on the corner: "To Miss Gilda Gorham, as an inadequate token of the author's regard. Angelo Casti." The signature was written twice as large as the dedication, and was ornamented with imposing flourishes of the pen.

"Why, thank you, Mr. Casti. That is very nice of you."

"I don't know if you are interested in phonetics at all. But in this little article I have upset a good many accepted ideas, by the simple process of laboratory experiment. There are certain people whose faces will be very red when they read this little article."

"I am sure of it."

"Of course, I have sent a copy to the President, but he is so busy I don't suppose he has time to do more than glance at the productions of the faculty. You are on good terms with the President, aren't you, Miss Gorham?"

"Well, we don't call each other by our first names. At least, not in each other's presence."

"But you are on good terms? I notice that he always stops

and gossips with you when he comes into the Library. Well now, if you could manage to glance through this article today, then at the President's reception tonight you might drop a word to him about it. Say you found it fascinating, or something of the sort. Of course, he will probably say: 'Ex-tremely int-a-resting! Ex-tremely int-a-resting!' and not mean a word of it."

"You really do the President very well, Mr. Casti."

"The phonetician's habit. It's my business to notice those things—the forced and faulty syllabication, the excessive value given to the dentals. The platform influence, I sometimes call it in jest."

"Well, I won't promise. But thank you for the offprint. I will put it with the rest of your works."

"Thank you. Now about that manuscript—the *Filius Getronis*. I was wondering—"

"Yes, I know. I am sorry, but Dr. Sandys doesn't think it should go out of the Library."

"So Mr. Hyett was just telling me. Well, I will have to get along with the microfilm. It is too bad, because some of the surcharged letters are not at all clear on the film. There are some laboratory tests I should have liked to apply. But I suppose I can consult it in the Library. It won't be quite the same thing. But if those are the rules, I shall merely bow to them. By the way—"

"Yes?"

"You haven't seen Mademoiselle Coindreau about, have you? There was—ah—something I wanted to see her about."

"She was in a moment ago. She went up in the stacks. I think you could find her in the Occulta. Or in the French Seminary. That's where she does most of her work."

"Poor dear Mademoiselle Coindreau! Hunting her radies-thésie, I suppose. You know, much as I like and admire Mademoiselle Coindreau, and much as I value the excellent work she is doing here, I do find it strange that anyone with her university training should be the dupe of pseudo-science! Of course, she went to Montpellier, and you know those provincial universities. I was born in the States, of course; but I took my doctorate at the Sorbonne, and I spent a year in the Institut de Phonétique. In France that is quite a different thing from the University of Montpellier."

"If you want Mademoiselle Coindreau, you could probably catch her now. I don't think she was going to stay here long."

"Thank you. I shall go and look for her. I shall put myself to her research, as we say in French. Ha-ha!"

Assistant Professor Casti departed. Miss Gorham dropped his off-print in her waste-basket.

"Gilda!"

It was Professor Parry again.

"Gilda, was that Casti I just saw going out?"

"Yes."

"He was in about the manuscript?"

"Yes. He was also looking for Mademoiselle Coindreau."

"That's interesting. Did he pronounce her name with a hushed and trembling voice, and with a far-away look in his eye?"

"I wasn't looking at his eye. But he seemed to me rather pettish about her."

"That's interesting, too. They have probably returned to normal."

"What do you mean?"

"What do you think? Lucie Coindreau, you know, is the

oomph-girl of the Romance Language Department. She arouses the beast in man. Did you know that?"

"No. Not to look at her—"

"Well, she's a beast-rouser. She's been reading French novels, scrofulous French novels, since she was twelve, and writing studies on Musset's Conception of Passion since she was eighteen. And I gather that for some time she's been ready to make the jump from literature to life. *Amour!* That's what she wants. And remember that *'amour,'* as used in the works of Alfred de Musset, is not exactly translated by the word 'love' as it appears in the works of Longfellow."

"Very prettily phrased. You think, then—"

"I think it's none of your business. But since you urge me, I will break a lifelong rule and tell a little gossip. Last spring she and Casti spent a lot of time in the Phonetics Laboratory, prolonging their research late into the night, and it is suspected that the time was not devoted exclusively to recording each other's vowels and consonants. But *voilà,* as we say in France! The trouble is that both of them are due for promotion to associate professor. And the Dean and the President both approve of Mademoiselle's excellent work with classes, and they think that Casti's ubble-gubble into phonographs is nonsense, and they just don't like him much anyway. So Mademoiselle will probably get an up, and Casti won't. He's a jealous little squirt, and he hates the idea of having a woman advanced over him. It is noteworthy that he has just bought a car, a massive late-Victorian model, but he doesn't seem to give poor Lucie any rides. So I think they have returned to a normal state of healthy rivalry and suspicion."

"You seem to be very well informed."

Miss Gorham rose and took down a volume of the *Deutsches Bücherverzeichnis* from her reference shelves.

"I *am* well informed. I am interested in human behavior, a subject which is relatively neglected in our curriculum. And I find the faculty a good field for observation. We're a funny lot. We are picked because we know something, presumably, and then they expect us not only to know, but to set an example of a beautiful life, which means a sexless life. We do our best to satisfy the trustees, but if you could really examine the minds of a lot of people around here, you would certainly be surprised. Or perhaps you wouldn't."

"And as for you, you might even be disappointed."

"I don't think so. You know, one thing I sometimes wonder about is how many of my colleagues are virgins."

"Why, Mr. Parry!" Miss Gorham blushed cherry red.

Professor Parry laughed his ringing, infectious, youthful laugh.

"What is so shocking about virginity, one of the chief of the Christian virtues? There is Hyett, mentally about as hard-boiled as they come. I'll bet he's a virgin. And Belknap, spending his life interpreting the behavior of all those very carnivorous rowdies of the Middle Ages, telling just what made them work. I think he'd learn more about their psychology by taking a floozie to Atlantic City than he ever will from his manuscripts."

"And how about Professor Parry, the rakish bachelor of the Department of Dramatics?"

Professor Parry bowed his head.

"That is a brutal and a painful question. Gilda—my dear Gilda, there is something I have to tell you."

"Well?"

"Something serious. Something that concerns you very close-ly. Will you permit me to say something very intimate, my dear Gilda?"

"Why—why, I suppose so."

"Your slip is showing."

"You rat!" Gilda's nervous giggle blended with Professor Parry's resonant boyish laughter.

He waved her a whimsical farewell.

Cameron, the janitor, entered the room, with a box of electric-light globes in his arms. He was a man in his middle sixties, with a certain faded distinction of manner. It was reported that he had come of a good bourgeois family, but had been impatient of education and had set off as a youth to see the world. It appeared from his conversation that he had followed many trades, as sailor, bartender, detective, electrician, and short-order cook. For fifteen years he had been the Library's head janitor and had served it well as a competent general handyman. The staff had learned to trust him; he had received only occasional reprimands when he was found in a quiet corner of the stacks, reading. His taste ran, apparently, to the more esoteric sort of books.

Cameron switched on the lights and found two burned-out globes. As he was replacing them, Assistant Professor Casti entered and glanced inquiringly about the catalogue room.

"Did you find Mademoiselle Coindreau?" said Gilda.

"No. She wasn't in the Occulta or the seminary."

"Well, she's probably somewhere around."

"Probably."

Professor Casti, with a troubled air, turned and left.

"She was there a couple of minutes ago," said Cameron to Gilda.

"Where? In the Occulta?"

"Yes. I was in the Wilmerding, making the rounds of the lights. She was in the Occulta. Talking to a man."

"Oh. Who?"

"I don't know. I couldn't make out his voice. They weren't talking very loud. But I did hear one thing. She called him a papoose."

"A what?"

"A papoose. You know, Indian baby."

"But that doesn't make sense!"

"I didn't say it made sense. I said she called him a papoose."

"You shouldn't listen to private conversations, Cameron."

"No. And you shouldn't listen to me when I repeat them to you, either."

"I guess you're right, Cameron."

"I guess I am right, Miss Gorham. There, that works all right."

Cameron moved away, grinning. He was clearly pleased with his repartee. He walked lightly, still lithe and erect for all his sixty-five years.

"Gilda!"

It was Parry again.

"Gilda! I've been thinking since I left you. Thinking about you."

"And what, pray, have you been thinking about me?"

> *"There was a young lady named Gorham*
> *Who behaved with extreme indecorum;*
> *She gave Mrs. Grundys*
> *A glimpse of her undies.*
> *First time I knew that she wore 'em!"*

Chapter III

ON THE campus, only two minutes' walk from the Library, stands the Faculty Club. The dining-room, smoking-room, and common rooms are on the ground floor; the three upper stories consist of two-room and three-room suites for the faculty. The University designed the building originally as a sort of housing project for poor married instructors. But the rents proved too high for the instructors' salaries, and no provision was made by the architects for nurseries. The instructors, fecund like all the lower organisms, remained in their quarters on the hot top floors of made-over frame boarding-houses in College Town. "The University's motto," said Professor Parry, "is: If you can't be chaste, be sterile."

The upper floors of the Faculty Club are therefore occupied by the bachelors of the staff. These are the aristocrats of the campus. They drive bright-colored convertible coupes, not the five-year-old black sedans favored by the married men. They travel in the summer; they buy books and bibelots; they have jolly dinners in hotels. They are regarded on the campus with mingled admiration and censure. "The University ought to burn out that nest of old bachelors and scatter them," said an irritated faculty daughter.

At eight in the evening the gentlemen of the Faculty Club were dressing for the President's reception.

In Apartment 1-B Dr. Sandys was carefully trimming his goatee with a pair of nail-scissors. He pressed his stomach against the wash-basin and leaned forward toward the mirror, making faces to get the goatee in various lights. Delicately he snipped at a gray hair. There were getting to be a good many gray hairs. Before long the total effect of the goatee would be nearer to gray-brown than to its previous rich and lustrous horse-chestnut. It would make him look really old. For the hundredth time he meditated parting with the goatee entirely. Where had he read that men grew beards as a symbol of concealment, of guilt? He frowned at the thought and prodded the shy chin beneath its cushion. It would be interesting to see his chin again, after twenty years. Perhaps people would admire him more without his goatee. Perhaps they would like him better. Those pretty creatures in the catalogue room. . . . That charming and intelligent Miss Gorham. . . . Not in her first youth, of course; all the better; old enough to have some sense, and certainly very attractive. . . . What would it feel like to be kissed on the actual spot now so well defended by the goatee? When he was a young fellow in the Hopkinson Library, there had been a girl who had kissed him there. That was before the trouble. . . . Some time on a summer vacation he would shave the thing off and have a real good look at himself. But not tonight, of course, just before the President's reception.

Dr. Sandys snipped an eighth of an inch from a protruding hair, dusted himself off, and put on his evening shirt. Great idea, these modern evening shirts, with only a single button. The trouble is, that button is in the middle of the back, where a stoutish man can barely reach. Dr. Sandys, straining hard, panted as he ran his thumbs up and down the middle of his back. He could not find the button, naturally, because the button was gone.

In Apartment 2-A Professor Belknap was also having shirt trouble. His proper collar was a fifteen, or even fourteen and three quarters. Anything larger than a fifteen and a quarter revealed entirely too much of his long, thin neck. With a fifteen and a quarter collar he could wear a fifteen and a half shirt. But even a fifteen and a half shirt had its bosom placed too high for his long body. What he really needed was something like a seventeen shirt with a fifteen collar. He buttoned his black vest. Standing close to the full-length mirror of his bathroom door, he could distinctly see the bottom of the stiff shirt-bosom above the top of the vest. He took off the vest, made a little fold where the vest fitted over the nape of the neck, and fastened the fold with a pin. Now the vest sat higher, and definitely overlapped the shirt-bosom. But below the vest was a white line isolating the vest from the trousers.

Women, damnable observant women, would notice immediately that his vest did not reach from his trousers to his shirt-bosom. Damnable tailors! Damnable shirt-makers! Damnable women, especially, always whispering to one another, interfering, ogling, spying on him! Damnable women, walking about nearly naked to swim in the University lake, or coiling on sofas as if they were in bed! He would like to—

But there was no use going on this way. And there was no use going to the President's reception merely to be laughed at. But no, to stay away would be weakness. He would not give them the easy triumph of saying that he was afraid to come to the President's reception. He was not afraid of them.

He pulled up the slides of his suspenders, raising his trousers to their painful limit. Carefully he adjusted his vest. He retreated slowly from the mirror. At a distance of about four feet the bottom of the shirt-bosom seemed to merge with the vest. He must simply keep well away from people, prevent them from getting so close that they could look down at his vest-top. And he must not reveal his mood by appearing sulky. He must think of something cheerful. He would think about good old Jakob Sprenger's *Malleus Maleficarum*.

He thought about the *Malleus Maleficarum*, about the agreeableness of the type and binding, and about his own generosity in giving it to the Library. He went on to think of old Sprenger's apt quotation from Seneca: "When a woman thinks alone, she thinks evil." He recalled his story of the man whose wife was drowned in a river and who persisted in looking upstream for the body. "My wife was always so contrary in life," he explained, "that doubtless she is still so in death!" That old Witch-Hammer was really quite a card.

Professor Belknap was soon very cheerful.

In Apartment 1-E Professor Parry muttered as he dressed. He had laid out his tails, a fine new suit made by the best tailor in town. He looked on them with affection. Only a dozen members of the faculty possessed tails, and half of the dozen bulged and puffed when they tried to wear their aged relics. Professor Parry slipped on the trousers, enjoying the kiss of the soft wool. He continued to mutter. He muttered:

> "'As to pants,' said a fellow in Putnam,
> 'It's a terrible bother to butnam—'"

He tested the suspenders over his gleaming shirt. "Utnam, butnam, cutnam, dutnam, futnam—"

He examined his pumps critically.

"Gutnam, hutnam, kutnam, lutnam, mutnam, quutnam, rutnam, sutnam. Sutnam. Shutnam. That's it! Shutnam!"

He slipped on his pumps with a shoe-horn.

"I'd hate to get shutnam. A terrible thing to get shutnam. Shutnam. Shut-in. Prison. Jail. Claustrophobia. Claustrophobia. Obia, bobia, cobia. So be yuh. No, be yuh? Know be a!

> *It may only, I know, be a—*
> *cute claustrophobia.*

Ha, I've got it!

> *'As to pants,' said a fellow in Putnam,*
> *'Though I wear 'em, I never will butnam;*
> *It may only, I know, be a*
> *Mild claustrophobia;*
> *But I terribly fear being shutnam!'"*

He laughed aloud. "There's a good one for Gilda!"

He washed his hands and put the pearl stud in his shirt. He carefully adjusted his white vest, a dainty thing of watered silk with an almost invisible design. It amply covered the lower edge of his shirt-bosom. But as he worked with deft fingers his smile faded and changed slowly into a frown. When his tail coat was snugly in place and he had surveyed himself from every reasonable angle, he went to his bureau. He opened the drawer which contained his shirts. From underneath the pile he drew two photographs. One was a portrait from a professional studio, showing the stiffly smiling face of Lucie Coindreau. It was inscribed: "For Francis. From Lucie." The other photograph showed a crudely painted airplane, the comic property of a cheap photographer, of the sort that thrive along the shabbier boardwalks. Peering from the grotesque airplane were the broadly grinning faces of Francis Parry and Lucie Coindreau.

Frowning, Professor Parry tore the photographs into small pieces. When about to drop them in the waste-basket, he thought better of it. He built a little fire in a broad standing ash-tray. The fragments were soon entirely consumed. Professor Parry, smiling again, closed his door and set forth for his appointment with Gilda. He muttered:

"'As to pants,' said a fellow in Putnam—"

In Apartment 3-D, the smallest and cheapest of the Faculty Club, Assistant Professor Casti had laid aside the somber costume of the day and was putting on the more somber hues of evening. Apartment 3-D was furnished with various pieces of maple, cherry, and golden oak. Each item of furniture had been bought at a remarkable bargain. The large and somewhat faded photographs of Paris on the walls had been discarded by the Department of Romance Languages. It was not so much poverty that had determined Professor Casti's choice of furniture and decoration as a ceaseless search for advantage. To find a good, though slightly shaky table underpriced in a second-hand store, needing only a few repairs he could make in his laboratory, gave him a lasting sense of delight. He felt that he was getting the better of a shiftless and incompetent world. He liked to tell his visitors the price he had paid for everything, and to revel in their polite astonishment. The money he saved went to repay his borrowings for his expensive years in French graduate schools. He would often complain about the economics of the professorate. He calculated that it had cost his parents and the state twenty thousand dollars to carry him to the end of his education, and that with the costs of research and publication a professor was lucky to pay off the investment in his professional preparation by the time he became emeritus.

His evening clothes, his shirt, tie, and shoes, had been bought at chain stores which give you the advantage of large-scale buying and low overhead. He had shrewdly checked the quality of each article. It would be hard to say quite what was wrong with the ensemble. There was a kind of meanness about it, enhanced by the wearer's mean satisfaction with his appearance. He seemed a collection of little advantages gained, but the collection did not make a total of anything.

Professor Casti proceeded deftly and efficiently with his dressing. He seemed abstracted; his brow was knit. When he had applied the last pat to his coat he went to his desk, an imposing roll-top from a bankrupt insurance office. He inspected the loose-leaf calendar pad. Five notes were written on it, in his careful, scrupulous hand:

> "Send off-prints to Ph. R.
> 10. See Miss G about Mss
> 2. See Dean about new kymograph
> 8.30. Pres. reception
> Settle matters with L. C. *Be firm.*"

Through the first three items neat pencil lines had been drawn.

He picked up a pencil and drew a line through "8.30. Pres. reception." He stared for a full minute at the calendar, then tore off the sheet, crumpled it, and dropped it in the waste-basket.

He patted his pockets, left the room, and locked the door. He descended to the parking-space behind the Faculty Club and gazed long and lovingly at a monumental Pierce-Arrow. He turned, and set off to walk the short distance to the Presidential Mansion.

Apartment 2-C would impress a visitor by its mingling of austerity and modest luxury. On the walls hung Piranesi prints of Roman ruins, and two fine portraits: one of Professor Hyett's father and one of his cousin, Dr. Pickard, who had been University Librarian until his death a year before. An eighteenth-century French *desserte* was adapted to serve as a small cocktail bar. The sofa and easy chairs, in dark green and brown, were comfortably overstuffed.

Professor Hyett was dressing. A half-empty glass of port stood on the *desserte*. On the desk, a gilt-scrolled eighteenth-century escritoire, lay open a little edition of the *Opera* of Johannes Secundus, printed in Leiden in 1651. Professor Hyett loved the lusty humanist writers of the Renaissance. Between shirt and tie he paused to read:

> *Hora suavicula, et voluptuosa,*
> *Hora blanditiis, lepore, risu,*
> *Hora deliciis, jocis, susurris,*
> *Hora suaviolis, parique magnis*
> *Cum Diis et Iove transigenda sorte.*

Smiling happily, he returned to his dressing. His coat fitted as well as it had ten years back. His figure was as trim as ever. Not like some of the colleagues, who seemed to let go suddenly amidships and get so sort of maternal-looking.

He gave his black felt hat a good brushing. Looking at his watch, he found that he still had ten minutes.

He finished his port, smacking it slowly. Then, a little irresolutely, he went to a cupboard beneath a bookcase and unlocked it. He selected a large volume with a florid Parisian binding. He sat down and turned the pages slowly, murmuring to himself and smiling.

Ten minutes later he returned the volume to its place with a sigh and locked the cupboard. He set out for the President's reception.

In the janitor's room of the University Library Cameron, the janitor, was sitting in an old easy chair with extrusions of doughty cotton seeping through many gaps of the upholstery. He was reading the Library copy of Conklin's *Principles of Abnormal Psychology*. Naturally he was not asked to the President's reception, and naturally he was glad of it.

Chapter IV

THE PRESIDENTIAL Mansion is a large, imposing, white-painted wooden building of about 1850, with a great two-story pillared portico that leaves the second-floor bedrooms in perpetual gloom, and with a series of magnificent parlors, twelve feet in height, that are, according to the Superintendent of Buildings and Grounds, hell's delight to heat.

On the evening of the President's reception, President Temple, Mrs. Temple, and the Commandant of the R.O.T.C. stood in the small reception room at the left of the entrance. As the guests entered, the Commandant inquired their names, which he then shouted to President and Mrs. Temple. Even President Temple could slip up on the name of a staff member he had not seen for a year, and poor Mrs. Temple was certain to forget everything in a crisis.

"Professor Anderson and Mrs. Anderson!" boomed the Commandant. Mrs. Temple welcomed the pair with more effusiveness than was fitting for an Assistant Professor of Mechanical Drawing. She realized, too late, that she had confused him with Professor Emeritus Henderson of Vegetable Crops.

"Hello, Anderson. Good evening, Mrs. Anderson." President Temple, large, bland, actor-faced, made for the couple a blend of hearty friendliness and condescension, as a theatrical spot-light operator blends his colored lights.

"Professor Casti!" announced the Commandant. Now Mrs. Temple was sure she had something.

"Oh, Professor Casti! I am so glad to see you! I hear such wonderful things about your psychopathic laboratory!"

"Phonetics laboratory, my dear," said President Temple. "How are you, Casti? Nice evening."

"Oh yes, phonetics laboratory, I mean. But you *do* work with pigs, don't you, Mr. Casti?"

"Well, in fact, you might call them so, he-he! Vile bodies, *corpora vilia,* anyway. As it happens, I have just sent off an article to the *Phonetic Review*—"

"Dr. and Mrs. Churchill and Miss Churchill," intoned the Commandant.

"Ex-tremely int-a-resting! Ex-tremely int-a-resting!" said the President, motioning Casti on, to yield place to Dr. Churchill, of the Medical Staff.

The guests, constantly displaced by new arrivals, drifted into the drawing-rooms.

"In President Darrow's time," said old Mrs. Eadie to Professor and Mrs. Anderson, "Mrs. Darrow had a divan here, where the two big chairs are."

"I don't like it so white," said Mrs. Anderson. "I think white walls are kind of ghastly, and everything shows on them so."

"Mrs. Darrow was an ideal president's wife. Every year she called on all the married professors and even the married instructors. Three calls an afternoon right up to Christmas. I declare, I don't know how she did it."

"My walls are all a nice oatmeal color. Never shows a thing, hardly. When you have children, you know, you've got to think about those things."

"Mrs. Darrow was so genteel! She used to ask the faculty to sit-down supper in groups of twelve during the winter. She asked them alphabetically, so as to break up cliques. Of course the faculty is a lot larger now. But the President gets an allowance for entertaining, you know. My husband always reads it to me out of the Treasurer's Report."

"I can't figure out how the President spends his entertainment allowance," broke in Mrs. Churchill. "I don't mean to suggest there's anything fishy at all, but I doubt if Mrs. T. is a very good manager. Now this kakemono here that they brought back from the Orient. I know something about silk, and I can tell just by feeling it that it isn't very good silk. But I'll bet you they paid a-plenty for it."

"I see people are going into the dining-room," said Miss Churchill.

"In President Darrow's time," said old Mrs. Eadie, "the dining-room was all paneled in solid mahogany. All ripped out now. To my way of thinking, that tinted wall looks downright cheap."

The party moved toward the dining-room.

"Sandwiches, cakes, ice-cream, and coffee," said Mrs. Anderson. "They look like Feltman and Gass's cakes."

"They have cigars in the Blue Room," reported Dr. Churchill, joining the group. "Just ten-centers."

The party mulled from room to room, testing, fingering, criticizing. Shirt-bosoms crackled, and bare bosoms itched under ticklish metals and semi-precious stones. The noise was deafening; the most intimate remarks were yelled across a two-foot gap, yet somehow they could not be heard a foot beyond the listener. It had become extremely hot.

"Might as well have a reception in the engine room of an ocean liner," shouted Professor Hyett to Dr. Churchill.

"What?"

"Might as well have a reception in the engine room of an ocean liner."

"What for?"

"I mean, it's so hot and noisy there."

"Well, it's hot and noisy here too," said Dr. Churchill, scornfully.

Professor Hyett looked away in disgust. Delightedly he perceived Mademoiselle Coindreau. She was wearing an evening gown of shimmering black, cut low, contrasting with the shimmering white of her bosom. Her high, full breasts stood up, clearly outlined in silk. There were Minoan statuettes of women wearing just such a costume, thought Professor Hyett. Curious how, in fondling them, one could feel a thrill of desire for a woman dead four thousand years! How brief and poor a thing is life in comparison with art!

"My dear mademoiselle!" he cried. "How beautiful you look this evening! And such an inspiring occasion! So, shall I say, uplifting! Do you, too, feel uplifted? If I may judge by a casual scrutiny of the advertising pages, uplift is the watchword of modern womanhood. And are you, too, a partisan of uplift?"

Professor Belknap, standing beside Hyett, turned away, his face hot. He would not listen to this smutty old man, embarrassing and shaming poor Mademoiselle Coindreau. But Mademoiselle Coindreau was bearing up well, hiding her shame under a smile. Professor Belknap surreptitiously reached under his vest and gave his shirt a smart pull downwards.

Dr. Sandys interrupted Professor Hyett in mid-persiflage. "How-de-do, Mademoiselle Coindreau? How-de-do, Hyett? Warm in here, isn't it? Oh, by the way, Hyett, question I wanted to ask you. When your cousin was Librarian, do you know if he ever had any personal trouble with the binder—I mean, the sort of thing that wouldn't appear in the files? I find him pretty difficult to deal with myself, and while of course the contract is all right—"

Lucie Coindreau abstracted herself from the discussion and joined Professor Belknap.

"Mr. Belknap, I wished to ask you something."

Professor Belknap looked at her in suspicious silence.

"I have just been reading your book on the Albigensian Crusade. I found it magnificent. So profound! So understanding!"

Belknap's face creaked in a smile. "It is accepted, at least, as authoritative."

"Such breadth of conception! We have a word in French: *envergure*—"

"Far-reaching, perhaps."

"Yes. I felt that. But there is one question of detail. You speak of Foulquet de Marseille, the Bishop of Toulouse, that cruel inquisitor. I admired especially your sketch of his early life as an amatory poet and as a person of a very relaxed morality. Your analysis of the conflict in his character was most subtle, most delicate. But you do not mention that Dante speaks of him in the *Paradiso*. Canto Nine."

"I was aware of it, of course. But I could not find that Dante added anything to the information given us by the chroniclers. There is a little book by Zingarelli—"

Professor Belknap was transformed. All his clumsiness had dropped away, and he spoke firmly and trenchantly, with that contained passion which had made of him a distinguished lecturer, whose courses were highly recommended by and for serious students. He seemed to be enjoying himself. Mademoiselle Coindreau listened entranced.

After a time they were conscious of Professor Casti by their side.

"Good evening, mademoiselle. Good evening, Mr. Belknap."

"Good evening, Mr. Casti."

"It is quite a reception, isn't it? Yes, quite a reception."

"Yes, yes. On the whole, it is."

"Do I interrupt an interesting conversation, perhaps?"

"Oh, no, no," said Professor Belknap.

"On the contrary, I found it extremely interesting," said Mademoiselle Coindreau.

"Oh. Could I get you some coffee and sandwiches, mademoiselle?"

"You are very kind. But Mr. Belknap was just going to fetch me some."

"Oh. Well—ah—see you again."

"He seems annoyed about something," said Professor Belknap as Professor Casti moved away.

"That is his right. It does not interest me if he is annoyed. Are you concerned?"

"No, no. Oh no."

"But perhaps you had better fetch me some coffee and sandwiches."

"Oh yes. Of course. Certainly." Professor Belknap steered for the dining-room. On the way he succeeded in pulling down his shirt. The voice of Mrs. Churchill clanged in his ears: "I figure they didn't spend more than sixty dollars on food, and with maybe twenty for service that makes eighty. If they give four receptions like this, that only makes three hundred and twenty. What do they do with the rest of the entertainment allowance? Answer me that!"

Professor Casti joined Mademoiselle Coindreau. For a time they talked, heatedly and rapidly, in French.

Against the couple Gilda Gorham and Professor Parry were thrust by a bulging of the close-packed throng.

"Hell-o, hello, mademoiselle," said Parry. "Hello, Casti. Everything passing off pleasantly?"

"Oh yes." Mademoiselle Coindreau smiled constrainedly. Casti did not reply.

"Well, we're going to force a passage to the food," said Parry. "Come on, Gilda; I'll buck and you kick. It's all right to strong-arm anything under an associate professor." He sketched a half crouch and pretended to ram the assemblage. Gilda followed on his heels. After a short struggle the two found themselves in the dining-room.

"Here, try one of these." Parry lifted the top layer of a sandwich, gazed at it dubiously, and took a bite. While chewing, he lifted again the top layer of the remaining morsel.

"What do you think it is?" he said. "Pemmican?"

"Kennel-ration, I should say."

"No, kennel-ration is richer and has more of a tang. This has a tougher texture. Some sort of plastic, maybe. Do you know the one about the old lady in Summit?"

"Francis! Not here!"

"Oh, this is a clean one, for the Presidential Mansion.

> *A toothless old lady of Summit*
> *Had to mash up her dinner and crumb it;*
> *And although she would groan*
> *When they gave her a bone,*
> *'Give it here,' she would say, 'and I'll gum it.'"*

"Francis!"

"Hot in here, don't you think? Let's take some ice cream out on the terrace. Very warm evening for September."

"All right. Let's try it, anyway."

As the two stepped out through the wide French windows, the great clock of the Library cleared its throat, struck ten mournful strokes, and sighed.

"Ten o'clock," said Parry. "How long are we supposed to stay at the President's reception?"

"Ten thirty. Then everyone rushes for the door, trampling on the women and children."

"Here's a couple of nice chairs in the dark. Cigarette?"

"Thanks."

The two settled themselves in wicker porch-chairs, which yielded with an angry groan.

"Lovely, isn't it?"

"Isn't it?"

"Gilda!"

"Yes?"

"We're good friends, aren't we?"

"Of course we're good friends, Francis. Always be kind to the faculty, is my motto."

"Please, Gilda. We get along beautifully, don't we?"

"Yes."

"We have a wonderful time together?"

"Francis, I think I see where these leading questions are leading. And I won't deny that I have been thinking a good deal about you lately. And one thing I think is this: that I really don't know much of anything about you. You are frank and open, and your heart is on your sleeve, and all that. But somehow you are never indiscreet about yourself. You don't keep other people's secrets; but maybe you keep your own."

"I would tell you anything you want to know, Gilda." Parry's voice was low.

"Well now, for example—last year, as you probably know, your name and that of Lucie Coindreau were, in that nice phrase, coupled. Was there anything serious between you?"

"Would it make any difference?"

"I don't know. I think it might."

"Well then—no."

It seemed to Gilda that the answer came a tenth of a second too slow. She shivered.

"You know, it is chillier here than I thought. Would you mind getting my wrap? Here's the check."

"Certainly, Gilda."

Parry reached over and pressed her hand. Then, with his buoyant step, he entered the house. Gilda crushed out her cigarette.

A moment later Lucie Coindreau emerged through the French windows. She had a black cloak on her arm. She glanced about and gave no sign of perceiving Gilda in her dark chair. She tossed on her cloak and went sinuously down the terrace steps to the black lawn.

Curious, thought Gilda. It could be only a few minutes past ten. Why should Lucie be going home early? And why not go out the front door, like anyone else?

Through the French windows came Professor Casti. He looked about the terrace and went irresolutely to the steps leading down to the lawn.

"Lucie!" he called. "Lucie!"

He paused a moment and re-entered the Presidential Mansion.

Gilda shivered again. She might warm herself by walking about a bit. And if she was going to walk, she might as well walk on the lawn as anywhere else. That Lucie Coindreau! What in the world could she be up to?

Gilda, trying to convey by her walk that she had been seized by a sudden whim, strolled down the steps and along the flagged path that led across the lawn. The path ended at a wicket-gate in the high cedar hedge protecting the Presidential grounds.

Someone was fumbling at the wicket-gate. It was a woman's figure in a dark and shimmering cloak. It was, in fact, Lucie Coindreau. She succeeded in opening the gate and passed through, closing it softly.

Gilda, still determinedly following her whim, went to the gate. She saw Mademoiselle Coindreau hurrying across the campus, directly toward the University Library, some two hundred yards distant.

"What is she up to in my Library?" thought Gilda, indignantly. All her sense of proprietorship rose up within her. A sense of duty, she would have called it herself. Without stopping to reason, she set off in pursuit of the hurrying dark figure.

She saw the figure enter the Library door. But when Gilda reached the wide tiled lobby, Mademoiselle Coindreau had disappeared.

And suddenly Gilda realized that all this was very undignified, to say the least; cattish, to say the most. And her own presence in the Library lobby, in evening dress, without a wrap, would seem at least curious. Fortunately the Library was almost deserted. The faculty were mostly at the President's reception. The graduates had not yet settled down to their dissertations. The undergraduates had not received their term reading assignments, and few of them were in the mood for browsing on this warm, summer-like evening. Still, Gilda preferred not to be seen. She sought woman's natural haven and refuge—the women's rest room, which opens conveniently off the Library lobby.

She looked at her watch. It was a quarter past ten. Francis was probably looking for her. Well, he could just look a little longer. Now that she was in the rest room, she might as well do a bit of primping.

After about five minutes' primping, she opened the door cautiously. A couple of students passed, preparing cigarettes to be lit the moment they should be outside the door. Then Dr. Sandys and Professor Casti entered. They said a word or two, and parted, Sandys turning down the short corridor that led to the Librarian's office, Casti going in the opposite direction toward the periodical room and the language seminaries.

This was awkward. Gilda felt very bare and shameless in her evening dress. It occurred to her that she had a raincoat in her locker in the catalogue room. If she had the raincoat she would at least look decent. And if anyone should ask her what she was doing in the Library at this time, she could answer bravely: "I was just getting my raincoat!"

The lobby was empty. Gilda darted to the catalogue room, unlocked it, turned on the lights, found the key to her locker, and took out her raincoat with a grunt of satisfaction. She paused to think. All this raincoat business was going to be hard to explain to Francis. Perhaps— She laid the raincoat on her desk. As she pondered she heard through the open door the buzzers that rang throughout the building at ten twenty-five as a warning that the doors would be shut in five minutes.

Immediately afterwards she heard a muffled, distant scream, or half a scream. The scream was broken in the middle by a crash. The sound came from the wing which held the Wilmerding Library.

The Library turned slowly upside down and began to describe a spiral. Gilda opened her mouth to scream. But she remained silent, with her mouth open. "Nonsense!" she said to herself. "Someone has dropped a dictionary or something! Enough to make any woman scream!" The Library ceased to spin and returned sheepishly to its foundations.

Still, the sounds demanded immediate investigation. A door, regularly unlocked, opened from the catalogue room to the stacks. Through this door and through the stacks Gilda hurried to the Wilmerding Library. As she entered she noticed that two or three lights were burning in the galleries. She snapped on the main overhead light.

Crumpled on the floor, amid splinters of broken glass, lay Lucie Coindreau. About her black hair was slowly spreading an ever-widening stain.

Chapter V

___

WHEN ONE enters the main door of the Library, one finds oneself in a large marble-floored lobby. To the left one mounts a
half-flight of stairs to the main reading-room, or one descends a
half-flight to a corridor leading to the periodical room and several seminaries, including the French Seminary. Opposite the
main entrance is a hall that gives entry to the various offices. To
the right is a stairway to the wing containing the Wilmerding
Collections.

The Wilmerding is the particular pride of the Library and
of the University, and Mr. Wilmerding is sanctified in the University's annals. Mr. Wilmerding made a great many millions in
railroads, during the third quarter of the last century. Retiring,
by the orders of his physician, from the collection of railroads, he
devoted all his magnificent energy to the collection of books. He
specialized in medieval manuscripts, fine bindings, philosophy,
Calvinist theology, the occult, and erotica. Books finally proved
more deadly than railroads. The ardor with which he collected
rarities hastened, if it did not cause, his fatal cerebral hemor-
rhage. In his will he left his collections to the University, with an
endowment for upkeep, and with the stipulation that the books

should be preserved in a separate collection, to be known as the Wilmerding Library.

His descendants later lost their fortune, which consisted mostly of railroad stock which the great financier had personally watered. Some threadbare members of the family still came occasionally to gaze vindictively at the treasures, and to tell the bored Librarian anecdotes about sitting on a Gutenberg Bible at the dinner-table when they were five years old.

The Wilmerding Library is a great deep well. Its floor plan is roughly that of a Romanesque chapel, cruciform, with deep rounded bays serving as transepts. The room is three tall stories in height. Two railed galleries make the complete circuit of the room, following the curves of the rounded bays. The railings are of wrought iron, coiled and twisted in incoherent designs. Books line the walls, from floor to ceiling. Occasional metal-scrolled wall-brackets jut out at the height of a woman's eye and of a man's teeth. It is a Library joke that the janitor can never get them quite clean of bloodstains. On the brackets stand mementoes bequeathed by Mr. Wilmerding: blue Bohemian glasses with his coat of arms, Dresden china vases with his portrait, bronze statuettes, by Augustus Saint-Gaudens, of his favorite trotting horse.

The Wilmerding Library is lit by several large ceiling lights, controlled by switches beside the main entrance door and the minor entrance from the stacks. Lights hang from cords, at five-foot intervals, along the line of the gallery rail, to aid searchers in the shadowed galleries. Spiral staircases at each corner and in the bays permit perpendicular circulation. On the ground floor of the north bay, or transept, is the main entrance. The top gal-

lery above the door is devoted to Occulta. The three levels of
the south bay, opposite, have been transformed into a locked
press. Here are kept the more valuable volumes of the Wilmerding Collection and the erotica. Heavy gratings run from floor
to ceiling of the locked press, flush with the main walls of the
south side. The only access to the locked press is by a door on the
ground floor. The two duplicate keys to the door are in the hands
of the Librarian and the Assistant Librarian, one of whom is
supposed to be present whenever the locked press is opened.

Within the locked press, against the south wall, stands a
great safe, once the property of a railroad. Mr. Wilmerding,
having by his astuteness emptied the safe of its valuables and
brought the railroad to bankruptcy, presented it to the Library,
for the protection of books excessively precious or astounding-
ly erotic.

On the ground floor of the north bay and in the crossing, or
center, of the room stand three show-cases. One contains several medieval manuscripts, another some rare incunabula and first
editions, the third some personal relics of Mr. Wilmerding, de-
posited there at the request of his heirs. There is a golden spike
which he hammered into place when the eastern and western
sections of the Chicago and Oregon met in the Rocky Mountains, and which, apparently, he immediately pulled out again.
There is a photograph of him shaking hands with the German
Kaiser, and one of him standing with his foot on the head of
a dead tiger, amid a swarm of flies; there is a wilted fur cap he
wore when, at the age of eighteen, he taught school in Apulia,
New York.

With all this *mise en scène* Gilda had long been affection-
ately familiar. She was fond of the Wilmerding; it was like the

old gentleman himself, she said: rich, tasteless, overpowering, a medley of wisdom and childish ostentation.

And now she was to find that mystery and blood could be at home in the Wilmerding Library, as it had in the man.

By the first of the show-cases, beneath the overhanging rail of the gallery, lay Lucie Coindreau.

When Gilda saw her, three conflicting impulses smote her simultaneously: to scream, to faint, and to be sick. For a small fraction of a second the three impulses fought for precedence. The scream won. It was a wild, full-throated scream. She then tottered, preparing to faint away from the body on the floor.

As she tottered, a steady arm caught her. "Easy there, Miss Gorham! Easy there! What's all this?"

It was Dr. Sandys. Gilda thought wildly that anyone should be able to recognize at a glance what all this was. But people have to say something, and you might as well say "What's all this?" as simply scream.

"I must see if she's dead—" said Dr. Sandys. "You all right, Miss Gorham? Stand against that case."

"I'm all right." Gilda suddenly knew that she was not going to faint or be sick. There were things that had to be done first.

Dr. Sandys knelt down and felt for Lucie Coindreau's heart.

"I can't feel anything. Looks as if she'd broken her neck. I've been afraid someone would go over those galleries. The first thing we want is a doctor. Miss Gorham, run down to the catalogue room—that's nearest—and telephone the President's house. Ask for Dr. Churchill or anyone else of the medical staff. Send him over on the run. Then get the President and tell him. Hurry."

Gilda took a step and almost fell. She seemed to have no sensation in her knees, and no control over her feet. "This won't do!" she said aloud. Angrily she forced her legs to work, as if she were just learning to walk.

She stepped on something small and round like a marble and steadied herself against a book-stack. Instinctively she stooped and picked up the object. It was Lucie Coindreau's little divining ball, her amulet of radiesthésie. Holding it by its string, Gilda wavered toward the door leading to the stacks and the catalogue room.

As she pushed the door open, Cameron brushed past her.

"Thought I heard a scream," he said.

Gilda gestured with her hand and went, with increasing sureness, to the stack entrance to the catalogue room.

She opened the door. The room was dark. She must have switched off the lights and shut the door automatically. Such is the power of habit.

At the telephone, she called the Presidential Mansion. Dr. Churchill, she found, was just leaving. She gave him her message. It took a little longer to get the President.

"I'll be right over," said President Temple. "And look here, Miss Gorham, don't touch anything and don't tell anybody. We can't have a lot of people barging in. Good-by."

Gilda hung up. Glancing around, she saw her raincoat on her desk. Untidy. Likely to cause comment in the morning. She put it away in her locker.

She felt a little stronger by the time she reached the Wilmerding once more. She saw Dr. Sandys and Cameron bending over the body. And there was a third figure—Francis Parry.

As she approached, Parry came to meet her. Silently he patted her on her bare shoulder. In the crook of his left arm he was carrying her blue-and-silver evening wrap. He threw it without a word about her shoulders.

Through the main door of the Wilmerding came Professor Casti, running. "Is it Lucie?" he cried. "I had a feeling—"

He looked at the body on the floor.

"Lucie!" he cried. He fell on his knees. "Lucie!" Gilda saw that he was weeping, in the horrible choking way that men weep. His right hand darted before his face. He was crossing himself.

Dr. Churchill entered through the main door. He bent down and examined the body. It did not take long.

"She's dead all right," he said. "How did it happen?"

"It looks clear enough," said Dr. Sandys. "She must have been up there, probably in the Occulta, on the top gallery. No doubt she was reaching up to turn on one of the lights. She's so short she could barely reach the key. Then she probably lost her balance and fell over."

"It could easily have happened that way," said Dr. Churchill.

"Those lights are strung out too far from the wall. But if you string them any closer, they will hit a tall man on the head. Probably we will have to put in higher-powered lights, fixed above the gallery runways, with wall-switches."

Gilda thought hysterically that in a crisis people seek to save themselves by taking a firm hold on the normal, as in a shipwreck one swims to safety on a kitchen table or something.

"What's that you've got in your hand?" Parry said to her.

She was still carrying the little divining ball.

"Here!" she said. "Here is Lucie's little radiesthésie gadget. I found it over by the Schopenhauer press."

"I'll keep it, if you like," said Dr. Sandys. "For—the authorities."

President Temple entered, bland, calm, and competent. Everything that could happen to a university president had happened to him. He knew what to do.

When the accident had been briefly explained, he took charge. "Violent death always has to be reported to the police," he said. "There has to be a coroner's inquest. Sandys, you call up the police. Casti, you go home. Cameron, you go outside the door there and stay on guard. We don't want a lot of people barging in here."

Everything was in good hands. And sudden acid fumes rose to Gilda's brain. Now she could faint. Now she was going to faint.

"Miss Gorham, you go home. Parry, you take Miss Gorham home. Come on, get out of here."

No, she would not faint after all. Parry took her arm and led her to the door and through the lobby. The fresh air blew through her thoughts.

"Can you walk to my car, in the parking area?" said Parry. "Or will you wait here while I get it?"

"I'd rather walk. I feel better."

They walked to the car in silence. In silence they drove to Gilda's apartment.

"Good night, Gilda," said Parry.

"Good night, Francis. . . . Francis!"

"Yes?"

"How did you happen to be in the Library?"

"Why, I got your coat, and then I looked for you at the Mansion for ten minutes or so. Then I got a little annoyed."

"But why did you go to the Library?"

"Well, if you must know, I wanted to go to the bathroom.

And the President doesn't make a very convenient provision for his guests. The Library was nearest, so I went there. And then I went out in the portico and lit a cigarette. It was such a beautiful night that I took a stroll around the Library. I had time enough to get back to the reception before ten thirty and, to tell the truth, I thought I would let you look for me a little."

"Did you hear the—the scream?"

"No. The exit bells rang, and it occurred to me that you might have run to your burrow in the catalogue room. I thought I would just take a look. So I went into the building and saw Sandys running up to the Wilmerding. Naturally, I followed."

"Naturally. Well, good night, Francis."

"Good night, Gilda. By the way—"

"Yes?"

"What were you doing in the Library?"

"Me? Why—why— Oh, let's not talk about it tonight."

"Certainly. Good night, Gilda."

"Good night, Francis."

Gilda shut the door and went to her bedroom. As she undressed it occurred to her that probably no one had seen her in the Library before her discovery of the body of Lucie Coindreau.

Chapter VI

THE FOLLOWING morning, Tuesday, September 30, Gilda woke
with a throbbing headache. She telephoned the Library that
she would not come in. She called the grocer, and spent the day,
thankfully, in a dressing-gown.

On Wednesday morning she attended, by command, the
Coroner's inquest, in a small room used for hearings in the
County Court House. Only a dozen chairs were disposed for
witnesses and visitors, and in fact not all the dozen were filled.
Gilda felt some relief as she looked about the room. If the town
had been whispering, or talking out loud, there would have been
an audience of drama-lovers.

She looked with approbation at the Coroner, Dr. Ingalls. He
was a hearty good fellow, elected largely by the co-operation
of his fellow members of the Lions, the Elks, the Moose, the
Oddfellows, and the Order of Red Men. Humanity's pal, he was
bound by many fraternal oaths to believe the best of mankind, to
boost, not knock. He was not one to go making trouble for folks.

The Medical Examiner testified that the deceased had come
to her death as a result of a broken neck. The fatal injury was evidently caused by a fall. The position of the body indicated that
the deceased had fallen from one of the galleries of the Wilm-

erding Library, had struck the show-case in her descent, and had landed on the back of her head, snapping the spinal column. Death had been instantaneous. No other injuries were noted, except some superficial wounds evidently caused by the body's striking against the show-case.

In response to a question from the Coroner, the Medical Examiner stated that a fall from either the first or second gallery might have caused the fatality. But the likelihood of the deceased's breaking her neck would have been considerably greater in the case of a fall from the upper gallery.

Lieutenant Kennedy of the city police was called. The lieutenant was a broad, hard-skinned, red-faced man with twinkling blue eyes. He had risen from the rank of patrolman by the merit or luck of never making a serious mistake.

Lieutenant Kennedy testified that he was called by telephone at ten thirty-seven p.m. That he had ordered the Desk Sergeant to call the Medical Examiner, and had arrived at the Wilmerding Library at ten forty-seven. He had examined the scene of the accident. The glass of the manuscript show-case was broken, but he was informed by Librarian Sandys that nothing was missing or disturbed. He had inspected the galleries. On the upper gallery he had observed a portable pair of steps, used, he was informed, for inspection or removing books on the top shelves of the book-presses. The steps were placed against the rail of the gallery, directly beneath a light which hung from the ceiling, on a line with the gallery rail. The light turned on and off by an ordinary key in the lamp-socket. This key was six feet eight inches above the level of the floor. The light was turned off.

This much was fact. When asked for an opinion, he replied: "This is only an opinion. A hypot'esis, you might say. Well now, this Miss Coindreau was just five foot one inch tall. She was dressed in a long skirt, which must have dragged on the ground. She couldn't hardly have reached the light standing on the floor. But if she put the portable step beneath the light, and then got up on the first or second step, and then had a dizzy spell maybe, or got her high heel caught in her gown, she could easily have lost her balance and tipped over the edge. That's the way I look at it, but it's just a hypot'esis."

Asked if he had noted any signs of her presence in the top gallery, he replied that he had found an evening bag, identified as that of Miss Coindreau, on the gallery floor, near the portable step. It was half open, but there was no sign of its being tampered with. He had further asked Mr. Cameron, the janitor, to make a check.

Mr. Cameron took the stand. He looked very distinguished in his neat blue serge suit. Though he was entirely respectful, there was something faintly supercilious, faintly mocking, in his manner. He reminded Gilda of something. After a minute or two she had it. He reminded her of an English country squire whom she had once visited. A thorough skeptic in the home, he had insisted on taking his house-party to the village church on Sunday, and, seated in the manor box-pew, had followed the service with the same air of not quite convincing reverence.

Cameron stated that he had found nothing amiss, except one trifling thing. A volume of the *Oracles of Nostradamus*, Paris, 1867, 4117 DP 808, was slightly out of place, being lodged between DP 812 and DP 813. Asked what this proved, he said that the misplacement showed only that someone had looked at the book since the summer checking and inventory. Asked if such misplacement was common, he answered that it was, very.

"How did Miss Coindreau get into this Wilmerding Collection?" asked the Coroner. "Is the door left unlocked?"

"Not usually. The main door, in the north bay, right beside where the body was found, is ordinarily locked. When I got there through the stacks, that door was open. I guess Dr. Sandys must have unlocked it with his key."

The Coroner picked out Dr. Sandys in the small audience. "Is this correct, Dr. Sandys?"

Dr. Sandys nodded.

"Then," said the Coroner, "there is an entrance through the stacks?"

"Yes, sir," replied Cameron, "on the ground floor of the Wilmerding. When there is a call for a Wilmerding book at the delivery desk, that's the way they send up a boy for it."

"Then you could get from any place in the stacks to the Wilmerding Library. How do you get into the stacks?"

"The main entrance is behind the delivery desk. But there are a dozen other ways of getting in. There are doors from the periodical room, and the reference room, and the catalogue room."

"Are those doors kept locked?"

"No, sir; there's a good deal of movement back and forth through them. And most of the seminaries open directly into the stacks, as well as into a hall. The seminary key opens any seminary door. So anybody with a seminary key can get into the stacks without being seen, if the seminary happens to be empty."

"Who has seminary keys?"

"I guess nearly all the faculty and most of the grad students. There are a lot more keys out than we can check on."

"Then Miss Coindreau could have gone into any of the seminaries without being observed, and through a door into the stacks, and up to this Occulta place without being seen?"

"Yes, sir. If it was me, and I wanted to get into the Occulta from the main entrance to the Library, I'd go through the Philosophy Seminary. You go up the same stair that leads to the main door to the Wilmerding, and then you go up two more flights and you come to the Philosophy Seminary. There's a door from that seminary that opens directly onto the third floor of the Wilmerding, where they keep a lot of philosophy books and such."

"Would there be anyone in the Philosophy Seminary who might have seen Miss Coindreau go through?"

"I've asked about that. The last person there was a Miss Labadie, a grad student. She went out at ten o'clock and turned out the lights."

"You seem to be very well informed, Mr. Cameron."

"I was interested. I guess I like to find out what goes on in this Library."

Cameron smiled apologetically. To Gilda, watching him closely, it seemed that his manner was condescending as well as apologetic.

Miss Gilda Gorham was called.

She described her discovery of the body, which she placed at ten twenty-six p.m., just after the ringing of the ten twenty-five exit buzzers. She volunteered the fact that on Monday morning Miss Coindreau had said she was going up to the Occulta, and that she was interested in Nostradamus. She told of the finding of the divining ball, and of Miss Coindreau's faith in radiesthésie.

The Coroner held up a small silvered leaden ball on a string.

"Is this the—er—radio-STZ thing?"

"It looks like it. It must be."

"Do you think Miss Coindreau could have dropped it easily?"

"Very easily. It was supposed to be held lightly by the knot in the string, between the thumb and finger."

"Perhaps she was performing some experiment and dropped it, and she was trying to turn on the light to look for it when she met with her fatal accident?"

"Possibly."

The Coroner seemed inclined to dismiss her. Gilda sighed with relief. He was not going to ask her how she happened to be in the Library. He was not going to uncover the fact that Gilda had followed Lucie there. Nor Lucie's surreptitious escape from the President's reception, and Casti's rather curious behavior. He was not going to bare the wild conjectures in Gilda's mind.

"Miss Gorham," said the Coroner, "there is one thing I want to ask you, purely as a matter of form, you understand."

Gilda's heart stilled and then beat more quickly.

"Do you know of any reason why Miss Coindreau might have wished to—ah—do away with herself?"

Gilda collected her swimming thoughts.

"None. She seemed happy and normal on Monday morning. As far as I know, she was perfectly well, and successful in her work."

"Did you ever hear of her being in financial difficulties?"

"Never. That would seem to me most unlikely."

"You don't know of any—ah—private or emotional troubles?"

"N-no."

"Thank you. You will understand that suicide is a painful possibility which must at least be considered. That is all, Miss Gorham."

Dr. Sandys and Dr. Churchill were then briefly examined. The Coroner retired, to consider the evidence. On entering his office, he picked up the morning paper, and read contentedly for fifteen minutes. He looked at the cross-word puzzle with a certain hankering, but resolutely laid the paper down. He returned to his small court and announced that after due deliberation he found that Miss Coindreau had come to her death as the result of an accident.

So that was that, thought Gilda. It was an accident. The Law had spoken. It was an accident, and thank God for that. Now she could stop thinking about it.

She went home to lunch, thinking about it.

After lunch she went to the Library and resumed the normal course of existence. The girls had got rather out of hand during her absence. She was obliged to put her foot down several times. An important auction catalogue had come in. Dr. Sandys wanted her opinion about an inter-library loan problem. Hillsville College, which had borrowed forty-seven books during the year, was making a fantastic fuss when asked to lend its one treasure, a first edition of *Moby Dick*.

About four in the afternoon the catalogue room fell into a sort of lull.

Gilda picked up her hand-bag and walked idly out of the room. But instead of turning left to the lobby and the women's rest room, she turned right to the stacks. She entered the Wilmerding Library, went up two flights of stairs to the upper gallery, and walked along it to the north bay, over the entrance door, over the display-case upon which Lucie Coindreau had fallen. She looked over the edge. There was no one in sight. It was a nasty drop; twenty-one feet from the gallery rail to the floor, she calculated.

Near by she found the portable steps which had apparently stood against the railing on the tragic evening. She carried the steps to the position they had then occupied. She mounted the bottom step and reached for the key of the hanging light. She was two or three inches taller than Lucie Coindreau. She touched the light-key and turned it without effort.

In imagination she was seized by a dizzy fit. She saw herself falling. . . .

She slumped down gently, well within the protection of the rail.

She tried it again, this time standing on the upper step. She dared to shut her eyes and sway a little She slipped down, inside the railing.

Of course this didn't prove anything. Naturally she wasn't going to fall over the railing just out of curiosity. And of course it was possible that, as had been suggested, Lucie had caught her high heel in her evening gown. Still—

Still, Lucie Coindreau didn't seem the type that had dizzy fits. She had boasted of climbing the Jungfrau and the Matterhorn in Switzerland. Women who are used to evening gowns and high heels don't often get them tangled up. Otherwise they would be tumbling down all over the place. Look at the way they walk up and down stairs without ever glancing down at their feet.

Gilda stood again on the step, trying to imagine that she was wearing a long gown and high heels, trying to imagine what would happen.

"Want a push, Miss Gorham?"

It was Cameron, who had come silently along the gallery.

Gilda attempted a freezing look. "Don't be impertinent, Cameron."

"Fresh is what the girls used to call me. I was watching you, Miss Gorham. You settled a point for me."

"You seem to be very much interested in this unfortunate accident."

"I was a detective once. Were you ever a detective?"

"Certainly not."

"Well, you act like one. You're reconstructing the accident." Cameron paused and surveyed the scene with a careful eye. "What's more, you're showing it's just like I thought. Anybody standing on that step and losing his balance would most likely fall inside the rail. Unless—"

"Unless what?"

"Unless they were pushed."

"But who would want to push Miss Coindreau?"

"That's just what I was wondering. Just like you."

"It seems to me, Cameron, that if you have any good reason to believe that Mademoiselle Coindreau's death was not due to an accident, but to—well, to being pushed, it's your duty to report it to the police."

"Maybe it is, but I ain't going to do it."

"It seems to me—"

"And I'll tell you why. In the first place, the police have got the case all nicely closed up, and they aren't going to open it up again just because I think maybe there was some funny business. After all, she *could* have tripped and fallen over, just like they said. But if they have to investigate a suspected murder, they've got to go poking their noses into the private affairs of half the people on this campus. They'll raise a stink you can smell from here to Chicago. Folks in Chicago will be saying: 'My, what's got into the stockyards today? They must be canning skunks today.' Well, that's the kind of stink they'll raise, but they probably won't find out who did the pushing.

"Then in the second place I won't say anything because I never did think much of Miss Coindreau, and if some guy pushed her over she probably deserved it, and I don't see it's going to help anything to have him go to the big house for the rest of his life, where they tell me the library is terrible."

"You don't seem to have much sense of your duty as a citizen."

"Maybe not. I never did like the cops much."

"But apparently you are trying to find out something about this—matter."

Cameron grinned. "I kind of like to know what's going on. Now, Miss Gorham, I know just what you're going to say."

"What?"

"You're going to say: 'You and me both, kid!'"

Gilda laughed, in spite of herself. Cameron walked away, showing his self-satisfaction in his jaunty manner.

After taking a few steps he turned around and came back.

"If you're going to be a detective, Miss Gorham, I'll tell you something. Maybe it's a clue. You know, Monday night the President told me to watch the door to the Wilmerding. Well, that Prof Casti came out, and he sure did look as though he'd been kicked in the belly. I watched him go down the stairs, but he didn't go out toward the lobby. He turned the other way. And I was just curious enough to follow him. I used to be a pretty good tail. Well, he went down to the French Seminary, and he went to the big table with the drawers in it assigned to the profs and grad students, and he took out a knife and pried away at one of the drawers. But he couldn't get it open, and after a while he left. I went down again later, and I saw the drawer had a label on it: 'Asst. Prof. Coindreau.'"

"You haven't opened the drawer since?"

"It wouldn't be right for me to open a private drawer," said Cameron, with an air of simpering virtue. "Anyhow, I would have had to make a false key."

"I think I had better have a look at that."

The two descended to the French Seminary. The room was empty. Cameron pointed out the drawer to Gilda. The lock was a cheap and simple one; its bolt extended upward, engaging with the solid framework of the table. The bolt was clearly visible in the gap of nearly an eighth of an inch between the top of the drawer and the table's frame. Around the bolt were fresh and jagged marks, such as a sharp knife-blade might have made.

"Umm," said Gilda. "This drawer should be reassigned to someone else."

"It is our duty to open it, isn't it, Miss Gorham?"

"Cameron, suppose you go up and ask Miss McDougal at the delivery desk if she hasn't a duplicate key to this drawer. It's number 14."

"Whatever you think is right, Miss Gorham," grinned Cameron.

In a few minutes he had returned with the duplicate key. The drawer was readily opened. In it Gilda found a lipstick, a photograph of a handsome young man in a pullover sweater, inscribed: "*Toujours*—Armand," half a dozen notes on "*L'Amour chez les poètes romantiques,"* a pad of thesis slips, two pencils, and a chocolate covered with a fuzzy gray deposit.

"I can't imagine what Mr. Casti would be wanting here," said Gilda.

"Maybe this Armand boy has got something to do with it. You would be surprised at some of the stories I could tell you."

"I don't think I could stand such surprises. I think I'll just keep this collection until something is done about the settlement of Mademoiselle Coindreau's estate. Then I'll turn them over to the proper person, of course."

"Even the chocolate?"

"You can have the chocolate. Here." She pushed the chocolate toward Cameron with a ruler.

"I never accept presents from ladies," said Cameron primly, pushing the object on into the waste-basket.

Chapter VII

Gilda returned to the catalogue room at about half past four and attempted to resume her unfinished tasks. After making three outrageous mistakes in three minutes, she gave up the effort. She made a negligent barricade of books on her desk, took out her pen, and tried to give the appearance of writing busily. She covered the sheet of paper with a series of comic faces in profile, all looking to the left.

Behind her defenses she meditated.

Just suppose that someone had, in fact, pushed Lucie. Who could possibly have done such a thing?

Under one of the grotesque faces she wrote the name: Casti. After a pause, she wrote another name: Hyett.

Motive and opportunity were what mystery-story detectives required. Better not go into motive at this point. Only a mind-reader could know the motive. Better restrict herself to opportunity. Who had opportunity?

She wrote down: Sandys. She thought a moment, and wrote: Cameron.

Anyone else? She had noticed Lucie talking earnestly to Mr. Belknap at the President's reception. Of course, that didn't prove much, but still—

She wrote down: Belknap.

Then, as if she were idly making marks on the paper, in a kind of automatic writing, she set down: Parry. She looked at the name and drew a firm line through it. And then she wrote again, with determination: Parry.

Then there was always the unknown. X, they called him. Gilda had absorbed a good deal of scholarly priggishness in the University. She would call him Ignotus. Under a horrible profile she wrote: Ignotus.

And then, half smiling, she wrote: Gilda Gorham.

Now what did she know about the opportunity of these people?

Perhaps it would be a good thing to make a time-table.

Where should she begin? What could she take as a starting-point, a *terminus a quo,* as Hyett liked to say? Perhaps the time when she and Francis had gone out on the terrace of the Presidential Mansion. As she tried to live again that moment, she seemed to hear the tolling of the Library clock. That was convenient. She wrote:

"10 p.m. Gilda and F. P. go out on terrace."

How long had they talked? Five minutes? It seemed like more than five minutes. Ten minutes? Less than ten minutes. She had smoked a cigarette. Once, in some sort of parlor game, she had been timed smoking a cigarette. She had thrown it away at the end of eight minutes. She wrote down:

"10.08. G. asks for wrap. F. P. leaves."

From then on, things were pretty clear.

"10.09. Lucie appears.

"10.10. Casti appears. G. follows L."

How long did it take to get from the Presidential Mansion

to the Library? A fast walker could do it in two or three minutes. But she was sidling along through the dark garden, following Lucie, who had seemed to be hurrying, without making very high speed in her high heels and evening gown. Five minutes. She had looked at her watch in the rest room, and it had been a quarter past. It all fitted nicely.

"10.15. L. enters Library. G. goes to rest room."

She must have been there about five minutes when Casti and Sandys had entered.

"10.20. C. and S. enter. G. goes to catalogue room.

"10.25. Exit bell.

"10.25. Tragedy.

"10.26. G. arrives on scene. Then Sandys."

She had then been sent to the catalogue room. And she passed Cameron on the way.

"10.28. Cameron arrives."

How long had she spent telephoning? Perhaps three minutes. And Francis had been present when she returned to the Wilmerding.

"10.28–10.30. Parry arrives.

"10.31. G. returns to Wilmerding.

"10.31. Casti arrives.

"10.33. Churchill arrives.

"10.34. Pres. Temple arrives.

"10.37. G. and F. P. leave."

That was about it. Probably some small errors here and there, but pretty close. Now what did it show, if anything?

She looked back at her list of names.

Casti. Gossip said that Casti had had an affair with Lucie, and that they were now on the outs, and rivals for advancement.

Casti was grimly ambitious, a scholastic go-getter. Perhaps he would be unscrupulous in attaining his ends, though Gilda admitted she had never heard any such specific accusation. Would he be capable, in a fit of anger, of giving his inconvenient rival just a little push? It wouldn't be a very sensible thing to do, for, after all, the chances were that Lucie would survive her fall, at least long enough to denounce her assailant. But no one said it was sensible.

Casti's actions on the fatal evening had been very peculiar. He had been talking with Lucie at the reception; he had come out on the terrace at 10.10, evidently looking for her. But she had left secretly at 10.09. Why? Was she escaping from him? Did she plan to meet someone in the Library? Whom? (Even in her thoughts Gilda said "whom.") Perhaps she planned to meet Casti there and had preferred to walk over alone, in order not to be seen with him.

Casti, on entering the Library, had gone in the direction of the French Seminary. Cameron had hinted that Casti was trying to get something out of Lucie's drawer. Was he working at the drawer before the tragedy as well as after? What was he hunting for? One of the miscellaneous objects she had found in the drawer? Or had he succeeded in prying out whatever it was he was after?

Then there was the very curious remark he had made on entering the Wilmerding. "Is it Lucie?" he had said. How did he know that anything had happened? He could have heard the scream if he had been near the Wilmerding, but not if he had been in the French Seminary. If he had heard the scream, why had it taken him—let's see—six minutes to reach the Wilmerding?

All very mysterious. Could he have been in the Occulta with Lucie at 10.25?

She looked at her time-table. Casti had gone to the French Seminary at 10.20. There was small chance that anyone else would be there at that hour. He could have gone into the stacks and followed a devious course to the Wilmerding without being seen. And then, after perhaps a brief quarrel, terminating in one fatal push, he could have gone back the same way, easily avoiding herself and Cameron. Certainly it was possible.

Except that it just didn't seem likely. Well, probably no murder seemed likely. In fact, it probably wasn't likely. Still—

Hyett. There was a pretty funny one. Sex-obsessed. A mental rake. But the campus agreed that the mental rake was harmless. You might as well expect to be struck by heat-lightning as by Old Harmless. Nevertheless, it is notorious that when men get to be about sixty, they sometimes go suddenly wild. The glands, probably. Mr. Hyett knew all about sadism and things like that. It might be possible that he had just boiled over, terribly.

But this was all speculation. Where was he at 10.25? At the President's reception?

Gilda made a mental note to ask when Mr. Hyett had left the President's house. Come to think of it, she was to have dinner with the Nobles this very evening. And Mr. Hyett was deputed to call for her. Maybe she could bring up the matter. Adroitly, if possible.

She looked at the sheet before her.

Sandys. Dear good Dr. Sandys! Why, that was just ridiculous!

She started to draw a line through his name, but held her pen poised. How about opportunity?

Dr. Sandys had gone to his office at 10.20, and there he had certainly been alone. A door opened from his office to the stacks. By that course he could get to the Occulta in about thirty seconds. Just supposing—. He could have committed the—thing at 10.25, and then have run down to his office through the stacks, and run back by way of the outer corridor and stairs, and entered the main door of the Wilmerding just after Gilda had arrived. Yes, it was possible.

With a guilty feeling, she raised her pen, leaving the name untouched.

Cameron.

He was a strange fellow, with a mysterious past. He didn't like the police. He said he had been a detective; but detectives work with the police, don't they? He was a good deal of a cynic, and was always completely self-assured. He was the sort of person who would not break down, and show weakness or remorse. If he had done something evil, he would be rather pleased with himself than otherwise. But why should he do something evil, something so frightfully evil? Well, men did do funny things sometimes. You couldn't read the books in a great library without knowing that.

Gilda shuddered. She thought of Francis's remark that Lucie was the sort that roused the beast in men.

And she recalled a recent report that had disturbed the campus. A young student and a co-ed, sitting on a stone bench late in the evening, perfectly innocently, or so they alleged, had been attacked from the rear by a man with a stick. Could that have been Cameron?

How did his actions appear on her time-table?

When Cameron was on duty in the evenings, as he had been on Monday, he made the round of the stacks, beginning at about ten o'clock, shutting the fire-doors that separated the various sections. He could have been in the Wilmerding at 10.25. When Gilda came running in through the door to the Wilmerding, he could have concealed himself, and then he could have merely gone out through the same door and waited, and then hurried in again after a proper interval. She remembered that he had brushed against her when she was rushing out to the catalogue room to telephone. That was 10.28, wasn't it? Yes, 10.28.

"No alibi for Mr. Cameron," she thought.

Then there was Belknap. There was really not much reason for putting him down. Except that he was a funny fellow too. A queer blend of force and shyness. She remembered a remark of Francis's: "He looks like a cross between De Valera and Upton Sinclair. I don't trust these tall, thin, stooping men, any more than Shakespeare did. That's the fanatic build. If they decide to live on nuts and roots, they would just as soon kill anybody that eats a steak."

But why? Why? What earthly reason would Belknap have for pushing poor Lucie Coindreau to her death? Not money, certainly. Not professional rivalry. Love, possibly? A lovers' quarrel? If Belknap had been carrying on with Lucie, the industrious campus FBI would have known about it. And then the idea was preposterous. Belknap was too genuinely austere, a priest of scholarship. Thirty years of devotion to historical truth had made a channel for his spirit, a channel from which he was not likely to be dislodged by some chance temptation. He had the piquant reputation of being a woman-hater, but woman-haters don't go so far as to destroy the female sex. They just run away. Come to think of it, there was Schopenhauer, who was quite a woman-hater. He attacked and maimed for life a lady who gave a coffee-party in the anteroom of his lodgings, without his permission. But that hardly fitted the present case. The worst you could suppose of Belknap was that he might fall foul of the Muse of History. Clio, wasn't it? That was really pretty good. She must tell that to Francis. A scholar who came from Ohio—. Belknap didn't come from Ohio, in fact; from Connecticut. But that was a small matter. A scholar who came from Ohio was so deeply entangled with Clio—. Francis would have to finish it. She could never get beyond the second line.

But where was Belknap at 10.25? That was something else she would have to find out.

Francis. Gay, frolicsome Francis a murderer? She felt ashamed even to formulate the thought. He took everything too easily, life, himself, herself. He would avoid with fastidious horror any tragic, terrible act. He was a talker, not a doer. She knew him through and through—

But no, come to think of it, she did not know him through and through, and had told him so only a few minutes before the dreadful happening. There were things he had never told her, parts of his life, parts of his thought, that he protected by a zone of laughter. He seemed to be very knowledgeable about women, but he had never mentioned a name, never revealed whether or not he had ever had a real love affair. Of course he must have had, a fascinating bachelor of forty. At one time campus rumor had said that he had fallen for Lucie Coindreau. But there was nothing tangible; they were seldom seen together, and never surprised in what is prettily known as a compromising situation. Naturally, it wouldn't make any difference to Gilda if they had had any kind of affair. After all, it wasn't normal for grown-up men to lead a monastic existence, without even the reward of monasticism, the hope of heaven. But he was almost too careful, too secretive. If she was going to—to marry Francis, she wanted to know all the truth about him.

Where was Francis at 10.25?

He had gone for her wrap at about 10.08. A minute to get her cloak. 10.09. He had said that he had looked for her for about ten minutes. That made it 10.19. Then he had gone to the Library, to go to the men's room. 10.21 to 10.23. He had gone out to the portico to smoke a cigarette, had walked around the Library, and had heard the exit bell at 10.25. Then he had re-entered the Library and had seen Sandys running up to the Wilmerding, at 10.27. He had not followed in hot haste, for he had entered the Wilmerding at least a minute or two after Sandys. That was like him, to pause and reflect a moment before acting, for fear of acting rashly.

But supposing he had not gone out to the portico at all? Supposing he had gone up to the Occulta, any time from about 10.21 on, and had settled matters with Lucie? It was possible. He could have escaped into the stacks, and out into the main corridors through one of the seminaries. The easiest way would have been to go through the Philosophy Seminary, and so down the stairs to the Wilmerding entrance door, as soon as Sandys was inside.

One thing would prove an alibi. If anyone had seen him in the portico, smoking his cigarette at the crucial moment, or entering just afterwards, he could not have committed any murder.

That was the whole list, wasn't it? No, there were two more names: Gilda Gorham and Ignotus. There was always Ignotus.

Well, Gilda knew she hadn't done it. She was in the catalogue room at the time.

But she was alone there. In fact, no one had seen her, so far as she knew, from the time Parry had left her at the President's house—let's see, 10.08—until she was found screaming beside Lucie's body at 10.26. That was really unfortunate. Supposing someone wanted to pin the thing on her, to frame her, as they said in mystery stories.

Certainly it would have been possible for her to give Lucie a push and then to run down one of the spiral staircases, to look at the body on the floor, and scream. It would have taken no longer, less long in fact, than the time she had spent in running from the catalogue room to the ground floor of the Wilmerding. She had, in short, opportunity.

Of course, no one could allege motive. There was no question of gain, or of ambition, or love, or jealousy.

Jealousy! Suppose someone was thinking about her at this moment as she had been thinking about her friends on the faculty! Suppose they said: "Gilda has been going around a lot with Francis Parry. And Parry was all tangled up with Lucie Coindreau a year or so ago. Maybe the two girls were fighting about a man, up there in the Occulta. And maybe one of them got pushed over. . . ."

But this was all nonsense! If anyone should make such a foolish statement, she would shout her denial!

However, there was no one else to support her denial. The only person who could deny it was dead.

It was silly of her ever to have got going on this train of thought. It would be even more silly of her to start in asking questions, making trouble. It wouldn't be impossible, if she began making trouble for somebody, for somebody to make trouble for her. Very terrible trouble.

Put the whole thing out of mind and come back to normal.

She looked up. The catalogue room was emptied of its staff. The girls had gone home. No doubt, in her abstraction, she had nodded good-night to them without even realizing it. It was already a quarter past five. She must be going home, to get ready for dinner at the Nobles'.

There was something else, though. On the morning of Monday, September 29, Lucie Coindreau was talking with a man in the Occulta. Cameron had heard them. Or he had said he had heard them. And Lucie had said something funny. She had said—what was it?—"papoose"!

Why in the world should she have said "papoose"?

Perhaps it was French.

Gilda got up and walked to the dictionary rack.

On the way she noticed Professor Belknap, in the alcove that contained the foreign library catalogues. He was looking up something in the new British Museum Catalogue.

"How do you do, Mr. Belknap?" she said. He nodded in reply.

There was no "papoose" or "papouce" in the dictionary. "Pappeuse," maybe; feminine for "pappose; downy. (*Bot.*)" Or "papuleuse"; feminine for "pimply. (*Fam.*)" It didn't seem likely that Lucie Coindreau would have exclaimed forcefully that something feminine and botanical was downy, or that some feminine noun was pimply in a familiar way. There was "papyrus." Maybe Lucie was mentioning a papyrus, and Cameron rationalized it into "papoose." But that didn't make much sense either.

Come to think of it, there was something else she wanted to know. Where was Professor Belknap at 10.25?

"Oh, Mr. Belknap!"

"Yes, Miss Gorham?" Professor Belknap was, as always, cavernously polite.

"What an awful ending to the President's reception!"

"Wasn't it, indeed?"

"But the President was wonderful! The way he took charge! I think I should have fainted if he hadn't controlled everything so magnificently."

"It must have been a very trying ordeal for you."

"What did they think at the reception when the President went rushing away?"

Professor Belknap smiled with his usual appearance of effort.

"I am afraid I cannot tell you. I had already gone home."

"Oh. I thought it a very pleasant reception, as they go. Such nice little sandwiches."

"Oh yes. Very. If one cares for receptions."

Professor Belknap stood with his finger in a page. He showed the slightest indication of impatience. Gilda nodded brightly to him and returned to her desk.

So. Belknap had gone home early. Unless someone had seen him in the Faculty Club, he had no alibi.

Professor Belknap left the catalogue room with a distraught nod.

Cameron entered the room, silently. He must always wear rubber soles, thought Gilda. Old quiet Cameron. He was shutting the office windows, on schedule.

"Cameron!"

"Yes, Miss Gorham?"

"Where were you on Monday night when you heard the scream?"

"Down in the stacks somewhere, shutting the fire-doors. I don't remember exactly where. Why?"

"I was just wondering."

"You're getting to be quite a detective, aren't you?"

"I wonder about things."

"So do I. For instance, I wonder how you happened to be in the catalogue room just before closing-time."

"I just stopped in to get something."

"Your raincoat, maybe? Your old black raincoat?"

"So it was you who turned out the lights in the catalogue room and shut the door?"

"Of course it was me. That raincoat must have looked kind of funny with your evening costume."

"Cameron, all this is certainly no business of yours."

"And all the time Professor Parry had your evening wrap over his arm. Wonder what was going on, exactly."

"What are you trying to get at, Cameron?"

"Nothing. I ain't a detective any more. But I was just thinking that if anybody should start stirring things up around here, they might stir up more than they intended. I don't hold with stirring up a row in this nice quiet Library. I like peace and quiet. Academic peace, like they say. Well, I'll be on my way."

And all this, thought Gilda, was clearly meant as a warning. A warning to keep out of trouble. A warning that she was in the trouble herself.

And Cameron could have murdered Lucie, and then have run to the catalogue room, perhaps to hide, naturally snapping off the lights and shutting the door. And then he could have thought better of it and returned to the Wilmerding to check in, as it were. It all fitted with her schedule.

This was serious. She would like to talk it over with some-one—someone she could trust.

Not with the police. That Lieutenant Kennedy would just laugh at her, tell her to go home and not get hysterical.

She glanced at her list. Not with Casti, Hyett, Sandys, Belk-nap, Parry. Any one of them might be the—the one.

There seemed to be no one she could trust!

She laughed, a little wildly, and looked around in a kind of desperation. She saw no one. But she did see that it was past six o'clock.

Heavens! She must be getting home to dress for the Nobles' dinner!

Chapter VIII

When, at a few minutes before seven, Professor Hyett called for Gilda, she was almost ready. With old-world gallantry, mingled with affectionate pats, he escorted her to his car. The two paused before the shimmering maroon convertible coupé at the curb.

"Why, that's a new car, isn't it, Mr. Hyett? What a beauty!"

"It is nice, isn't it? Would you like the top down? Such a warm evening for the season."

"Oh, I think it's all right as it is."

But Professor Hyett started the engine, pushed a lever, and proudly watched the top fold itself neatly, pack itself away, and tuck itself in. He laughed with glee.

"Wonderful! But I'd really rather have it up. Windblown hair, you know, only goes with tweeds and long tramps over the moors with the faithful bird-dogs."

"No trouble at all." Hyett pulled the lever, and the buried top stirred, peered forth, shook itself out, groped aloft, climbed over their heads, and fumbled at the windshield top, struggling, apparently, to fasten itself on.

"Eleven seconds!" exclaimed Hyett in triumph.

He talked of cars for several blocks. Gilda sought in vain

for an opening. Finally, at a pause before a traffic light, she decided to dispense with a neat transition and come to the point.

"I had to go to the inquest on Lucie Coindreau this morning," she said.

"My dear Miss Gorham! What an experience for you!"

"It was pretty terrible, from first to last."

Professor Hyett made a noise indicative of sympathy and encouragement to forget and lead a new life.

"You didn't see her after the—accident, did you?" said Gilda.

"No. In fact, I didn't hear of it until next morning, when I opened my paper."

"Oh. You weren't at the reception at the time, then?"

"No. Fact is, rather a funny thing occurred. I happened to look into the small reception room, and the President and Mrs. Temple and Colonel Sloan were standing there all alone. And I thought it a shame that everyone should desert our poor President at his own reception, so I stepped up and murmured something to Mrs. Temple about its being a lovely party. She turned on me with a start—you know how distraught she is—and put out her hand and said: 'Oh, I'm so sorry, Mr. Hewlett!' And then there was nothing to do but shake her hand and say goodnight to the President."

Gilda laughed. "That must have been right in the middle of things?"

"Oh yes. I don't suppose it was much more than ten o'clock."

"And no one brought the news of the accident to the Faculty Club?"

"I don't think there was anyone around. I went right to my room, myself."

"So," thought Gilda, "if this is true, and it can easily be verified, Hyett has no alibi."

The car turned down one of the campus roads and stopped in front of Professor Noble's residence.

The Nobles' house was built in the eighties, in an apparently unpremeditated combination of brick, stone, stucco, and wood. It was spacious and comfortable, in its wide-arched, wide-windowed, golden-oak manner. True, its component parts were now separating, and in winter jets of icy air blew on the backs of callers' necks. The original occupant, obviously sentimental about his home, had carved mottoes celebrating peace on the stone fireplaces and on wooden panels. "Peace rules the day, where reason rules the mind"; "Be blest with health, and peace, and sweet content"; *"Über allen Gipfeln ist Ruh."* The appropriateness of the mottoes had passed with time, for Professor and Mrs. Noble notoriously fought like tigers, largely about the economic interpretation of history. Professor Noble was an orthodox economist, while Mrs. Noble, who had her Ph.D. also, was a more radical thinker. At the mention of Pareto or Veblen the Noble children began to cry, knowing that all hell was about to break loose.

The dinner was in honor of Professor and Mrs. Sparhawk, of the University of Rhode Island. Professor Sparhawk was being looked over for the vacant chair of Money and Banking. He was the devout, earnest type of professor; he tried to organize his life on economic principles. Aware of the outrageous cost of tooth-powder, he bought the ingredients wholesale and mixed them. He had nearly half a barrel of tooth-powder in his cellar, with a queer sort of mushroom growing in it. He deplored the waste of household time spent in washing dishes, and had given his wife a hundred gross of paper dishes for a wedding present. He tried to put in practice his theories, about the benefit of the barefoot life, about the edibility of alfalfa. His wife, a wholesome, homey woman, abjectly admired his giant intellect, while treating him in the house as an imbecile child. For the rest, the pair were painfully poor, since Professor Sparhawk put all his surplus into the stock market, testing out his convictions on the behavior of money. He was always right, he insisted, but so far never at exactly the right time.

Professor Sparhawk had passed his preliminary tests, on scholarship, publications, and teaching record. The social qualifications remained to be settled, for in the close-knit college community it is important that the relations of husbands and wives of a department be harmonious, or at least not openly hostile.

Gilda and Professor Hyett saluted their hostess and host, and were presented to the guests of honor. In a moment Professor Parry entered, bringing Miss Cornwell, from the Library.

Gilda understood all about the party immediately. The hostess had been anxious to lift the pall of Social Studies for the evening. Parry and Hyett had been asked because they were amusing and would make any party go. She was included because she was bright and pleasant and knew what people were talking about, and Irene Cornwell because she was an extra girl. The party was limited to eight, because that is the best number for general conversation, and all that one girl in the kitchen can handle. Parry, of course, had been asked to call for Irene, as Hyett had been told off to get Gilda.

Cocktails and canapes appeared. There was some small talk on subjects of common scholastic concern. Professor Sparhawk gazed meditatively at his cocktail, for which he could find no justification in a rational society. Deciding, however, to accept the social mores of his host, and to get the thing out of the way, he drank it off. His wife, watching him closely, gratefully sipped at hers.

"Very refreshing, very prophylactic," said Professor Hyett. "Tell me, Noble, what are you doing about the vermouth situation?"

"I still have some of the French. The domestic is passable, I think, but it certainly isn't the same thing."

"I don't see why we can't make a good substitute for vermouth in this country," said Professor Sparhawk. "Vermouth is just a white wine exposed to the sun, fortified with alcohol, and flavored with herbs. To me the flavor is not unlike that of bay rum. It would be interesting to try baking some white wine to approximate the effect of the sun, and then mix it with a little bay rum. It might prove very satisfactory."

"I'll just take a dash of Flit in mine!" said Professor Hyett, shuddering.

Mrs. Noble, noticing that Professor Sparhawk's glass was empty, refilled it. He protested feebly. He definitely didn't like the stuff. But he was proud of doing disagreeable jobs immediately and scrupulously. He up-ended his glass and set it down on a table.

Professor Hyett found himself pocketed with Mrs. Sparhawk. "What nice weather for golf!" she said. "Are you fond of golf, Mr. Hyett?"

"I used to play a little. But I found it a very morbid game."

"Morbid? I'm afraid—"

"It is an introspective game. In any other game, such as tennis, the player is always thinking about his opponent. 'What is that fellow going to do? Where is he going to put the ball?' And one extroverts, to the good of one's soul. But in golf one is always thinking: 'How are my feet? My hands? My stance? My swing? Yesterday I got a five on this hole. Can I, today, beat myself, yesterday?' It is significant that in golf one must always keep one's head down, one's eyes on the ground. Never look up! All this is very unhealthy. The popularity of golf is symptomatic of the introversion that is the curse of the modern spirit."

"I think golf is a very nice game."

"Golf?" said Mrs. Noble, passing with a cocktail shaker. She noticed that Professor Sparhawk's glass was empty and filled it full. "Golf? Whenever I pass the golf course, I am shocked to see that great stretch of arable land going to waste. It would make two subsistence farms. There must be twenty men who do nothing from morning to night except take care of that grass, so it will be just the right length for grown-up men to play on! Hah!"

Professor Sparhawk perceived the full glass beside him. He was under the impression that he had just emptied it. Well, he must have been mistaken. The best of us make mistakes. He drained the glass hardily.

"The reason I gave up golf," said Professor Hyett, "was not fear of introspection. It was because my ball was so constantly in the rough. I grew tired of taking as my motto: *'Per aspera ad astra.'*"

He looked around quickly. Nobody was smiling. He translated hastily: "Through the rough to the stars."

Still nobody smiled. "These economists!" thought Professor Hyett. The unlettered hinds in our modern universities! How his little joke would have rung through the common rooms of Oxford or Cambridge! Oh dear, why wasn't he born in England?

Mrs. Noble noticed that Professor Sparhawk's glass was again empty. She frowned. But she knew her duty as a hostess. Grimly she refilled the glass.

"Golf?" said Professor Parry, joining the group, with Gilda at his side. "You know, Hyett, I have a fine idea for a murder."

Gilda, with her eyes on Hyett, saw him stiffen and cast a quick look at Parry.

"You know," pursued Parry, "the problem of the murderer is always what to do with the body. You can't just leave it kicking around. And you can't bury it most places without leaving one of those telltale mounds of fresh-turned soil. So do you know what I would do?"

"I can't imagine, my dear fellow."

"Bury it in a sand-trap. Easy to dig, and when you are through, you just smooth the sand over it again, and nobody knows the difference."

"I am glad I gave up golf. I should hate to try a deep explosion shot some day and bring up a big toe."

"I think you could take the shot over without penalty. Temporary obstruction, you know. But when I bury 'em, I bury 'em deep!"

Gilda looked sharply at Parry, and looked away.

She noticed that Mrs. Noble, tight-lipped, was refilling Professor Sparhawk's glass.

Dinner was announced. Professor Sparhawk looked at his glass with an appearance of great surprise. He lifted it to his lips and tossed it off.

During the soup Professor Sparhawk fell into a brown study. Mrs. Noble, at his left, tried to bring him out on current problems of the gold supply and international barter. He answered in solemn monosyllables.

During the roast, a crown roast of lamb, always so safe, Professor Sparhawk spoke, compellingly.

"I hear you had an accident here. A sad accident. A sad, sad accident." His lips worked with emotion.

"Roger!" said his wife sharply. He snapped to attention.

There was a moment of silence. Almost a ritual silence, thought Parry, like the moment when the faculty stands mute in faculty meeting, in respect to a dead colleague.

"I wonder what they are going to do in the department?" said Mrs. Noble. The question could properly be discussed in public two days after a death.

"Oh, I think Casti will get his raise to Associate," said Professor Noble. "For the student-contact work, they'll probably bring in a younger person, an instructor, maybe. Thus the administration will be able to make a net reduction in the departmental budget."

"Casti has published a sufficient number of pages," said Professor Hyett. "I confess that I cannot understand them; the language of phonetics is one that I have never thought it necessary to learn."

"Mademoiselle Coindreau, I believe, was not a producer," said Mrs. Noble.

Parry turned to Gilda, at his side. "You aren't taking part in settling the affairs of the Department of Romance Languages?"

"No. I don't feel like it."

"A bit ghoulish, eh? And you were fond of Lucie?"

"N-no. Not really fond of her. But I am shocked."

"And maybe a little puzzled?"

"Are you?"

"Well, naturally, a little. No one has ever fallen over those railings before. I wonder how she happened to do it."

"That's what I was wondering." And to herself Gilda said that she wondered, also, what Francis really thought, and what he really knew. She was aware that he was not going to tell her. He was really too secretive.

Dessert appeared. It was fruit, and crackers, and a mound of ominous blue-veined cheese.

"This is a domestic Roquefort," said Mrs. Noble. "Not quite like real Roquefort, of course, but we think it's very good."

"No, thanks," said Miss Cornwell. "I'm afraid I don't like goat's milk cheese."

"But Roquefort is made of ewe's milk, I believe."

"We are very restricted in our cheeses," said Professor Hyett. "The Romans prized ass's milk cheese very highly."

Professor Sparhawk roused himself from meditation. "In Lapland, reindeer cheese is one of the principal staples. The yak butter of Tibet is fermented, and might be called a cheese. There is no reason why cheese can't be made from any mammal."

"Imagine trying to milk a giraffe!" said Miss Cornwell with a pretty shriek.

"Or a whale!" added Professor Parry.

"The milk of the whale is not drawn forth by a vacuum process, as in the case of the cow," said Professor Sparhawk, with an inspired air. "The mother whale actually ejects the milk into the mouth of her offspring."

Parry was delighted. "It would be necessary to deceive the

mother whale, perhaps by means of a small submarine built in the form of a baby whale. The mother whale probably couldn't bend round far enough to see what was milking her."

"But how are you going to locate your whales in the first place?" said Hyett.

"A nice question. Obviously it would be awkward and expensive to chase them all over the Antarctic. If we're going into the whale-cheese business commercially we must have our whales always available, to ensure regularity of output. I would transport the whales to some deep salt-water lake."

"How about the Great Salt Lake?"

"No," said Gilda. "I've been to the Great Salt Lake. It's so salty that you just float on it. The whales wouldn't be able to submerge, and it's so hot and dry that they would get sunburned."

"I have it!" said Parry. "Did you ever see Cayuga Lake, in central New York?"

"No."

"Well, it's handy to the New York luxury markets, and it's a convenient size and depth. The New York State College of Agriculture is in Ithaca, at the head of the lake, with fine facilities for the study of dairy industry, fish culture, animal husbandry, and veterinary science. And there are salt works along the shore. There are great salt beds under the lake bottom. All we would need to do would be to open the lakes into the salt mines, until they reach the proper saline solution. Then we would stock the lake with sea food, marine mollusks, floating crustaceans, jellyfish, and what not. Then put in your whales, and build a great whale-cheese factory by the shore. Put on a big advertising campaign to make America whale-cheese-conscious. There are millions in it!"

"Jonah apparently throve," put in Hyett. "Whales are probably full of vitamins."

"I don't think I would like whale cheese," said Miss Cornwell. "Probably taste like cold oyster stew. I don't like oyster stew."

"Cheese can be made from the milk of any mammal," said Professor Sparhawk, emerging from secret thought. "It would be interesting to try human cheese." He looked calculatingly at his wife.

"Let us take our coffee in the drawing-room," said Mrs. Noble, rising. "President Temple may be dropping in. He said he would try to make it, between the Religious Work Organization Banquet and the Nutrition Get-Together."

The party rose and removed to the drawing-room. Professor Sparhawk walked with great dignity and precision.

When coffee was barely finished, President Temple entered, radiating vitality and goodwill. He saluted everyone with a hearty hand-clasp, and fastened on Professor Sparhawk.

"Glad to see you, Mr. Sparhawk. I enjoyed our little talk this morning. You have some interesting views."

"How was the Religious Work Banquet, Dr. Temple?" said Mrs. Noble.

"Splendid. Inspiring. Everybody in agreement. What this country needs, as well as this campus, is a spiritual reawakening."

"What this country needs is to go barefoot," said Professor Sparhawk, fiercely.

"Barefoot?"

"Half the sickness of modern man has its origin in the feet. Feet distorted and crippled by cramping, fashionable shoes. Men's shoes, causing pressure on the delicate bony structure, provoking myriad maladjustments in the system, and giving no free play to toes. Women's shoes, with their high heels, causing faulty posture and unsettling nervous system of spine. Ought to go barefoot."

"I'd hate to go barefoot. My feet would freeze," said Miss Cornwell.

"You're pradicly—practically barefoot now," said Professor Sparhawk, looking contemptuously at her feet. "I wouldn't be in your shoes!" He laughed loudly and coarsely.

"The natives of the Syrian mountains," contributed Professor Hyett, "go barefoot all their lives, through the terrible cold of their winters. They wrap up their faces, but they leave their feet bare. Never get frost-bitten."

"That's right; never get frost-bitten," said Professor Sparhawk, eagerly. "Never, never get frost-bitten. I haven't worn shoes, except in public, for fifteen years. I take off my shoes and socks just soon I enter the house. Result is, my feet—" He reached for his shoe-strings.

"Roger!" said his wife. Professor Sparhawk hesitated.

"Dear me, I must be going," said President Temple. "I'm already late for the Nutrition Get-Together. I had no idea it was so late. Well, good night, Mr. Sparhawk. Good night, Mrs. Noble. Good night, all." He waved a fatherly farewell.

"I was going to say, about my feet—"

"Dear Mr. Parry!" said Mrs. Noble. "I hear you have a perfectly killing recitation in dialect. The one you did at the Halseys'; they say it was perfectly killing. Couldn't we persuade you to give it to us?"

"Well—"

There was a chorus of urgent demands.

Professor Parry rose. "This is a little memory rhyme. For, let

us say, one of our metropolitan students who has difficulty in remembering the order of the Presidents of the United States:

> *Washington, Edams, Chefferson, Medison,*
> *They was the foist in the country who led us on;*
> *Monroe, and Jake U. Edams, and Jeckson,*
> *Each in the Prasident's uffitz he checks in;*
> *Von Büren, Harrison, Tyler, and Polk*
> *Was Prasident then, and did okey-doke;*
> *Taylor, Feelmore, Piertz, and Buchanan,*
> *Foist in whatever elections they ran in;*
> *Lincoln, Chonson, Grent, and Hayes,*
> *All fine fellas who went quite a ways;*
> *Garfield, Arthur, Cliffland, Harrison;*
> *So what is the everage man by comparison?*
> *Cliffland, McKinlich, Rosefelt, Teft,*
> *They did big business before they left;*
> *Wilson, Hardink, Coolitch, Hoover,*
> *They all did many a smart maneuver.*
> *Now irregardless what friends and foes felt,*
> *We give a hurray for Frenklin Rosefelt!"*

There was much applause, and cries of "Encore! Do another!
More!"

"Oh, I'm afraid I haven't any more parlor tricks."

"You might tell them some of your limericks, Parry," said
Professor Hyett, with a sly look.

"Oh yes! Limericks!" was the general cry.

"The one about the clergyman out in Dumont would be safe,"
suggested Gilda.

"The clergyman out in Dumont!"

"Well, I don't mind, really.

> *A clergyman out in Dumont*
> *Keeps tropical fish in the font;*
> *Though it always surprises*
> *The babes he baptizes,*
> *It seems to be just what they want."*

This was much enjoyed by the party. "Tell us another!"

Professor Sparhawk rose carefully to his feet.

"I know a limerick. Very funny limerick. Now, how did it go? There was a young lady of Lucca—"

Professor Parry began to shout. "I am afraid we must be going. I had no idea it was so late. It was a wonderful party, Mrs. Noble. Such a delightful evening! Come on, Miss Cornwell, I'm taking you home."

Everyone crowded around Mrs. Noble, muttering about the delightful evening and the lateness of the hour. Gilda glanced at her watch. It was a quarter past nine.

Once more in the convertible coupé, Gilda and Hyett laughed about the remarkable evening and that incredible Mr. Sparhawk. They discussed the guests of the evening.

"That Miss Cornwell," said Professor Hyett. "She is a nice creature, isn't she?"

"Yes. I think she found the evening pretty awkward."

"I am sorry. It was I who suggested her to Mrs. Noble. Lucie Coindreau was originally asked, and I happened to see Mrs. Noble, and she said she couldn't think of an extra girl."

"Lucie Coindreau! Poor Lucie!"

"Yes, poor Lucie indeed!"

The car had come to the door of Gilda's apartment building. There was a question she wanted very much to ask. She wanted to make it sound offhand. But as she framed it in her mind, it didn't seem offhand. Well, too bad, she was going to ask it anyhow.

"Oh, by the way, Mr. Hyett, there was something I wanted to ask you."

"Yes, my dear Miss Gorham?"

"On Monday night, after the President's reception, you didn't happen to see Mr. Belknap anywhere?"

Professor Hyett sat silent for a moment before replying.

"No. No, I didn't see him. Why?"

"I was just wondering."

"I can guess what you are wondering about. Now let me tell you something, my dear Miss Gorham." Hyett had entirely dropped his customary tone of banter. "I am old enough to be your father, and I am going to give you a little fatherly advice. You just stop wondering. And stop asking questions. You can't do any good, and you may do some harm. Real harm."

Professor Hyett handed her to her door.

"Good night, Miss Gorham. Stop wondering."

"Good night, Mr. Hyett."

Gilda turned the key in her door. She sat down in her easiest chair, lit a cigarette, and sat there for a long time, wondering.

In the Noble household, Professor and Mrs. Noble emptied ashtrays, aired the rooms, obscured the spoor of the party, and gave the maid a hand with the dishes.

Professor Noble, having removed his shirt and collar, was putting away the bottles.

"I wonder what was the matter with Sparhawk?" he said.

Mrs. Noble pursed her lips. "The man's a drinker!"

"I never heard that before."

"Well, he drank five cocktails. When everyone else was just sipping at theirs, he was emptying his at a gulp. I never saw such a thing. He's a dipsomaniac."

"He has done the best book there is on the history of monetary theory."

"No matter. We can't have a drinker in the department. That's the end of Mr. Sparhawk!"

Professor Noble yawned. He was in no mood to start an all-night battle.

As far as the University was concerned, it was in fact the end of Professor Sparhawk.

Chapter IX

ON THURSDAY afternoon Gilda was in Dr. Sandys's office, discussing with him the departmental appropriations. Social Sciences was complaining again, demanding more money; Slavonic had a large unexpended balance from the previous year. The Professor of Slavonic, who was building a house, was too busy even to read the book catalogues. Dr. Sandys wanted Gilda's advice about transferring the Slavonic surplus to Social Sciences.

"And about the arrangement of the Wilmerding," he said. "Do you think we should raise those railings? Or alter the lighting system? It would be pretty expensive."

"I don't think we need to make any alterations."

"We don't want any more of these terrible accidents."

"There has never been one before, in about fifty years. And people are going to be careful from now on."

"You are so sensible, Miss Gorham! But I somehow feel that we ought to do something."

A nervous knock sounded on the office door. "Come in!" shouted Dr. Sandys.

It was a cadaverous young man with a twitching little yellow mustache.

"I'm Elmer Drexel," he said. "Assistant in Classics. Mr. Hyett told me to come and see you."

"Oh yes. I've seen you around. Sit down."

Gilda wondered for the hundredth time how it happened that from these unhealthy, decayed-looking graduate students were recruited the faculties of America, rather distinguished in appearance, on the whole. The charm of youth was very much overpraised. A repellent lot, mostly.

"I have something rather curious to tell you, Dr. Sandys. I was in Mr. Hyett's workshop, looking over some of his collections in a merely desultory way. And I happened to notice on his desk a microfilm, with a Library label: 'MS. B 58. Hilarius: *Filius Getronis*.' Well, I had been hearing about it, of course, and out of curiosity I put the film in Mr. Hyett's reader. You can imagine my surprise when I read, in the first frame, the words: 'Thou shalt do no murder!'"

"What do you mean?"

"Just what I said! The words: 'Thou shalt do no murder,' in English, written in large capitals."

"But that can't be part of the manuscript!"

"I don't see how it could be."

"What is this? A joke?"

"I don't know. Maybe it's a joke. But it isn't my joke."

"You didn't bring the film with you?"

"No, sir. Mr. Hyett came in while I was looking at it, and he told me I'd better come right over and report it to you."

"I think I'll run over and have a look at it. Come on along. I'll see you later, Miss Gorham."

The two left, and Gilda went soberly back to her work.

Half an hour later she dropped in at the Librarian's office.

"What did you find out?" she asked, without introductory pourparlers.

"It's a funny business, Miss Gorham. A very funny business. I looked at the film and saw nothing of what was reported to us. The film began with the first folio of the manuscript. I asked the assistant, Drexel, to point out the frame with 'Thou shalt do no murder' on it. He looked at the film and could not find it. He seemed genuinely surprised. I noticed that Mr. Hyett was tapping his forehead in a significant manner. Mr. Hyett said that he had examined the film and had seen nothing peculiar about it. I think I may say that we were all nonplussed. Nonplussed indeed."

"Could such a frame have been patched in between the trailer and the film proper?"

"Certainly. It would be very simple. Someone could have written the words on a big sheet of paper, and then photographed them, and patched in the frame after the trailer. But if Hyett is right, it is all an invention of the student's."

"But why should the student have told such a story?"

"A hallucination, perhaps. Or a hoax. But I am nonplussed. I was just trying to get the psychiatrist of the Medical Department. He may be able to tell us something. Ah, the telephone. Probably that is Dr. Reed now." Dr. Sandys picked up the receiver.

"Dr. Reed? This is Sandys, at the Library. Dr. Reed, I have a question to ask you. Rather a curious thing has been reported to me by a student. Elmer Drexel, his name is; Assistant in Classics. Almost an incredible thing. I wonder if you have any record of this Drexel. Has he shown any—ah—instability? . . . Oh, you know him, do you? . . . Yes. . . . Yes. . . . But exactly how serious is that? . . . Would it affect his credibility? . . . Yes, I see. . . . Thank you. Yes, I understand that this is entirely confidential, and I will keep it under my hat, as the boys say. Thank you very much, Dr. Reed."

He replaced the receiver.

"Dr. Reed says that this Drexel has been under observation by his office. He had some sort of breakdown in his senior year, and withdrew for the second term. A mild psychotic condition, brought on by overwork and strain. He thought he was persecuted by Mr. Hyett, because he only got 85 in some course at mid-years. Not insane, Dr. Reed said, or at least not too insane to be a professor." He laughed. "That I took to be a quip."

"What do you make of it, Dr. Sandys?"

"Oh, a hoax, I imagine." Dr. Sandys laughed comfortably. "The students love these hoaxes. I remember when I was a student we dressed up a doll in baby clothes and left it in a basket at the door of the Dean of Women. With a rather suggestive sign on it." He laughed again.

"No doubt you are right, Dr. Sandys."

Gilda retreated to the catalogue room.

She had hardly sat down when Francis Parry phoned, urging her to dine quietly with him in the country. Gilda declined, alleging a headache, one of those invaluable headaches. The headache would give her an opportunity for quiet and consecutive thought.

In her cosy living-room, after dinner, she prepared her favorite setting for meditation. She sat in her easy chair with a drawing-board before her, laid across the chair's arms. On the drawing-board lay a pad of yellow paper and two soft pencils. On the table at her side were cigarettes, matches, an ashtray, and a tall glass of mixed ginger ale and grape juice, amply iced.

On the yellow pad she wrote:

1. Hoax.

2. Hallucination.

3. Genuine.

1. Hoax.

It was true that students were forever getting up hoaxes, some of them elaborate, some of them pretty funny, some of them in dreadful taste. Like that Royalist Party of America, which had provoked stern editorials in the *New Republic*. Who was it they had proposed for King? W. C. Fields, wasn't it? The point of the hoax was usually brutally clear. It was intended to befool some person or group, by making them confess publicly to swallowing some absurdity. But this hoax, if a hoax, was not clear. It would give no opportunity for gloating publicity in the college paper. It did not seem to fit the rules of the type.

Perhaps the assistant, Drexel, having some suspicion about Lucie Coindreau's death, was trying to scare Mr. Hyett. He hadn't seemed to be playing a part, nor did he appear to be the sort who could play a part convincingly. And then, why in the world should he have come running to Dr. Sandys? Having succeeded in scaring Mr. Hyett, he should have avoided the complications which would follow upon his telling his story to others. He could have returned to Mr. Hyett with the report that Dr. Sandys was out or in conference or something. But then, people often don't act very logically.

Perhaps this Drexel, who had suffered from delusions of persecution, had made up the whole story in order to point suspicion at Mr. Hyett? But in that case the suspicion would disappear as soon as people inspected the microfilm and found no warning written on it.

No, the whole hoax hypothesis didn't seem to fit the facts.

2. Hallucination.

According to medical testimony, the student was neurotic, to say the least. If for some reason—not clear—he was haunted by the idea of murder, he might easily see the sixth commandment written on a wall, in the sky, or on a microfilm. That sort of vision was a commonplace of religious mysticism and of abnormal psychology. But in the circumstances it was a coincidence, and *ipso facto* suspicious. Also, it was what Mr. Hyett was deliberately trying to suggest. Perhaps Mr. Hyett had good reason for making the suggestion. Perhaps, perhaps!

On the whole, the hallucination explanation was possible, but pretty far-fetched.

3. Genuine.

If Drexel had actually seen the commandment, and if later it had disappeared, what implications and inferences could she find?

Gilda wrote on her pad:

    A. How was it prepared?

    B. Who removed it?

    C. Who prepared it?

A. How was it prepared?

Probably you could write directly on a square of film. But that would be pretty awkward. And you would have to use some sort of crayon, a lithographer's pencil or something, to hold on the film's surface. That would be difficult too. Dr. Sandys's explanation was better; someone had written the words large on a sheet of paper and had photographed the sheet. He had developed it and patched it into the microfilm. Thus whoever had done it had a miniature type of camera and had the knowledge, and the opportunity, for doing photographic work. But that meant practically everybody nowadays.

B. Who removed it?

Hyett, obviously. It was no job to cut out a frame and patch the preceding and following parts of the film together. And since the warning had appeared between the trailer and the microfilm, probably patched together in any case, you couldn't tell anything by looking at the film in its present state.

C. Who prepared it?

Gilda wrote, in a column, the names:

Hyett
Belknap
Casti
Parry
Sandys
Cameron
Ignotus

Hyett was the obvious suspect. He made superb photographs, stills and movies, plain and colored. He gave illustrated travelogues, in aid of properly patronized charities, on "Fabled Isles of the Ægean," on "Highways and Byways of the Peloponnesus." The microfilm was in his office. He had every opportunity.

But what motive? Surely he wasn't trying to teach himself moral lessons?

Probably he was planning to frighten somebody. By putting the film in the hands of someone who had reason to be frightened, he would give that someone the scare of his life.

Who was that someone? Most likely Hyett planned to substitute his prepared film for the film in someone else's hands. The films were all exactly alike, with identical Library labels on the reel.

Belknap, Casti, and Parry had the other films.

Belknap? Did Hyett have some reason to suspect that Belknap had committed murder? Specifically, the murder of Lucie Coindreau?

But that brought her back to the question why Belknap should have murdered Lucie. Gilda had gone over all this before and had found no reasonable answer.

She thought, with a smile, of Francis's speculation on the virginity of Belknap. She would like to bet that he was, shall we say, unsullied. He was a perfect example of the successful sublimation of the sex-instinct, if you wanted to be Freudian. She could not believe that there was some sort of emotional relation between him and Lucie. Love, in his case, would be as obvious as—as eczema. It was just ridiculous.

Casti? That earnest little fellow? Certainly the disappearance of Lucie cleared the way for his advancement. Ambitious people, she knew, had murdered for ambition. There were some very exalted examples in history, ancient and modern. And in this case only a single impulsive push was required. Still, it was hard to believe. The contrast between the terribleness of the deed and the meanness of the end was too great. No, it wasn't likely.

But there was more to it than that. There was the story that Casti and Lucie had had a love affair, a passionate, thoroughgoing love affair. Love turned to hate. That was enough to satisfy a writer, or a reader, of mystery stories. Enough to satisfy a jury.

And still, it didn't seem likely. . . .

Parry?

Nonsense, nonsense, nonsense!

But she wished she knew a little more about Parry. Not so much what he had actually done as what he actually was. He was like an open house, in a way, in which everyone was invited to wander at will, to make oneself at ease, to pick up and examine the objects of art. But there was one room you must never enter. Bluebeard's secret room, she thought with a shiver.

Parry had not been very convincing in his denial that he had ever had an affair with Lucie. Of course, she didn't really care if he had. She wasn't a prude, she hoped. But she did wish he weren't so careful. And that she could be sure he was telling the truth.

Supposing, now, he had had an affair with Lucie. And that she was jealous. And making trouble. How far would Francis go with someone who was making trouble?

She didn't know.

But nonsense, nonsense!

Then there was Sandys. Could Hyett have been trying to frighten Sandys? He had, to be sure, no copy of the microfilm. But Hyett could have found some pretext to get him to look at one.

In fact, come to think of it, Sandys had been the first person to be informed of the mysterious warning. True, it had disappeared by the time he had reached Hyett's workshop. Why had Hyett removed it? Cold feet, perhaps. Or a taste for mystery. Or perhaps merely because he had achieved his purpose, of alarming Sandys.

But why should Sandys have murdered Lucie?

If there was any motive, it was hidden.

Cameron? Cameron was out.

But not necessarily. Cameron, the general handyman of the Library, had made the microfilms in the first place, in his workshop in the Library. Hyett could have planned to send him the film, with a request that the trailer be lengthened or something. While working on it, Cameron would inevitably have seen the warning.

Motive? Only the horrible motive she had already thought of. But that was possible, certainly.

Then there was Ignotus.

Perhaps the assistant, Elmer Drexel? He might have patched in the warning, in order to frighten one of the others. Or, being somewhat on the skittish side mentally, he might have been frightening himself. Possible. But not very.

There was another possibility. Suppose one of the five, or Ignotus, had prepared the warning and put it on Hyett's desk, in place of Hyett's own microfilm? According to this supposition, Hyett, recognizing the warning, had immediately removed it from the film.

Possible. Anyone might have heard or seen or merely suspected something and have chosen this melodramatic means of alarming Hyett. For the means was melodramatic, certainly. If the suspicious person had been willing to do the simple, obvious thing, he would merely have sent his warning as an anonymous letter, by mail.

Gilda got up, realizing that she had been sitting on her right leg, which now felt as though it had been frozen up to midthigh. She shook herself, walked around the room, lit a cigarette, and sat down.

There were some other queer things that came into it. Casti and the drawer in the French Seminary. Papoose. How did a papoose get into it?

Well, there didn't seem to be any answer. She would try to stop thinking about it. Get a little music, calm down, go to sleep.

She crumpled the paper and threw it in the waste-basket. She turned on the radio and found a station that was broadcasting old favorites from the operas, interspersed with anxious, motherly appeals to music-lovers to correct their stomach acidity.

The music did not soothe her. Someone was trying to tell her something. Was it the soprano, trumpeting her arias? Or an interloping voice, doing its best to ride the waves of ether to her ear? Or was it something deep in her memory, struggling to rise to the surface of her conscious mind?

She snapped off the radio, went to the waste-basket, and fished out the crumpled sheet. She smoothed it out and stared at it for a long time. Then she crumpled it again and threw it viciously into the waste-basket.

Chapter X

IT WAS the custom of the members of the Faculty Club to gather (or, as some preferred to say, to "forgather") in the smoking-room after dinner. There the events of the day were reviewed, and light, digestive conversation indulged in, to the accompaniment of sucking pipes.

On this Thursday evening several of the bachelors, with certain of the married men whose wives were out of town and whose maids were taking maid's day out, were there gathered, or forgathered. The early comers picked up the popular magazines and glanced at them casually. The later comers appeared, looked for the popular magazines, saw them lying unregarded in the laps of the talkers, and waited patiently or impatiently. From time to time someone drifted in or drifted out. According to the custom of the smoking-room, greetings and farewells were dispensed with.

"I hear you made a Doctor of Philosophy this afternoon," said Professor Caleb of Education to Parry.

"Yes. A woman named McGee. Majors in English, minor in Dramatics. She had a thesis on the length of the sentence in certain modern authors. She has been counting the words in sentences since 1935. She proved conclusively that some authors use longer sentences than others. But I forget which."

"How did the exam go?"

"Very well. Mr. Gosse, the big Milton man, you know, asked some brilliant questions, and Mr. Bury, the big Chaucer man, shone in his cross-examination. He made the candidate cry three times. Of course, it wasn't like that great Doctor's Oral three years ago, when he brought the candidate to a fit of hysteria. I didn't do so badly myself, though I felt I wasn't quite at the top of my form. I asked several questions that neither the big Milton man nor the big Chaucer man could have answered, though they pretended they could."

"Did you pass her?"

"Certainly. We were all very pleased."

Professor Belknap, who hated Parry's tone of levity about serious matters, changed the subject.

"I hear that two girls have been quietly dropped by recommendation of the Dean of Women."

"What for? Spots on their morals?" asked Professor Hyett.

"I imagine so."

"What gripes me," said Professor Coffman of Psychology warmly, "is that they don't drop the young men who are presumably involved. Why take it out on the poor girls? It probably isn't their fault."

"It has always been presumed to be their fault," said Professor Belknap. "The lawgivers, and society too, have always said that the woman is to blame. If a man attacks and a woman yields, the woman is to be punished for yielding, while the man becomes a kind of hero."

"And you think that's right?"

"Not according to your theories about the equality of the sexes. But it must be right according to the judgment of history. Men in all times and places have felt it to be right, by an instinct deeper than logic. So it is right. Women offend against society by being temptresses."

"Women offend against society by being women, then? That's nonsense, my dear Belknap!"

"I don't think so. I think it is a truth too profound for the Department of Psychology."

"Well," said Professor Hyett, feeling the need for appeasement, "women do have a good deal to answer for. Look at Eve. I suppose, Belknap, if you had been Adam, you would never have been tempted?"

Professor Belknap smiled. "No. I would have put Eve in her place. And saved the race a lot of trouble about Original Sin."

"He probably would have fixed it by bringing the race to a full stop right there," said Hyett to Parry, *sotto voce*.

Another conversation was rising to the surface.

"Have you been out on the links at all, Caleb?" said Professor Casti.

"I played nine holes yesterday. The leaves are beginning to fall, and you spend half your time hunting your ball. If this goes on, some day I'll have to get a caddy. I would have done pretty well, though, if I hadn't taken four shots to get out of the sand-trap on the seventh. I had to burrow for my ball like a mole."

Professor Hyett chuckled. "Parry has a great idea for a murder! He's going to bury the body in a sand-trap, where Caleb will uncover it with his niblick."

Professor Parry smiled with much satisfaction.

"But how are you going to get your corpse in the first place?" pursued Professor Hyett.

"Well, I haven't given the matter much thought. But I think I'd try to find something simple and obvious. None of these elaborate gadgets or mysterious poisons you read about in detective stories. Too much research necessary, and I have enough of that to do in my own field. What I think is this: we are so well protected by society and our own hygienic habits that we don't realize we are protected. For instance, we're so used to getting purified water that we drink any water that's offered to us, provided it is in a glass. A little really foul water would destroy us. If we open a can of something, we immediately empty it out; never leave it in the can, for fear of poisoning. Well, I would leave some canned meat in the can for a week, and then mix it in my victim's hash."

"I don't think I would eat much of that hash," said Professor Hyett.

"Well then, I'll get you good and tight some night and take you for a ride in your car to cool off, and when you pass out I'll shut all the windows and leave the motor running. And everyone will say you did it yourself, in a fit of remorse for your evil life."

"I never get tight, and I never pass out. And I will remember to keep the top down, if I want to cool off."

"Well, there are lots of ways. I don't want to give away my really good ones. Anyway, I think there's too much fuss about ingenuity in murder nowadays. Perverse, I call it. I like the casual, offhand murders of the old aristocracy. There was a great chap in Dublin at the end of the eighteenth century. He killed a servant in his club, and ordered that the fellow should be put on his bill, at two hundred and fifty pounds. Buck English, his name was."

Professor Casti spoke up. "There was a very good method used in the famous *Affaire des Poisons,* in the seventeenth century."

The smoking-room looked to Professor Casti politely.

"There was a noble lady named, if I remember rightly, Madame de Poulaillon. She impregnated her husband's undershirt in a solution of arsenic."

"Did it kill him?"

"No. But it made him very sick for about three months. She finally had to hire some soldiers to kill him. And the soldiers took her money and denounced her to her husband."

"What do you make of that, Parry?" said Professor Hyett.

"I make of it that it is a mistake to wear an undershirt for three months."

"We have some contemporary pamphlets on the *Affaire des Poisons* in Criminology," said Dr. Sandys. "I think they might give some ideas to some of our mystery-writers."

"There are some good recipes in the medieval *grimoires,*" said Professor Belknap.

"What are they like?"

"Most of them are very complicated. The trouble is that the properties are very difficult to obtain. You have to have a lot of things like candles made of human fat; strange herbs mixed with the blood of a goat, a bat, and a mole; four nails pulled out of the coffin of a man who has been tortured to death; the head of a cat which has been fed on human blood for five days, and preferably the skull of a parricide."

"You see? It would really be easier just to strangle your man," said Professor Parry.

"But there is one simple one which I think would be workable. Let's see. On a Saturday you buy a beef-heart, and you must not haggle over the price. I don't understand at all the reason for that provision about not haggling, but there it is. Perhaps an old folk-feeling that the devil acts like a grand gentleman, magnificently. You take the beef-heart to a cemetery and bury it in a deep hole on a bed of quicklime. You prick the beef-heart with large needles, each time uttering the name of your victim. Fill in the grave, and recite over it the first chapter of the Gospel according to Saint John. Every succeeding day recite the same chapter while still fasting, and with all the malevolence possible. The victim will feel horrible pains, and will soon waste away and die."

"It seems too simple," said Professor Hyett. "I don't think it would work."

Professor Belknap smiled slowly. "If you had really the scientific attitude, you would not venture a conclusion until you had made an actual experiment."

"It's funny, the vogue for supernaturalism in our scientific age," put in Professor Coffman of Psychology. "Look at all these books about witchcraft and the beliefs of primitive peoples. For instance, about Haiti and their zombies, who are brought back to life with their brains removed entirely."

"That explains something. I have two of them in my Drama 10," said Professor Parry.

Dr. Sandys had something to contribute.

"There was one of the Emperors of Russia, Thomas Basilides, I think; yes. He had the novel idea of sewing up his victims in bear-skins, and then setting a pack of fierce mastiffs on them."

"Impracticable," said Professor Parry.

"There was a curious case in my home town," said Professor

Coffman. "It wasn't in fact homicide, but it might just as well have been. A fellow who worked in a filling-station or something was suspicious of his wife; thought she was cutting up with a lodger in his house. A very jealous fellow, apparently. Well, one morning after he had left the house he turned around and came back. He entered the house very quietly, and sure enough, he found his wife and the lodger in, shall we say, a compromising position, in the living-room. He pulled a pistol out of his pocket and threatened his wife and the lover. The wife distracted his attention and the lover sprang on him. The two men grappled with each other and fought for the pistol. The lover succeeded in pointing the pistol downward and fired it through the floor, wounding in the leg a meter-reader from the gas company, who had been listening with great interest. It was only a flesh-wound, but he might easily have been killed."

"That reminds me of a story I heard," said Professor Caleb. "One of the boys was telling it at the Ethical Education Convention. How did it go now?—There was a traveling salesman—"

Professor Hyett raised his voice a little and brought the conversation back to its track.

"How would you commit a murder, Casti?"

Professor Casti pondered. He seemed to take the question seriously.

"I wonder," he said, "how far hypnotism would go? I don't remember ever reading about a case in actual fact. But I should think if you could establish absolute hypnotic control over another, the victim would go even as far as suicide. Especially if the action was not so clear and shocking as to break the hypnotic spell. For instance, you might order your subject to go swimming in a place you knew to be dangerous. Or to go and sit for an hour in a kitchen in which you had turned on the gas stove."

Suddenly everyone felt that the note was wrong. If this was joking, it was too gruesome for the Faculty Club smoking-room.

"I'll tell you one of my better ways," said Professor Parry. "Supposing, for instance, I want to murder Coffman, here. I will dress up with a silk hat and a tennis blazer and an umbrella, and I will walk into his classroom while he's giving one of his famous lectures on psychology, and I'll shout: 'You are the man who stole my wife! Take that! And that!' And I will shoot him in his tracks. And then naturally all the class will sit back and sneer, and say: 'Aw, that old stuff! They try it on us every year!' And I will calmly walk out, and take off my costume and hang it up in the Dean's anteroom, and go back to my own class. The point is that you psychologists have proved over and over again that when you give such a surprise test in observation, none of the students ever describe what happened accurately. Since they always get everything wrong, I will be perfectly safe."

There was a satisfactory amount of laughter.

"I would kind of miss old Coffman," said Professor Caleb. "Couldn't you murder someone else, Parry?"

But Parry, for some reason, was tired of badinage. He shook his head.

"No," he said, "I don't think I could. Let's talk about something more cheerful."

But Professor Coffman had something to say first.

"I don't think you could either, Parry. It's the simple people, like that filling-station man I was telling about, who proceed from the simple cause of jealous hatred to the simple result of shooting with a pistol. We teachers think too much, and thought paralyzes the motor responses. The uncomplex person answers an offense with a blow; we answer it with an analysis of the case. And when we have got the case analyzed, it is too late for the blow. Therefore what we have on this campus is a large number of situations painful and menacing. But they never result in action. Or hardly ever. The situations just go on until the persons concerned in them die, or become emeritus and move to Florida."

"I don't agree with you," said Professor Caleb, warmly. "I will grant, with you, that the campus is a mass of repressed emotions. Most professors, like most people, sublimate their repressed emotions successfully. But some do not. When you repress, or suppress, or compress anything, whether it's emotions or gases, you are likely to get an explosion. And you know perfectly well that every now and then some respected leader of American education blows up with a loud bang."

"Oh, of course, anything can happen," admitted Professor Coffman. "Probably in time everything does. But people on the faculty as a rule know enough about psychology, including their own, to diagnose their own troubles. We work off our crimes in conversation, or in imagination, or in reading. That's what love stories are for. And murder stories. Here's a motto for the faculties: Read a good book and keep the commandments."

Professor Hyett spoke in a strangely hollow voice.

"Thou shalt do no murder!"

Everyone was quite startled.

Chapter XI

ON FRIDAY morning, as soon as Library good form permitted, Gilda went to Dr. Sandys's office. She had an idea.

Dr. Sandys was sitting slouched in his desk-chair, staring out the window. His morning mail lay before him untouched, like a bad child's breakfast.

"Good morning, Dr. Sandys."

"Good morning, Miss Gorham."

"If you will permit me to be disagreeable, you aren't looking very well, Dr. Sandys. You look tired. Aren't you sleeping well?"

"Oh yes, I'm sleeping all right," said Dr. Sandys, wearily. "Just a little worried, perhaps."

"About that hoax?"

"Yes. That hoax. And other things."

"Well, I was thinking about the hoax. We assumed, without question, that the mysterious sixth commandment was patched into the film, unless the boy made the whole thing up. There is at least one other possibility: that the commandment was written on the fly-leaf of the manuscript, and was properly photographed with the rest. I think we ought to take a look at the manuscript."

"That is true. Perhaps we should. Suppose we do it immediately."

Dr. Sandys seemed glad of a reason for action. He unlocked a drawer of his desk with a key from his key-container. He took from the drawer a Yale-type key, attached to a small block of wood.

The two proceeded to the ground floor of the Wilmerding. Gilda glanced at the second-hand of her wrist-watch. The time from the Librarian's office to the Wilmerding was twenty-six seconds.

They crossed the Wilmerding to the locked press in the bay of the south side. Dr. Sandys turned his key in the lock and pulled open the heavy grilled door.

Gilda pointed with her finger and made a queer gobbling noise, half scream, half an effort at speech.

Inside the door, sitting on a chair, was Professor Hyett. His shoulders had slid a little sideways, and rested in the angle formed by one of the projecting uprights of the book-shelves and an extra-illustrated set of Casanova's *Memoirs*. His noble-Roman head leaned forward in a reverent attitude. His face was gray. The wispy white hair on his skull stood up with an air of comic surprise.

Dr. Sandys sprang to his side, pulled open the coat, and burrowed beneath it with his hand.

"This is too much," he said, inadequately. "This is too much."

"Is he dead?"

"Yes. Stone cold."

"But how?"

"Maybe a stroke. A heart attack or something. I don't see any blood."

"This is a case for the police. I'll go and call them."

"Come to my office. There's no reason to rouse the whole catalogue room."

The two left the locked press. Dr. Sandys slammed the door, and the spring lock engaged. He removed the key.

"How did he get into the locked press?" said Gilda.

"I don't know. There are only two keys: this one and the Assistant Librarian's. But if that were missing, Mr. Dickson would have reported it to me immediately. At any rate, the police will no doubt find a key on him."

"No doubt."

"This is too much," said Dr. Sandys.

He called the police station and was connected with Lieutenant Kennedy. He told his story briefly. The telephone rasped; the Lieutenant was probably very angry. His ideal, to which he would possibly attain in heaven, was a city without sin, but with a steady flow of traffic violations. He directed Dr. Sandys and Gilda to wait for him and to stay away from the locked press.

The two sat in silence.

"Should we tell him about the—the hoax?" said Gilda.

"I suppose so. It may have some bearing. Though I must say I don't see—"

"Neither do I."

Again silence.

"You know," said Gilda, "I wonder if this has anything to do with the death of Lucie Coindreau?"

"I don't know," said Dr. Sandys, miserably.

"One thing seems to lead to another. What is that phrase of the detective stories?—'the ever-widening stain.' Crime seems to make more crime, and bloodshed makes more blood. The ever-widening stain."

Dr. Sandys looked at her with wide eyes.

And again silence. Gilda gave up any effort to understand.

It was a relief to hear the police car slide to a stop and park in the no-parking area in front of the Library's entrance.

Lieutenant Kennedy entered, storming, with the Medical Examiner, a nervous young man from the District Attorney's office, and the Detective Sergeant, who did the stenography, fingerprinting, and photography, and helped out the traffic squad on Saturday afternoons.

Dr. Sandys led the party to the locked press. Gilda was directed to remain in the Librarian's office for questioning. She spent there an interminable half-hour, trying to think, trying not to think, her mind mostly occupied with longing for a cigarette. Smoking was certainly no vice for a librarian.

At last the party returned. A few minutes were spent in routine telephoning.

"What's the answer?" said Gilda, in an aside to Dr. Sandys.

"The answer has not been divulged. The medical man says that he died of strangulation; that, to judge from certain superficial signs, someone choked him, facing him and pressing on the windpipe with his thumbs. It must have happened somewhere around midnight, but he can't tell very closely, after this lapse of time."

"But who did it? And why?"

"Maybe the police will find that out for us."

"Maybe." Gilda looked doubtfully at Lieutenant Kennedy.

"Now, Miss Gorham."

Lieutenant Kennedy, seated in the Librarian's desk-chair,

glared at her. Whatever he had learned as an investigator he had learned by bullying, shouting, and occasionally slapping down. His favorite device was to stare silently into space, then to turn suddenly on his victim with a roar.

"Now, Miss Gorham, I got some questions to ask you. Just some little questions. Routine, you might say. Don't get scared. Make yourself easy, Miss Gorham."

His voice rose to a bellow. "How you happen to go into that there locked press this morning?"

"I was curious about a certain manuscript, and I asked Dr. Sandys to let me see it."

"Ho, a certain manuscript! We heard about that manuscript already. How you happen to get so interested in this manuscript all of a sudden?"

"Some of the faculty were working on it, and I wanted to compare it with the microfilm."

"Ho, the microfilm, hey?"

He stared moodily at the ceiling. With an abrupt convulsion he shot a finger at her and shouted: "Didn't have any reason to suspect something funny going on in that locked press?"

"No."

"No, hey?" His tone was heavily sarcastic.

"No."

Lieutenant Kennedy brooded for a moment. He turned to his Sergeant. "Write down she says no," he directed. He swung on Gilda.

"How many keys was there to this locked press?"

"So far as I know, two."

Dr. Sandys spoke up. "My own was in my desk this morning, locked up. And Mr. Dickson has already told us that his own was locked in his desk, and the drawer has not been tampered with."

Lieutenant Kennedy seemed not to hear. Contorting his face terribly, he snarled at Gilda:

"Djever hear of another key?"

"Never."

"Never?"

"Never."

"Um, never." He settled back in his chair, with an air of profound thought. He roused himself to say to the Sergeant: "Write down she never heard of another key."

He wasn't so terrible after all, thought Gilda. She plucked up her courage to ask a question.

"You didn't find a key on him, then?"

"No. He had a big knife on him with tools on it, scissors and things, but you couldn't force a Yale lock with scissors. So how in hell did he get in?" There was something plaintive in the Lieutenant's ferocity.

The young man from the District Attorney's office spoke up. "It looks to me as if—"

"Well, young feller?"

"—as if the murderer let him in. Or else he had a key, and let himself in, and left the key in the lock. Going into a place like that, it would be natural to leave the key in the lock until you come out. And then the murderer took it away with him."

"You're learning, young feller," said Lieutenant Kennedy loftily. "Prof Sandys, you ever turn over your key to a locksmith to be reproduced?"

"Oh, no."

"Anyone ever borrow your key, or that other key of Prof Dickson's?"

"Never. However, it occurs to me—"

"You just answer my questions. If I want to know what occurs to you I'll ask you what occurs to you."

"Oh, very well."

But Gilda was learning that the police will answer questions if you simply ask them politely. She tried to fill her eyes and voice with humble admiration.

"Lieutenant Kennedy," she said, "would you have to be a locksmith to reproduce such a key?"

"Naw. They ain't hard to reproduce, if you got the original. You can get the blanks anywhere, and if you're handy with tools, you can cut or file one down. But you'd have to be careful. Them tolerances is pretty small."

The Lieutenant fell into one of his fits of musing. He turned his swivel chair sideways and felt in his pocket. Suddenly he swung the chair a full half-turn toward Dr. Sandys and Gilda and whipped from his pocket a white slip, which he held close before their eyes.

"Djever see this before?" he thundered.

On the card, a three-by-five thesis slip, the words were typewritten in capitals: THOU SHALT DO NO MURDER.

"No," said Gilda.

"No," said Dr. Sandys. "But only yesterday—"

He stopped, remembering Lieutenant Kennedy's objection to volunteered information.

"Go on. What's the matter with you? Can't you talk?" shouted the Lieutenant.

Dr. Sandys told the tale of the mysterious microfilm.

"I'll have a look at that film," said Kennedy. "And at the manuscript too. But first—"

"Where did you get the slip?" asked Gilda.

"Found it in his pocket. Nothing else of interest. He had about forty dollars in his pants. 'Twasn't robbery. Now I want to ask you two something. Do you know of anyone who had a grudge against this Prof Hyett?"

"No." Dr. Sandys and Gilda both seemed sure.

Gilda tried to run over in her mind the names she had written the night before. Belknap, Casti, Parry, Sandys, Cameron. Only five names now. She was still sure.

"Do you know of anyone who would profit by his death?"

"No."

"Any life insurance? Who are his heirs?"

Dr. Sandys and Gilda did not know.

"Well, we'll find out. And we'll get to the bottom of this business pretty quick. But it does beat all hell. . . ."

Lieutenant Kennedy knew his own weakness: a too ready confession of his own mystification. He pulled himself together and put on his look of professional confidence.

"Let's have a look at this here manuscript."

Obediently Dr. Sandys led the way to the locked press. He unlocked the grilled door. The body of Professor Hyett, Gilda saw with relief, had been removed.

The party filed into the press. There were five aisles, each lined from floor to ceiling with books, either precious or indecent. A queer fellowship, thought Gilda: Saint Francis de Sales and Aretino, *Pilgrim's Progress* and the *Memoirs of Fanny Hill.* A superb morocco binding might contain an Eliot Indian Bible or the fetid fancies of Felicien Rops. And, after all, there was some sense in their association. They were all books that must be defended from public curiosity, books so valuable, or so perverse, that some people might want them too much. Some people would become thieves for their sake. They were dangerous books. For all our talk of knowledge, there are things too high and too low for us to know. Some things should be hidden; some things belong in the dark.

Murder belongs in the dark. It was appropriate that murder should take place in the dark, in this locked press, the home of secret and forbidden things.

Dr. Sandys went to the great safe against the wall. He spun the combination: left, right, left, right, left. He pulled the bar that opened the ponderous door, and switched on a light inside the safe. The walls of the safe were lined with books and manuscript cases. Some were of sumptuous leather; some were in the original bindings of the Middle Ages and the Renaissance, vellums more enduring than brass; some, tattered and disreputable, preserved the cheap nineteenth-century bindings in which they had first appeared, poor, humble little books, destined to glory.

Dr. Sandys put his hand confidently toward the third shelf in the right-hand press, and stayed it in mid-air.

"It's gone!" he cried.

"Not B 58!" cried Gilda.

"Maybe it's out of place," suggested the young man from the District Attorney's office.

The same thought had occurred to Dr. Sandys. He went methodically along the shelves.

"Maybe it's in behind the others," said the young man.

"No, the shelves aren't deep enough. There is no other place in the safe it could be. It's gone."

"Just what is this manuscript, anyhow?" said Lieutenant Kennedy.

Dr. Sandys tried to speak, in vain. He went out in the locked press and sat down on the chair on which Professor Hyett had sat, dead.

But Gilda found herself surprisingly calm. She recited what sounded to herself like a memorized lesson: "It is a miracle play of the twelfth century, in Latin rhymed verse, evidently by the wandering scholar Hilarius, who is supposed to have lived and worked in Angers. Several of Hilarius's plays have been published, the *Suscitatio Lazari*, for instance. But his *Filius Getronis* has been unknown. It was Professor Belknap who attributed it to Hilarius and recognized its importance. It tells the story of a miracle of Saint Nicholas, who restored a Christian boy, held captive by the pagans, to his parents. The manuscript itself is in a fine clerkly hand of the thirteenth century. It has some very remarkable miniatures, illustrating the methods of production of miracle plays. It is bound in blue morocco by Trautz-Bauzonnet of Paris."

"Worth a lot of money, hey?"

"Mr. Wilmerding paid twelve thousand dollars for it at the Montucla sale in 1885. What it would be worth now could only be determined by an auction. But a dealer wouldn't think of asking less than a hundred thousand."

"That ain't hay!" Lieutenant Kennedy whistled. "How would a fellow sell a job like that?"

"I really don't know."

"Hey, Prof Sandys, how would a fellow sell a job like that manuscript?"

Dr. Sandys wiped his brow with his handkerchief and rejoined the group.

"Sell it?" he said. "Why, it would be difficult and dangerous.

He might find a wealthy and unscrupulous collector who would buy it. But the collector would get little satisfaction from it. He would hardly dare to show it to many of his fellow collectors, for fear of being denounced."

"But someone might buy it without knowing it was hot?"

"Anyone who would be likely to pay a large sum for such a manuscript would demand an authenticated history of his purchase, for fear of its being stolen goods."

"Maybe a fellow would steal a manuscript like that just for himself, just to have it around?"

"That could happen. There are some very peculiar things that happen in the world of books." Dr. Sandys smiled wanly. "A few years ago, I have been told, there was an instructor in English here who was working on Carlyle. He took a strange dislike to Jane Welsh Carlyle, and he went through all the Carlyleana, effacing references to her, adorning her picture with mustaches, and writing insulting and even obscene references to her in the margins. Of course he was a little insane."

"We never got any report on that."

"It was never reported to the police. It was hushed up."

"Try and hush this up!" Lieutenant Kennedy meditated sourly. He tried a new tack.

"Who knows the combination to this safe?"

"Presumably I am the only one who knows."

"What happens if you get bumped off?"

"The combination is recorded in a sealed envelope, which is kept in the Treasurer's office."

"Have you got it written down somewhere?"

"No."

"Did you ever tell it to anybody?"

"Certainly not."

"You never get a little tight, maybe, and talk too much?"

"Good God, no!"

"No offense. Some people do. The safe shuts, I suppose, by just spinning the knob?"

"Yes."

Lieutenant Kennedy brooded for a moment. Then he burst out in a deafening roar. "Hell! A guy murdered in a locked room! A manuscript gone out of a safe! A girl jumping off on her head! And two years before I go on a pension!"

Chapter XII

BACK IN the Librarian's office, Lieutenant Kennedy meditated massively in the Librarian's desk-chair. He turned to Dr. Sandys.

"How many people had copies of this here microfilm?"

"Professor Belknap of History, Professor Casti of Romance Languages, and Professor Parry of Dramatics."

"Get 'em over here."

"They may be in class now."

"Get 'em out of class then. I'll lecture these profs for a change."

Dr. Sandys left the room to telephone from his secretary's office.

Lieutenant Kennedy scowled at Gilda.

"How'd this murderer get out of the Library?"

"I don't know."

"Don't know, hey? How many doors are there?"

"Three; the main entrance, a side entrance to the periodical room, and the service door."

"What kind of locks they got? Ordinary spring locks?"

"No. The front door and the periodical room have big, ponderous old-fashioned locks on them; you just turn the key in the lock. But there are also bolts. When the janitor locks up at night, he shoots the bolts. Then he goes out the service door."

"What kind of a lock on that?"

"A Yale-type lock. But all three doors are connected with an alarm device. The janitor sets it when he leaves. It rings a warning in the office of the Campus Patrol, if any of the doors are opened between closing-time and a quarter to eight in the morning."

"Who locks up at night and opens her up in the morning?"

"The janitor, Cameron, or one of the assistant janitors. They take turns. They are all old employees, and we have perfect confidence in them."

"Who was on duty last night?"

"Cameron, I think. Yes, Cameron."

"Alarm bell didn't ring last night?"

"Certainly not. If it had rung, the campus cops would have come over on the run, and everybody would have been informed."

"How about jumping out a window?"

"All the ground-floor windows are sealed shut. The windows on the upper floor open, but they are too high for anyone to jump out of."

"Don't people ever get locked in at night?"

"Oh yes, once in a while. They usually telephone to the Librarian, and he informs the Campus Patrol and then he comes over and gets them. Once or twice people have broken a window on the ground floor and got out that way. And sometimes it appears that they have spent the night on the couch in the women's rest room."

"No windows broken this morning?"

"No."

"Huh."

"I suppose," ventured Gilda, "it is clear that Mr. Hyett was killed after closing-time?"

"No, it ain't clear. Nothing is clear. Doc says he could have died any time from about ten to twelve at night. Say—"His voice rose to a roar. "Who's asking questions around here, anyhow?"

He ruminated for a moment, and shot a new question at Gilda.

"Djever hear of any of these professional book-thieves?"

"Oh yes. There was a case at Williams College a year or so ago. A fellow came in with a forged letter of introduction and asked to see a First Folio Shakespeare, I think it was. He had prepared a dummy that resembled it exactly, and when he went out he put the genuine book in his brief-case and simply returned the dummy at the desk. Later he sent back the book, but I don't know whether it was from remorse or whether he couldn't dispose of it. Then there was another case; somebody was talking about it just recently. It was a long time ago, in the Hopkinson Library in California. A very valuable book disappeared. I seem to recall that it was the Paris Donatus of 1451. Yes, that was it. In that case, too, the book was returned by mail."

"Well, that gives us a precedent, anyhow. Now lookit here, Miss Gorham. Out of your special knowledge, have you got any ideas how this Prof Hyett could have got into the locked press?"

"No."

"Or how somebody could have opened the safe?"

"No."

"Or who might have had some reason to take that manuscript and rub out Prof Hyett?"

"N-no."

"Well, we'll catch him all right. Don't you worry. If we can find out how it was done we'll find out who did it. And vice versa. We'll get this guy; you can bet your bottom dollar on that."

But the tone of the Lieutenant's voice suggested that he would not venture his own bottom dollar.

"Dja get those fellows?" he said to Dr. Sandys, who had returned from his telephoning.

"Yes. They'll be right over."

Dr. Sandys sank wearily into a chair. He was taking this very hard, thought Gilda. And no wonder; when a responsible librarian sees his good friends and guests of his library murdered, and when precious manuscripts disappear out of his safe, he has a right to feel depressed.

"While we're waiting, let's talk to this Cameron," said Lieutenant Kennedy.

"I knew you'd want him; I have him in the outer office," said Dr. Sandys.

Cameron was summoned. He entered, suave and smiling, like the guest of honor at a party.

"Sit down, Cameron. We want some information out of you. Sit down and make yourself easy. And don't get excited. We ain't suspecting you of anything."

"Certainly, sir."

"*Where was you at ten o'clock last night?*"

"I was making my round of inspection and shutting the fire-doors."

"Go into this Wilmerding place?"

"Yes, sir."

"See anything out of the way?"

"Nothing. The Wilmerding Library was empty when I made my rounds."

"When d'you leave the Library?"

"It must have been about quarter to eleven. But I didn't notice particularly."

"Lock up all right, did you?"

"Of course, Lieutenant. I went out by the service door, and set the alarm device as usual."

"Um. Any sign this morning that the alarm device was tampered with?"

"No, sir."

"I'll have a look at it myself. Any other way a fellow could have got out after hours?"

"No, sir. I have made the rounds of the windows this morning, and I don't find that any are forced."

"Could anyone have jumped out of one of the second-floor windows?"

"No, sir. All those windows are locked; anyone escaping that way would have had to leave a window unlocked. And I don't find any signs of anyone landing on the ground or bushes below."

"I'll take a look at that too. A guy could have spent the night in the Library and walked out early this morning without being noticed?"

"Certainly, sir. I believe it has been done."

"Now about the locks on those doors—"

Cameron corroborated Gilda's evidence at every point.

Lieutenant Kennedy meditatively felt in his pocket, and drew forth a package of cigarettes. Cameron, Gilda, and Dr. Sandys cried, almost in chorus: "No smoking in the Library!"

Kennedy returned the cigarettes to his pocket, embarrassed.

He found a stick of gum, somberly peeled it, and thrust it in his mouth. Again he felt in his pocket.

"Djever see this before?" he shouted, whipping forth the thesis slip and holding the message: THOU SHALT DO NO MURDER, six inches before Cameron's eyes.

Cameron started back. After all, thought Gilda, it is entirely natural to flinch if a police lieutenant suddenly thrusts his big fist right in your face. But was Cameron's flinch a flinch of recognition? You couldn't analyze things so closely. Anyone would be scared to death by the Lieutenant's technique. He ought to be examining witches, with that book of Mr. Belknap's, the *Hammer of Witches,* for his manual!

Cameron collected himself immediately.

"I've seen the sixth commandment before, if that's what you mean. But I've never seen this particular slip."

"Ho." The Lieutenant relapsed into gloom.

"You make the microfilms for the Library?"

"Yes, sir."

"Remember making one of a Latin manuscript, called, now, uh—"

"Filius Getronis," supplied Dr. Sandys.

"Oh yes," said Cameron. "B 58. I did that only two or three weeks ago."

"You see this business: 'Thou shalt do no murder,' anywhere in the film?"

"What! Certainly not, sir."

"You didn't patch it into the film yourself, for a joke, like?"

"No, sir. I would never have done such a thing." Cameron seemed genuinely shocked.

"Well, somebody did. Unless everybody's lying around here."

The Lieutenant glared balefully about. He seemed to be searching for a masterly question to ask. Finding none, he took another stick of gum.

"I beg your pardon," Dr. Sandys interrupted tactfully. "I see that Mr. Casti is in the outer office."

"All right. That'll be all, Cameron. I'll let you know when I want you again. Don't go on any week-end trips."

"Thank you, sir." Cameron bowed respectfully and left the room.

He was very convincing, thought Gilda. He had given a perfect demonstration of how to behave when being questioned by the police. Almost too perfect. If anything could be almost too perfect. She remembered inconsequently how she had been lectured by Mr. Bury, the big Chaucer man of the English Department, for saying "too perfect," since perfection admits of nothing more or less. And "almost too perfect" would probably send Mr. Bury into a frenzy. But come, come, pay attention.

Professor Casti was nervous. His face and fingers twitched. He collided with the desk and the chair, and had difficulty in sitting down. His state seemed to cheer Lieutenant Kennedy.

"Take it easy, prof; take it easy. Make yourself at home. You heard about the death of Prof Hyett?"

"Yes, of course."

"Well, I just called you in for a little routine questioning. You don't need to get excited. Just a little routine questioning." He rolled and smacked his gum ominously, as if preparing to devour the witness horridly.

"Where was you at ten o'clock last night?"

"Why, why— At ten o'clock? I was in my apartment, working on a little problem. Yes, I was in my apartment, I think."

The Lieutenant's voice dropped to a bellow. "You just think? You don't know?"

"Why, if you put it that way, I suppose I know, I think. Or I mean I do know. Because I went up to my apartment after dinner. And I just stayed there working."

"Didn't go out at all?"

"No. Or yes, yes! Come to think of it, I did go out. I was tired of working, so I went out for a little walk."

"What for?"

"Just to clear my brain."

"Put down he went out for a walk to clear his brain," said the Lieutenant to the Sergeant, in a tone of heavy sarcasm. To Professor Casti: "Did you see anybody while you was clearing your brain?"

"No; no. I don't think so. I don't remember. I looked into the smoking-room when I stepped out, to see if there was anybody there. But the room was empty."

"Well, that was certainly too bad. The room was empty. About what time was that?"

"I don't know. Really I don't know."

"What time would you guess it was?"

"Oh, maybe ten o'clock or so. Because I walked around for perhaps half an hour or so, and then I came back to the Club and puttered around a little and went to bed, and I usually go to bed about eleven or a little later."

"You don't look at your watch when you go to bed?"

"Yes. But I didn't notice the time especially. So I suppose it was about the usual time."

"Ho. And you didn't see anybody?"

"No."

"Didn't see Prof Hyett around anywhere?"

"No."

"What time you get up this morning?"

"Why, at seven. I always get up at seven. I have an eight o'clock class. French 3."

"What time you have breakfast? And whereabouts?"

"In the Club. At half past seven. I always have breakfast at half past seven."

"All alone?"

"No. I had breakfast with Mr. Caleb of Education. There were several others in the dining-room. I didn't notice particularly."

Lieutenant Kennedy was feeling in his pocket. He pulled out the thesis slip and flashed it close before Professor Casti's eyes. Casti recoiled, nearly upsetting his chair.

"What's that? What's that?"

"Suppose you tell me."

"I don't know. I never saw it before."

"It seemed to surprise you."

"Of course it surprised me. I thought you were going to hit me in the face. And when I saw it—well, of course I've been thinking about murder since I heard about poor Mr. Hyett."

"You never saw nothing like it before?"

"No."

"That microfilm of yours; you've examined it closely?"

"The *Filius Getronis*? Certainly."

"Nothing like this on the microfilm?"

"Oh no, no. Dear me, no."

"Um. You and this Prof Hyett, you was pretty good friends?"

"Oh yes. Very good friends, I would say. I have been deeply afflicted by the news."

"Do you know anybody who might have wanted to do him in?"

"No, no. It's quite incredible."

"Well, I guess that'll be all. You got any questions, Mr. Wither?" He turned to the young man from the District Attorney's office.

Mr. Wither had no questions.

Professor Casti was dismissed. As he left he bumped into the side of the door.

"Hey!" shouted Lieutenant Kennedy. "If you see Prof Belknap or Parry out there, send them in."

Professor Casti smiled weakly.

Professor Belknap entered, courteous but annoyed. He sat down, fingering his Phi Beta Kappa key like an amulet. It was soon evident to Gilda that he regarded the Lieutenant as a dull fellow, one of the bores he was accustomed to enduring in the way of business. He made Gilda think of the professors she had interviewed when, a naïve sophomore, she had been a competitor for the college paper. The same air of polite fortitude. The way the Sphinx looks at tourists.

He reported that at ten the previous evening he had been in his rooms, reading. He had seen no one; he had gone to bed, according to his custom, at about half past eleven. He had come down to breakfast at about a quarter to eight. He had breakfasted alone, reading his newspaper, as was his invariable habit.

"But if you want a corroborating witness," he added, "I can refer you to the student waiter, and to several others of the faculty who were having breakfast. Mr. Parry was there; and Mr. Coffman; and I could probably think of several others."

"We don't question your word at all, prof," replied Lieutenant Kennedy. "Just routine, you know; just routine."

"Certainly. Just the routine examination of suspects in a murder case." Professor Belknap smiled.

Lieutenant Kennedy's dramatic presentation of the thesis slip with its injunction against murder was, relatively, a failure. Professor Belknap started, indeed, at the Lieutenant's gesture; he was not disconcerted. He denied that he had ever seen the slip before, and that a similar warning had appeared on his microfilm.

"You know, that suggests something," he volunteered. "Early yesterday evening, just after dinner in fact, quite a group had forgathered in the smoking-room. We were talking about murder, but rather in a tone of badinage. And Mr. Hyett suddenly exclaimed, in a very strange manner: 'Thou shalt do no murder!' I think we were all somewhat taken aback."

Lieutenant Kennedy's gum was stilled during a moment's meditation.

"Well, that's something! So it looks like this Prof Hyett was making a warning! And maybe he wrote out this here slip for a warning, too. And then he got choked to death for his trouble!"

"There is another possibility," said Professor Belknap, mildly. "Maybe this warning was directed to him. And his curious remark in the Faculty Club: 'Thou shalt do no murder,' may have been prompted by remorse."

"Remorse for what?"

"Remorse for murder."

"What murder?"

"Don't you know?"

"Well, I guess you're talking about that Coindreau accident

case. And you're trying to suggest that this Prof Hyett did in this Miss Coindreau, and then he got sorry and wrote himself warning notes, which he photographed and patched into films of a manuscript, and then he busted into the safe and took the manuscript and ate it and strangled himself!"

"Someone else could have written the warning note to him, and inserted the warning in his copy of the microfilm. And someone else could have strangled him, in revenge for the death of Mademoiselle Coindreau."

"And how did he open the locked press? And the safe? And what for? One thing, we'll soon find out what typewriter this note was written on. Um. *What's happened to that manuscript, young feller?*"

"What, you don't mean the *Filius Getronis*! Is it missing?"

"Where is it, I'm asking you?"

"The *Filius Getronis*! It couldn't be! It was in the safe!"

"It ain't in the safe now."

"But this is appalling! The *Filius Getronis*! We must get it back! Dr. Sandys, we must make every effort to get it back!"

Gilda was interested to note that Professor Belknap was so much more excited about the loss of the manuscript than he had been about the loss of Professor Hyett. Dr. Sandys uttered something like a groan.

Lieutenant Kennedy champed his gum.

"Well, I guess that's all, prof. You got any questions, Mr. Wither? No? Prof, if this Prof Parry is out there, send him in."

Francis Parry entered, his jauntiness barely subdued by a solemnity proper to the occasion. He informed the Lieutenant that he had spent the previous evening in his rooms, reading, correcting early themes, and writing letters. He had not gone

out after ten o'clock. He had seen no one. When the Lieutenant flashed the thesis slip at him, he was taken aback, but
not overcome. When questioned, he remembered the scene in
the smoking-room, and Professor Hyett's exclamation of "Thou
shalt do no murder!" which had seemed rather peculiar at the
time. He had no theories about the death of Professor Hyett.
He was shocked to hear of the disappearance of the manuscript,
but could give no helpful suggestions toward the solution of the
mystery.

"Well, I guess that's all, prof," said the Lieutenant.

Parry rose and nodded good-by. He turned toward Gilda and
made a gobbling grimace.

"Hey, what you doing?" cried the watchful Lieutenant.

"I was inviting Miss Gorham to lunch."

"Miss Gorham regrets," said Gilda.

The Lieutenant chewed moodily.

"Say, just to make it complete, where was you, Prof Sandys, at
ten o'clock last night?"

Dr. Sandys roused from his thoughts.

"Me? Why—why—I was working here in the Library. I
dropped in here from the Faculty Club. I stayed on until nearly
closing-time."

"All alone?"

"Yes. All alone. I met some people going out. Mr. Noble of
Economics. We were in the lobby when the exit bell rang at ten
twenty-five. I remember he made some joke about escaping in
time. Then I went back to the Club."

"Um. How about you, Miss Gorham?"

"I was home. Reading. All alone."

"How about this morning?"

"I got my own breakfast. I came up on the bus at a quarter to nine. I suppose I could have strangled Professor Hyett, rifled the safe, and spent the night at the Library. Then I could have rushed to my apartment at eight, changed quickly, and caught the eight forty-five bus. But I would have missed my breakfast."

"Huh. Well, I guess that's all for now. We got a lot of routine work to do, hey, Mr. Wither? We'll just get going on this case. None of you folks leave town."

He spat his gum into the Librarian's waste-basket. Probably the first time in a hundred years there was gum in the Librarian's waste-basket, thought Gilda.

Chapter XIII

Before entering the catalogue room, Gilda paused. Most of the staff and some of the faculty were certainly gathered there, putting their imaginations together. The girls would have done practically no work during the morning, and what they had done would have to be done over. Her entrance would assemble the whole group about her, demanding news. Her gorge rose at the thought. She didn't feel like going over the whole dirty business in detail. And she was tired of noise and bluster. What she wanted was peace and quiet.

It was nearly lunch-time. She could run over to the University Union. Fortunately she had clung to her bag throughout the morning.

Without a hat? Certainly without a hat. If anyone wanted to worry about it, they would take her for one of the free spirits from the Graduate School of Social Studies.

She put on her luncheon face and strolled to the Union. She dismissed the idea of feeding in the cafeteria, where long lines of students and staff members prodded one another in the kidneys with aluminum trays, and where they ate placidly amid the piled refuse of previous feeders. She dismissed the Blue Room, where one was served with Economy Specials on bare tables, with paper napkins. She entered the restaurant popularly known as the Tablecloth Room, which was commonly deserted, except for visiting parents, guests of the University, and a group of fastidious professors who liked to believe that linen napkins enhanced their morale. Here she had a table to herself, and quiet.

She experimented briefly with the first course, Tomato Juice Delight, an invention of the College of Home Economics, a blob of peach ice cream in tomato juice. And she let her thoughts run on their way.

Whoever had done the deed—why not call him the murderer?—had had access to the locked press and had known the combination of the safe. That suggested immediately Dr. Sandys. It meant that Dr. Sandys was rifling his own safe and ruining his own career. Perhaps he was interrupted by Mr. Hyett, and he strangled the intruder. Perhaps. But aside from the fact that Dr. Sandys had always seemed the soul of uprightness, a jealous guardian of his Library's treasures, and just not the sort of person to commit murder and grand larceny, Gilda felt certain that the crime was somehow connected with the death of Lucie Coindreau. And if Dr. Sandys was implicated in that, he must be a homicidal maniac. All right, maybe he was a homicidal maniac. Homicidal maniacs exist; they are just like ordinary people until their mania seizes them. Dr. Sandys, as well as anyone else, might be one.

The second course appeared. It was another creation of the College of Home Economics: a combination of sweet potatoes, bananas, and peanut butter, wrapped in bacon, crowned with marshmallow, and crouching on a leaf of lettuce.

"Would you rather have a chop?" said the sickly-looking student waitress, dully repeating the usual formula.

"No; I don't care; just bring me some black coffee," said Gilda. She separated the dainty into its component parts and ate them separately with rolls and butter. She avoided the surprise in the center of each roll: a ball of cheese, a piece of ginger, a maraschino cherry. She recalled a remark of Francis's, that he wouldn't be astonished to find a Black Widow spider in the middle of a Home Economics roll.

Supposing the murderer was not Sandys. Maybe he was a professional safe-robber, who could feel the tumblers of the lock with sensitive fingertips, pared to the blood. Why don't they use a stethoscope some time? Or one of these laboratory devices that amplify sound a thousand times? But this was mere fancy. Much more likely that the thief had learned the combination of the safe from Sandys. Did Sandys talk in his sleep? Had he in some access of folly told the combination to another? Had someone wormed it out of him by threats or bribes? Not likely, certainly; but after all, a possibility.

Of course, the previous Librarians had known the combination. Perhaps they had told—

Ah! The last Librarian was old Dr. Pickard, the cousin of Professor Hyett! They had been very close friends. Hyett had practically nursed Dr. Pickard through his final illness, a year ago. Perhaps in a moment of sick and aged folly the old Librarian had told Hyett the combination, and had given him the opportunity to duplicate the key to the locked press. Hyett was—had been —very handy with tools; probably he had plenty of equipment in his workshop to cut a blank key down to size.

This was good; this was excellent. Perhaps then Hyett had gone into the locked press and opened the safe and removed the manuscript, for some purpose of his own. And the thief had followed him, murdered him, and taken the manuscript.

Why? For gain? Or driven by the overpowering lust of the collector? Or, possibly, as a blind, to conceal the true reason?

In other words, was the murder a by-product of the theft, or the theft a by-product of the murder?

No answer.

There was another possibility. Perhaps the thief had known that Hyett possessed a key to the locked press and knew the combination of the safe. An incautious remark in the Faculty Club might have revealed Hyett's knowledge. And the thief could have forced Hyett to open the safe, and could then have killed him, on the principle that dead men tell no tales. Or again, the thief, knowing the combination, could have been surprised at work by Hyett and could have taken his grim revenge.

Hyett certainly had suspected something, or known something. Gilda remembered his warning to her, on the night of the Nobles' dinner, to keep out of the Library mystery. But what he had warned her about was inquiring into the death of Lucie Coindreau. So, as her woman's instinct (a detective instinct) had told her, the two deaths in the Wilmerding Library were connected. How?

The waitress brought her dessert, a fruit salad heavily lathered with whipped cream. Gilda carefully scraped off the cream into a little puddle at the side of her plate.

There was also, she thought, the whole question of time. The murderer, Ignotus, could have done his deed any time between ten and midnight. No one had an alibi for those hours. Not Sandys, Casti, Belknap, Parry, nor Cameron. Nor, in fact, Gilda

Gorham. Except that she would hardly be suspected of choking a man to death with her bare hands. Not that it was impossible, however. She could have got a good grip on that soft elderly neck, with her thumb-knuckles on the windpipe, and simply pressed. Brr-rr! She realized that she was crooking her thumbs and slowly strangling her napkin.

Supposing Ignotus had done his work after closing-time. How, then, did he escape from the Library? If his method was to wait till eight in the morning and then walk out, Ignotus was not Casti, nor Belknap, nor Parry, who had breakfast alibis; nor Sandys, who was outside the Library at closing-time. That left Cameron.

And Cameron, come to think of it, could have committed the murder after closing-time, and could then have calmly walked out the service door, setting the alarm device at any time he pleased.

Cameron!

He had testified, as had Gilda herself, that the only exit from the Library was by way of the three doors. It seemed curious that a great building like the Library should be so well sealed. Was there nothing they had overlooked, or concealed? A coal-chute, for instance? No, for the building was heated from the University steam plant. How about the ventilating system, whose tortuous channels ran through the entire building?

Perhaps there was a vent of the system in the locked press! Could a man have crawled through it into the press? Or out again?

She must look into the ventilating system.

She rose and went to pay the pallid cashier, who was shaking some digestive tablets into a glass of water.

"Here, give me a couple," said Gilda. "You ought to pass those out after every meal like after-dinner mints."

The cashier smiled drearily.

The trouble with these Home Economics meals, thought Gilda, is that they have lost touch with humanity. They aren't on the human scale. They are full of fancy and imagination, but they really demand some new organ to digest them. And maybe even that wouldn't work. What was that awful limerick of Francis's?

> *A phenomenal fellow of Weston*
> *Has about fifty feet of intestine;*
> *Though a signal success*
> *In the medical press,*
> *It isn't much good for digestin'.*

Chapter XIV

AFTER LUNCH Gilda stopped in at the Librarian's office.

"Dr. Sandys," she said, "I have an idea. I wish you would let me into the locked press."

"Certainly, Miss Gorham."

Dr. Sandys took the key from his desk drawer. He escorted Gilda up the stairs to the Wilmerding Library. She glanced about; no one was visible. Dr. Sandys unlocked the locked press and the two entered.

"I was wondering about the ventilating system," she said. "Is there a vent in the locked press? And if so, is it large enough for a man to crawl through?"

Dr. Sandys laughed. "Miss Gorham, I think your idea is a little fantastic. But let's try it, anyway. Let me see; yes, here is a vent in the wall. You see this grille. I should say it is about twenty inches square. A small man could conceivably wriggle through it. But notice that the grille is screwed over the vent, and there are no fresh marks on the screws. Besides, the air passage must run down vertically at some point. No, I'm afraid it's no soap, as the boys say."

"I'm afraid you're right," said Gilda, reluctantly.

"You aren't going to suggest that the killer had a trained mongoose or something?"

"No. A mongoose couldn't choke a man to death. Maybe a boa constrictor, which was educated to wrap itself around the victim's neck and constrict."

Both laughed. Curious how soon one could laugh about a thing like this.

"You know," said Gilda, "there is another thing I was wondering about."

"Yes, Miss Gorham?"

"I have never strangled anyone myself, nor been strangled. I was wondering how it is done. When the strangler gets his thumbs on the stranglee's windpipe, I should think the stranglee would be able to wiggle free, or at least hit and kick enough to leave a mark on the strangler. That is, unless the victim was knocked out first by a lead pipe or something."

"That is indeed a problem."

"Would you feel like trying to solve it?"

"How?"

"Let me try to strangle you."

"Bet you a nickel you can't strangle me!"

Gilda noticed with amusement that Dr. Sandys was actually playful.

"I'll bet you a nickel I can!"

Gilda reached suddenly for the Librarian's well-fleshed neck. Her hands were too small to clasp the neck; her thumbs found the windpipe beneath the beard and slipped on the short clipped bristles. Dr. Sandys raised his arms sharply and knocked her hands away.

"I didn't get a good hold that time! Of course, you were on your guard! Let me try again."

Dr. Sandys let Gilda settle her hands well in place. Smiling, he wound his arms over hers, drew her hands against his breast, and held them there imprisoned with one arm, while with the other hand he gave her nose a tiny tap. Gilda realized that his arms were extremely powerful, for a sedentary man.

"I won't try to strangle you! But it isn't fair. You're too strong!"

"Now I'll bet you a nickel I could strangle you!"

"All right."

Dr. Sandys's hands shot out and gripped Gilda by the throat. The thumbs rested lightly on her windpipe; the strong fingers pressed the back of her neck. Almost in earnest she raised her hands to fight. Dr. Sandys's elbows bent and forced her hands against her chest. His thumbs and fingers tightened, and he raised her from the floor. She kicked with foot and knee, but, being held close against his body, she knew that her kicks had little force.

"Enough!" she tried to cry. No sound emerged from her lips, not even a gasp. The world swayed, her mind raced and dived. Dr. Sandys's face slowly enlarged to more than life-size. There was a strange, hot gleam in his eyes.

She shook her head. At least she could shake her head. But would it do any good? Would anything do any good?

Dr. Sandys set her down and removed his hands. He was red in the face and breathing fast. He rubbed his brow with the back of his hand.

"Well," he said lamely, "I imagine I won my nickel."

"You won about twenty dollars, I should say." Angrily Gilda

patted her mussed hair. "You didn't need to prove the case so thoroughly."

"I am sorry. Something came over me. I suppose I—was rather captured by the spirit of the thing. You are all right?"

"Oh yes. Quite all right."

"Miss Gorham—Miss Gorham, no doubt it's very foolish of me, but there is something I think I ought to confess to you."

"Confess?"

"Dr. Sandys! Dr. Sandys!" A voice, with the intonation of a paging bellboy, sounded from the entrance to the Wilmerding.

"Yes," replied Dr. Sandys.

Cameron approached from the door. "Dr. Sandys, they're looking for you in your office. President Temple is there. Wants to talk over the shocking event."

"Oh, all right, Cameron. I'll be right along. That is all—ah—you wanted to consult me about, Miss Gorham? Then we can close the locked press."

He ushered Gilda out of the press, snapped the door shut, and hurried away to his office.

"Get what you wanted, Miss Gorham?"

"Certainly, Cameron," said Gilda frigidly. She could feel a hot blush rising to her face. She hoped Cameron had not seen it. Nor anything else.

Gilda decided that she needed a cigarette before returning to the catalogue room. She walked out the main Library door to the entrance porch, where busts of Socrates, Dante, Shakespeare, and Mr. Wilmerding look down with distaste on the cigarette butts flecking the stone floor. She lit a cigarette, adding her burnt match to the litter underfoot.

Perhaps the murderer had come out this way, only a few hours before. Or one of the other doors—

Why not stroll around and look at those doors? It would take less than the length of a cigarette to make the circuit of the Library.

With what she intended to be an idle, musing air, Gilda sauntered around the Library walls. The University's landscape gardener had tastefully surrounded the building with shrubs and bushes. Gilda looked in vain for vines stout enough to enable a courageous criminal to descend from an upper story.

She stopped short. A door! An inconspicuous door in the basement level, which she had never noticed, or which, at least, she had forgotten.

On one side of the door was a heavily grilled window. On the other side a large, stout grating was set in the wall. From the direction of the grating came the sound of a rhythmic *whank!* *whank!* *whank!* and the ground-bass of a motor.

But of course! It was the intake of the ventilating system! It was by way of the door that the machinery had been installed, and it was here that the mechanics entered to service the motor.

She peered through the heavily grilled window beside the door. She could see the large motor, connected by a fan-belt (going *whank!* *whank!* *whank!*) to the axle of the enormous fan in its metal housing. Beyond the motor she could see dimly into the Greek Literature stacks.

Of course! Between the machinery and Greek Lit was set an open grille, by means of which the motor was cooled, and an odor of hot oil wafted through Greek Literature. She remembered poor Mr. Hyett's complaints; he had said that the smell of hot oil was, after all, classical, and that he wouldn't object if only the administration would add a whiff of garlic.

She tried the door. It was locked.

But Cameron must have known of this door! And he had not mentioned it to the police Lieutenant!

To be sure, the door did not really give entrance to the Library, but only to the room that housed the machines. The grille separating the machinery room from the Library stacks was fixed irremovably in place. Or, at least, that was her recollection.

Gilda walked quickly around to the main entrance and descended two flights of iron stairs to the Greek Literature section. She inspected the grille. It was securely screwed into its frame. And the screws were on her side.

She peered through the grille at the external door. She could see the lock, an ordinary Yale-type lock.

Well, no one had escaped this way last night. Or—yes, there was a possibility. The culprit could have unscrewed the grille, walked out the door, and returned this morning with a screwdriver, to replace the screws.

She looked carefully at the screws. They were not dusty. The grooves in the screw-heads had been slightly abraded on both sides; hence they had been unscrewed as well as screwed in. But that proved nothing at all. There were no marks that looked unmistakably fresh, no litter, no tracks on the metal floor.

Well, she hadn't really discovered anything. But she felt she had not wasted her time.

There was something else she had mentally noted, to be further investigated. What was it, now?

Gilda's mind was admirably indexed. Ah, here it comes! The Hopkinson Library! The book-theft at the Hopkinson Library!

Someone had been talking about it not long ago, at the time of the Williams College theft, in fact. And whoever it was that told the story had mentioned that the theft had taken place during the war that we called, in our simplicity, the Great War. Gilda was just a kid then, of course, and totally uninterested in libraries.

She went to the periodical room and took down the *New York Times Index* for 1914. Under "Hopkinson Library" she found a few items about the acquisition of sensational book-treasures at sensational prices. Nothing about a theft. No luck in the Indexes for 1915 and 1916. But in 1917 she read: "Hopkinson Library: Theft of rare book. Jan. 12, 14:6. Cont'd, Jan. 13, 24:1. Book returned, Jan. 20, 11:4."

Nodding to the periodical-room librarian, she went behind the delivery desk and into the newspaper stacks. The *New York Times* was bound in enormous volumes, one to a month, and disposed in tiers according to the year. January was at the top, well above Gilda's head. Everything she had to look up in the *New York Times* seemed to have happened in January. She worked the volume out of its shelf and tipped its back toward her. When it began to slide like an avalanche, she succeeded in catching it on her head, her breast, and her knee on its descent to the floor. The next Library murder would probably be that of the editor of the *New York Times* by a librarian, using the *New York Times* as a lethal weapon. A blunt instrument, assuredly.

Gilda put her foot under the back, and tried to lift the mighty volume to a newspaper reading-desk, and then decided to consult it on the floor.

Here was January 12, page 14, column 6. Two paragraphs. The first told of the disappearance of the Paris Donatus of

1451 and of the mystification of the authorities. The second described the book. Its value was estimated at a hundred thousand dollars.

January 13, page 24, column 1. Everyone continued to be mystified. A summary of the examination of the Librarian, John Morrow, of the Reading-Room Superintendent, McCutcheon Voigt, of the messenger of the Rare Book Room, William Sandys—

William Sandys! Not our William Sandys, surely!

She looked at January 20, page 11, column 4. The book had been returned by parcel post. There was no clue to the sender.

William Sandys!

Gilda left the *New York Times* on the floor. At the periodical-room desk she told a weedy working student, who was employed by the Library at twenty-five cents an hour, to return the volume to its place. He rose with a sigh.

Gilda went to the reference room and took down *Who's Who*. She turned to Sandys, William. She read:

"SANDYS, William Bentley, librarian; *b.* San Francisco, June 18, 1893; *s.* William Henry and Dimple (Cummings) S.; A.B., U. of Calif., 1914; A.M., 1916; Ph.D., Columbia, 1924; unmarried. Enlisted U. S. Army 1917; commissioned 2d. Lieut. Inf. . . ."

Well, that was interesting! If our Dr. Sandys was the Hopkinson Library messenger of 1917, he had omitted to put in *Who's Who* the beginning of his library career. And he failed to mention what he was doing between the taking of his A.M. in 1916 and his enlistment in 1917.

No wonder he had been shocked to discover that the *Filius Getronis* was missing! But then, he would have been shocked anyhow. He had seemed, in fact, on the edge of collapse. But that didn't prove anything. The trouble was that nothing proved anything!

It was high time she was getting back to the catalogue room. She returned the *Who's Who* to its place, which is more than most people do.

In the lobby she met Cameron. He was carrying six rebound volumes of the *Encyclopædia Britannica*.

"Cameron!" she said sharply.

Cameron halted. "Yes, Miss Gorham?"

"I have just been looking around a little. And I noticed the door of the ventilating apparatus."

"Yes, Miss Gorham."

"In your testimony to Lieutenant Kennedy, you didn't mention that door."

"He didn't mention it either."

"You should have suggested that it was a possible means of escape for a criminal."

"Oh, but, Miss Gorham, there's a fixed grille there! No one could get out that way."

"They could if they had a screwdriver."

"Yes, but Miss Gorham, all the screws were in place this morning. I looked specially."

"Would you swear to that?"

"Certainly."

"Anyhow, I think you ought to mention it to Lieutenant Kennedy. Or I will myself."

Cameron slowly set down his burden of *Britannicas* on the floor.

"Now look here, Miss Gorham, do you really think it's a good thing to go and tell everything you know to the police?"

"Of course."

"I think that just bothers them. I think it's better to wait until people ask you something. That's my advice to you, Miss Gorham, and I used to be a detective. Wait until you're asked."

"If I ask you something, will you give me an answer?"

"Why, of course, Miss Gorham."

"Who do you think murdered Mr. Hyett?"

Cameron waited several moments before replying.

"Well now, I tell you, Miss Gorham. When I was a detective, I found out that most crimes have something to do with money. 'Cherchez la femme,' they say, but the cops say: 'cherchez le jack.' About the first thing the cops do is to investigate what they call the financial status of the people involved. It don't usually prove anything, but it gives them an idea where to look."

"I presume they will do so in this case."

"Yes. But they may not have all the opportunities of some private individuals. Some people don't like to go around blabbing everything they know to the cops. But they do tell things to their friends. For instance, I happen to know that there's an organization in town called the Excelsior Personal Loan."

"I've heard of it. A shyster money-lending outfit."

"That's it. But they're very confidential. A lot of people go to them who don't want to be seen borrowing money from a bank. For instance, your friend Dr. Sandys borrowed a thousand dollars from Excelsior when he came here in July, giving a lien against his salary as security."

"How do you know this?"

"I'm a director."

Cameron smiled, with a deprecating air of triumph. "But I think it would be a shame to bring all that up to the police, don't you? So, as I was just suggesting, better not go telling them things until they ask you. See?"

"I think I see."

"Well, I must be getting my exercise. We all ought to keep in trim. I get pretty near enough exercise around the Library. I don't have to do any calisthenics. If I do need to, maybe I could join you in the locked press? You and—"

"Cameron!"

Cameron smiled sweetly, picked up the six volumes of the *Encyclopædia Britannica* with no appearance of effort, and walked lightly away.

Chapter XV

GILDA ENTERED the catalogue room. She was conscious that all the bright, inquiring eyes of the staff were fixed upon her. She sat down at her desk with a flounce and seized a handful of communications in her Incoming basket.

A letter from an alumnus saying that his wife had picked up a very ancient book with the covers gone, a school arithmetic of 1830, and asking if it was, possibly, of great value. An offer from another alumnus to bequeath his library to the University, with the remark, apropos of nothing, that his brother had just been made an honorary LL.D. by Allegash College. She glanced down the attached inventory of the library. Allen and Greenough's *Latin Grammar; Le Voyage de Monsieur Perrichon; David Harum; Graustark. . . .*

No, no, no. She didn't have to do this sort of thing, with people dropping dead all over the place. She wanted to think, and, by golly, she had a right to think once in a while.

She rose, went to the south stack, and down two decks to the ground level. At the top of a circular iron staircase she snapped on the lights of the crypt.

The crypt was the Library's basement, storehouse, junkyard, and dungeon. In the tall presses were stored those unhappy books condemned, barring a special pardon, never to see the light of day. A collection of duplicates; a file of U. S. Patent Office records; the Wilmerding Time-table Collection; the Mosher Collection of Stereoscopic Slides; and all the old odds and ends which, for one reason or another, it was inexpedient to give away or destroy. It was always cool in the crypt, and always quiet; and always, too, ghostly, secret, and melancholy. Gilda liked it.

She chose an alcove lined with a set of Siamese classics presented by the King of Siam. She found one of the kitchen chairs which are standard library equipment. It would be nice to have a cigarette. . . . But no, that would be too dreadful. She smiled, recalling that Cameron had once caught a trustee smoking in the stacks. Cameron, standing just out of sight of the trustee, had tactfully shouted: "Come on there, boys; no smoking, or out you go on your ear!"

Let's get down to business. She had two new facts, if they were facts. She had obtained them, to be sure, at a cost. She had made a tacit bargain with Cameron not to mention the door to the ventilating apparatus. Her new facts were: that Dr. Sandys had once been questioned, and probably suspected, in the case of a book theft; and that he was in financial difficulties. But why? He certainly had a good salary, probably of seven or eight thousand, and he lived very modestly, in simple bachelor style. He probably didn't spend more than two or three thousand a year. Where did it all go, then?

Family obligations? Some relative with an expensive disease? Blackmail?

Was somebody living comfortably off his past sin, or indiscretion?

No answer.

There was also the curious excitement he had shown in the strangling test in the locked press. The bizarre idea had already occurred to her that he might be a homicidal maniac. That idea she had lightly dismissed. Nevertheless, she was ever more impressed, as she grew older, by the lurid things that are hidden by the outward decorum of individuals, and of society. To take even a mild case: there was a professor in Entomology who, after twenty-five years of blameless married life, had arranged a divorce from his wife, a theosophist who lived mostly on raw carrots. And he had married a totally brainless little knee-flaunting sophomore who had sat in the front row of his lecture course. The public announcements in the case had been flat and formal, and the professor himself seemed a stodgy fellow, God knows. But a thorough psychological and pathological record of the case would reveal a fantastic tale of passion and folly. It would have to be kept in the locked press. In the card-catalogue she would put a see-also card under Sin.

Perhaps she hadn't been thinking about this murder business sufficiently under the heading of Sin.

What were the seven deadly sins, now? Pride, envy, anger, sloth, avarice, and—hum—gluttony, and—what was it? Oh yes—lust.

Pride. Pride is the most sinful sin of all, the one that Dante puts on the lowest shelf of purgatory. Dante got around a good deal; he ought to know. And yet, in the present case, it was hard to see how Pride could have caused the death of Lucie Coindreau and Mr. Hyett, and the theft of the *Filius Getronis*.

Strike out Pride.

Envy. Of course, there was Casti! He was afraid that Lucie would get the associate professorship he coveted. Perhaps he was secretly jealous of Hyett. Jealous enough to kill him? Even if so, that didn't explain the theft of the manuscript. But before the theft Casti had been pulling every string to get the manuscript in his hands by legitimate means. He wanted it badly. Perhaps he was surprised by Hyett while he was in the act of stealing it.

Fairly good. How about Anger?

Sandys, maybe. That sudden rush of blood to the head when he was pretending to throttle her. Then there was that funny business, a couple of weeks ago, when a man had attacked with a stick a boy and girl sitting on a bench behind the Library. Nothing like that had ever happened before Sandys's arrival. Perhaps he had had such an access of rage toward Lucie Coindreau. Perhaps, again, he had been rifling the safe, and had been discovered by Hyett, and had strangled Hyett in fear and fury. There was that other book-theft at the Hopkinson. People are consistent; they don't learn by experience. Exposed to the same set of stimuli, they always exhibit the same responses, and act accordingly. That's psychology.

How about Belknap, under Anger? He was one of those repressed boys, an adrenalin-secreter. And if at some point he couldn't control his adrenals, he might burst forth into frantic violence. Yes, but why should he commit two murders and grand larceny?

Or how about Casti, for that matter? He was an Italian, and they were famous for their thoroughgoing vendettas. *Vendetta* means "revenge," in Italian. Could revenge come in?

Why, yes! Suppose that Hyett had murdered Lucie, in a burst of senile dementia or something. And Casti, secretly in love with Lucie, murdered Hyett, and took the manuscript for good measure. But that scenario would fit Belknap, Sandys, or Parry just as well. And it was all just fancy, anyway.

Sloth. Well, murder was no job for a lazy man. Strike out Sloth.

Avarice. Sandys, again. Or Cameron? The fact that Cameron was mixed up in the Excelsior Personal Loan revealed something new. He had money, he was fairly unscrupulous about making more. He was likely to know how to dispose of a stolen manuscript to his advantage. He had told her, gratuitously, a fact which cast suspicion on Sandys. Why? Only to divert suspicion from himself? Or was there a deeper purpose?

Put down Cameron for Avarice. Or possibly Casti? Possibly. Certainly not Belknap or Parry.

Gluttony?

Gluttony is an obsolete vice. It was a reality to Dante, in the Middle Ages; it is the vice of hungry races and haggard times, when to feed full is to rob the starving. Strike out Gluttony.

And Lust? Well, perhaps in the case of Lucie's death. Any one of the five men could be suspected. But it was hard to charge the second murder and the theft to Lust. Unless they were the results, in some way, of the first crime. Or unless the two crimes were committed by different people.

Of course, she hadn't put in Ignotus anywhere. There was always Ignotus, who was probably a victim of all the seven deadly sins.

Maybe also there were some new sins that Dante didn't know about. Morality seems to be subject to constant revision, in the light of new ideologies. Murder itself, for instance.

"Miss Gorham! Oh, Miss Gorham!"

It was Dr. Sandys's voice, calling from the circular staircase that led down to the crypt.

Gilda felt that she did not want to be bothered by Dr. Sandys, especially if he was in his throttling mood. She made no answer.

What did Dr. Sandys want with her, anyway? And why did he suspect she was in the crypt?

He had a funny voice, she reflected. A sort of rasping huskiness in it that was not unpleasant. Gilda smiled, and tried to imitate it. "Miss Gorham! Oh, Miss Gorham!"

Not very good. Casti could do a better imitation of it. Probably got the phonetic values right, the proper number of vibrations per second.

Could the voice she had just heard have been Casti imitating Dr. Sandys?

There were getting to be too many mysteries around this Library.

"My dear Miss Gorham!"

It was Francis Parry, beaming at her.

"Why, Francis! Were you calling me?"

"Yes."

"Why did you imitate Dr. Sandys?"

"I thought it would sound more official, sort of."

"Showing off your stage technique. How did you know I was down here?"

"Cameron told me. He said it was your favorite hideaway. And I wanted to see you. I wanted to ask you to go to the concert tonight."

"It's Giulia Thalmann, isn't it? Oh, I should like to hear her."

"Good. I'll stop and get you. Dinner first?"

"No. I won't have time to do it comfortably."

"Cosy down here, isn't it?"

"Francis, there was something I had on my mind to tell you."

"Yes?"

"What was it, now? Oh yes! I started to make up a limerick about Mr. Belknap. And I got stuck, so I wanted you to finish it. It went—let me see—

> *A scholar who came from Ohio*
> *Was deeply enamored of Clio.*

But then what?"

"That's quite a problem. There isn't much that rhymes with Clio. There's a place near Paris called Chaillot. And there was a Spanish scholar named Menéndez y Pelayo. But I don't see how to drag them in."

"I was thinking of 'heigh-ho.'"

"No. That makes an impure rhyme with 'Ohio,' and in a limerick you must above all things be pure. There is 'trio.' But I don't see how to do anything with 'trio.' Wait a minute. . . . Here comes something. . . . Quiet. . . . Absolute silence. . . .

> *A scholar who came from Ohio*
> *Was consumed by a passion for Clio.*
> > *I dunno what you use*
> > *When you ravish a Muse,*
> *But you never can tell till you try-O.*"

"Mild."

"Not one of my best efforts. But I didn't have time for meditation. A good limerick is produced by meditation, labor, and prayer."

"What, a mere limerick?"

"Scorn not the limerick. It is our commonest and most be-loved verse-form. It has its own perfection. Try making any al-teration in its structure; every alteration is for the worse. Like all art, the beauty of a perfect limerick arises from the fitting of a beautiful, gem-like thought to a strict and difficult pattern. I call it the 'poor man's sonnet.'"

Gilda laughed.

"It's the only important verse-form which the English have invented. And the strange thing is that it did not come into the open in English poetry until about a hundred years ago. How could it have escaped Shakespeare, for instance? Or Milton?"

"Edward Lear invented it, didn't he?"

"No. He took it from an anonymous collection of verses for children entitled: *Anecdotes and Adventures of Fifteen Gentle-men*, which was published about 1820. My own theory is that it was developed from nursery rhymes. 'Hickory, dickory, dock' is in limerick form, and is probably very ancient. It suggests in its wording an old gypsy spell, which begins: 'Ekkeri, akai-ri, you kair-an.' And that suggests the numerals in Sanskrit, and also the very ancient Anglo-Cymric score, by means of which the shepherds still count their sheep. Fascinating how things hook up. 'Dance a baby diddy' is a limerick too, come to think of it. Well, I imagine that the illustrious, though unknown, writer of the *Anecdotes and Adventures of Fifteen Gentlemen* realized the possibilities in the thumping rhythm and brought it for the first time into literature."

"Didn't Lucie Coindreau have some theory about the lim-erick?"

"Yes. She had turned up a couple of examples, one from the Ménagiana, I remember, of the mid-seventeenth century. It had the right rhyme-scheme, a a b b a, but lines three and four were the same length as lines one, two, and five. I had to tell her it was an improper limerick."

There was a short silence. Gilda suddenly decided to try Lieutenant Kennedy's technique.

"Speaking of Lucie," she said, "did you ever have an affair with her?"

There was a longer silence.

"You asked me that once before, Gilda. And I said no. After all, a man is supposed to say no."

"Not to a girl he wants—well, not to me."

"Maybe. Lucie is dead now, and what I say can't affect her. It can only affect me. Well then, I did have an affair with her."

"Oh. Why didn't you marry her?"

"I didn't really love her. It was what she called a *passade*. She was pretty angry because that is all it was. She was apparently fonder of me than I was of her. No doubt this is all very boorish of me, if not caddish, but you wanted the truth and I am telling it to you. We went for one week-end together to a shore resort. And then we didn't go again."

"Why not?"

"Well, the fact is, she had too much temperament for my chill northern blood. Besides—"

Though Parry's mood had been tensely serious, he permitted a gradual smile to develop on his face.

"The fact is, our week-end cost about a hundred and fifty dollars. And at that time I wanted to buy a set of the *Encyclopædia*

Britannica. And when the question of a second week-end came up, I thought it all over and decided I would get more lasting satisfaction out of the *Encyclopædia.* I tried to explain tactfully to Lucie; I described the *Encyclopædia* in most glowing terms, and suggested that we should sit side by side, reading it aloud to each other. I showed her the advertising brochure. She nearly murdered me with it."

Gilda might have been amused had it not been for Francis's last phrase. Someone had actually murdered Lucie, out of love or hate, such love or hate as Francis had hinted beneath the humorous surface of his tale. No doubt he had told the truth. But he was too inclined to shy away from the really important, the really serious, and turn it into a joke. And also, come to think of it, he was a very good actor. He could express his feelings very well; he could also disguise them. She sat impassive, trying to reveal none of her thought.

She shivered, and rose from her chair.

"Come on, Francis. I must be getting back to work."

Francis's long arms shot out. One hand caught her by the neck and drew her imperatively toward him. With a little cry she twisted sidewise, out of his grasp. Then she laughed.

"Francis! I thought you were going to strangle me!"

"My idea was that I would kiss you!"

Again his arms reached for her.

"Francis! No! Not now! Not here!"

"Why not?"

"Not in the Library!"

The tense, ridiculous pout of a man about to kiss disappeared from Francis's face. He laughed.

"I see. No desecration of the temple. Amour in the stacks strictly forbidden. Well, all right, my dear Gilda. Back to work. You go first. I'll see you this evening, anyway."

As Gilda climbed the circular stairs Francis, close behind her, amused himself by pinching her ankles, just above the shoe-heels.

Chapter XVI

WHEN FRANCIS Parry called for Gilda that evening, he seemed to have something on his mind. He showed her into his car, a natty convertible, and set his course for the Lancaster Memorial Auditorium.

Gilda was reminded of a recent ride in another natty convertible.

"I wonder what will become of poor Mr. Hyett's car, and the rest of his things," she said.

There was no answer. She looked at Parry in surprise and saw him staring somberly through the windshield. He caught her look.

"What? Sorry. I was thinking of something else."

"Has anything happened?"

"Well, yes. Your friend Lieutenant Kennedy and his merry men have been in, searching the Faculty Club. Purely a matter of routine, he explained."

"Don't they have to have a search-warrant or something?"

"I believe so. But he put his visit on such a friendly man-to-man basis that I didn't ask to see the search-warrant. After all, if I objected I might become a major suspect, and then he would drag me off for questioning and search the rooms anyhow."

"But they wouldn't suspect you, Francis, would they?" Gilda glanced slyly at him.

"I don't know why not. If I were Lieutenant Kennedy I'd suspect me. There are moments when I even suspect myself. Anyway, he found out one thing. He tried out all our typewriters. He wanted to find out who wrote that card, you know, 'Thou shalt do no murder.' Well, he discovered that it wasn't written on mine."

"I wonder whose it was written on."

"It was written on Hyett's. Kennedy just couldn't help telling me. For a sleuth, he doesn't seem to carry reticence to a fault."

"So! On Hyett's typewriter! That proves that the words were written by Hyett as a warning to someone else, and not by someone else as a warning to Hyett!"

"I suppose so. Unless someone else had access to his typewriter."

"Possible but not probable. It suggests further that Hyett knew or suspected something about the death of Lucie Coindreau."

"Are you going in for solving murder mysteries? Isn't that a little dangerous, my dear Gilda?"

It was dangerous, Gilda recognized. It was particularly dangerous as long as the name of Francis Parry was not crossed off her list of suspects. She changed the subject.

"Did they find the manuscript?"

"No." Parry grinned. "But they found something else in Hyett's rooms. They found a peerless collection of dirty pictures. Judging by Kennedy's pop-eyed description, they were mostly things with some sort of classical or artistic justification. Art at ten dollars a volume, Greek vase-paintings, wall-paintings from the lupanars of Pompeii."

"Lupanar! That's a pretty word."

"It's a beautiful word, now that you mention it. Swinburne was probably crazy about it. It belongs in the rich, syrupy poetry of the 1890's.

> *Why is my soul unpopular,*
> *A leper in a lupanar?*

If Oscar Wilde or Ernest Dowson didn't write that, it's because they never got around to it."

Parry seemed to have recovered all his good spirits.

"Look! A parking-space!"

Parry sped toward a vacant space by the curb, but was beaten by a station-wagon. For fifteen minutes all his attention and Gilda's were taken by the parking problem, that gigantic game of pussy-wants-a-corner which occupies so large a part of America's time and energy.

The two entered the Lancaster Memorial Auditorium, a great melancholy hall used for such functions as the University Music Series, commencement exercises, and the productions of the Motley, student musical comedies which derive their only humor from the fact that the chorus girls are large hairy-legged males, singing bass.

Francis and Gilda settled in their seats, nodded to friends, and opened their programs.

"I see that Giulia Thalmann is going to demonstrate this

evening that she can pronounce five languages," said Francis.

"I'm glad we're early. I always enjoy reading over the English translations of the songs. Here's a pretty bit, for instance. S. Rachmaninoff: 'Sorrow in Springtime.'

> *In the springtime when joy's in the air*
> *And the brightness of hope fills the land,*
> *How my spirit in anguish doth moan,*
> *And my soul is bowed down with its pain!"*

"Sad. My spirit moans with sympathetic anguish. And here's more woe, if you can stand it. Respighi's 'Nebbie':

> *I suffer far, far away,*
> *The creeping, dreamy mist*
> *Rises from the silent plain.*
>
> *From the air to the crude gnawing*
> *The suffering bodies*
> *Offer, praying, their naked breasts.*
>
> *How cold I am! I am alone;*
> *To the gray, limitless skies*
> *The dying groan ascends."*

"A bleak picture indeed," said Gilda. "How these singers do suffer!"

"It's the contraltos who suffer. A soprano is relatively bright and gay, but a contralto never has any fun. They're nothing but human cellos."

Francis and Gilda sniggered together, drawing some reproving glances from music-lovers who took their music as a sacrament.

"Here's a tasty bit, too," said Francis. "'Cäcilie,' music by Richard Strauss, words by Heinrich Hart:

> *If you but knew, sweet, what living is,*
> *In the creative breath of God, Lord and Maker,*
> *To hover, upborne on dove-like pinions*
> *To regions of light—if you but knew it,*
> *Could I but tell you, you'd dwell, sweet, with me.*

If I understand that, Herr Heinrich Hart is trying to tell his girl friend that if she will move into his apartment she will have the happy experience of living in the creative breath of God, Lord and Maker. Heinrich Hart must be quite distinguished in his way. But he finds it impossible to tell her so. Why can't he tell her, since he seems to make it clear to the casual reader?"

"Probably she is too dumb. Or maybe her mother has told her to look out for Herr Heinrich and his dove-like pinions. 'Very pretty, Herr Heinrich,' she says, 'but by me it is *Äpfelbrei*.'"

"What is *Äpfelbrei*?"

"Applesauce."

Bells rang in the corridors. The student ushers closed the auditorium doors. The lights dimmed. The velvet curtains of the stage parted, and Giulia Thalmann appeared.

She was a queenly woman, in the great tradition of the opera. Tall and massive, she posed in a circle of light. Her low-cut evening gown, with sweeping train, was white and bespangled, sparkling like a stop-sign. Her eyes and teeth sparkled also, as she greeted her audience with what seemed an enormous collective kiss. Her great bosom, mat white in the midst of the sparkle, rose and fell gently like a sea of milk.

"She certainly has a great pair of lungs," whispered Francis to Gilda.

Gilda slapped his hand.

Giulia Thalmann gleamed at every quarter of the auditorium, and glanced at her accompanist, who had furtively slipped in to the piano. Her tongue made the circuit of her lips. The accompanist brought down his hands. The upper part of the singer's face assumed an archly infantile air, while her mouth followed the rules of efficient voice-production. She sang a song of Ad. Jensen's, words by Heyse:

> *As so oft before I've listen'd,*
> *I shall hear him tell his yearning,*
> *Tell his love so hotly burning*
> *For my eyes that starlike glisten'd,*
> *As his "little snake" I'm christen'd;*
> *Yet he slumbers, breathing low,*
> *Yet he slumbers, breathing low.*
> *Shall I wake him now?*
> *Shall I wake him now?*
> *Ah no! Ah no!*

As she questioned whether or not she should wake the hotly burning lover, she seemed to plead with the audience for an answer. Her voice assumed a thrilling, penetrating quality that would have roused anyone else, though he were dozing in the lobby. *"Ach nein! Ach nein!"* she boomed, and the packed auditorium breathed with relief that the loved one could continue in his sodden slumber.

Six thousand palms smacked their approval. Francis and Gilda joined in. There are few who dare to refrain when the world is applauding, thought Gilda. Hence the universality of the Nazi salute, in the Dark Continent. Anyway, Giulia Thalmann was really a very fine singer.

"Why do you suppose that sleepy lover called her his little snake?" Gilda whispered. "'Little hippopotamus' would have been more appropriate."

Francis smiled. But he seemed abstracted. Gilda noticed that his lips were moving, in a barely perceptible way.

The concert continued. Giulia Thalmann proclaimed, in English, French, German, Italian, and Swedish, that she would fain be a lark, a dove, a storm, a dew-drop, even an apple blossom. She dealt mostly with love, in its aspects of unsatisfied longing and despair. After each revelation of her woe she turned her glittering smile and her heaving breast to the audience and dropped little coquettish curtsies, to the multitudinous patter of the palms.

Francis was still abstracted. He drew a pencil from the pocket of his dinner coat and wrote with it in a blank space of his program. Giulia Thalmann was thundering, with a dreadful grimace of the upper face, while the mouth went steadily about its business:

> *Joyful and grieving, or buried in thought,*
> *Longing and fearing, with agony taut. . . .*

(Words by Goethe, music by Schubert.)

Francis passed the program to Gilda. She read:

There's a singer in Long Island City
Whose form is impressively pretty;
* She is often addressed*
* By the name of "Beau Chest,"*
Which is thought to be tasteful and witty.

Gilda snorted, tried to bury the snort in a cough, and produced a horrible strangling noise. People for several rows around turned to her, frowning, their lips pursed in reproof. Gilda turned red and redder, and strangled again. Even the singer contrived to dart a fierce glance in her direction, without altering her facial mask of sweet despair. Francis, beaming, pretended to be totally occupied with drinking in the music.

In the intermission half of the three thousand auditors tried to crowd into the lobby, to smoke a cigarette. Francis and Gilda, rammed against a pillar, exchanged greetings and commentaries with their friends and breathed the mingled incense of innumerable cigarettes. Dr. Fox, head of the Department of Music, worked his way to and fro, picking out a few of the musically minded to be honored with an invitation to drop in at his house after the concert and meet the singer. He had noticed Gilda's misbehavior; he passed her with an unseeing eye.

The learned criticized Giulia Thalmann's breathing, voice-control, and tone-production. Nearly everyone else talked about the murder.

Dr. Sandys forced a determined way toward the pair.

"Good evening, Miss Gorham. Good evening, Parry. Wonderful, isn't it?"

"Wonderful," said Parry. "Wonderful. Is there any news?"

"If there is anything important, I haven't heard it. They haven't learned, apparently, that anyone profits especially by the death of poor Hyett. His property goes to some female relatives in Cincinnati."

"I wonder what they will do with his art works. Have them framed for the parlor?"

Dr. Sandys frowned and glanced at Gilda. "I'm sure I have no idea. You've heard that they have identified the typewriter that wrote: 'Thou shalt do no murder'?"

"Yes. Miss Gorham points out that evidently Hyett was warning somebody. Maybe you or me. Or Miss Gorham herself."

Dr. Sandys frowned again.

Gilda decided to try once more the method of the direct question.

"Dr. Sandys," she said, "who do you think did it?"

"I have no idea."

"Who might have stolen the manuscript?"

"I don't know. But I think it will come back of its own accord."

"Why?"

"They usually do. The thief finds out that a unique treasure of that sort is practically unsalable. And it is too dangerous to keep, with the police searching everywhere. And if the—ah—culprit is an academic person, he will hardly be able to bring himself to destroy the only known text of a medieval miracle play."

"Well, I hope you're right. There's the bell."

The bell rang, the lights winked. The smokers did their best to find, amid the flicker of silken legs and billowing gowns, a patch of floor on which to crush out their cigarettes. They filed back to their seats, while a blue cloud of smoke gushed into the auditorium.

The lights dimmed. Giulia Thalmann again made her majestic entrance. She beamed at the applauding audience, now old acquaintances. With a condescending gesture, she drew the audience's attention to the accompanist, as if he were an imbecile cousin whom one has to have around.

She launched into the aria from *Thaïs*: "Qui te fait si sévère?" She was Thaï's, blasting Athanaël with her violent reproach. One of the dimmed electric-light bulbs in the ceiling shivered and burned out. Through the whole tirade she managed to preserve something of her smile.

Gilda let her thoughts stray a little. And suddenly she knew something. She knew the meaning of "papoose."

She knew who had been in the Occulta section of the Wilmerding with Lucie Coindreau, on the morning before she died. She knew how and why Lucie had died.

And as she pondered, she knew why Hyett had died.

She knew everything.

Chapter XVII

GILDA DID not get to sleep till late that night. On Saturday morning she woke, to the alarm-clock's snarl, feeling drugged and unsteady. She put on the coffee, mixed a hasty potion of orange-juice, and began to resume human shape.

She took in the college daily from her door. She liked the college paper, for its information about campus activities and for the appealing youthfulness with which the news was misunderstood and misrepresented.

The front page was plastered with news of the murder. Well, she knew all about that. That was not the mild digestive she needed with her breakfast. This was more the idea: a description of the new insect exhibit at the College of Agriculture. The housefly shown in all stages from the egg onward. Microscopic views of bedbugs and other vermin. Examples of various bugs, spiders, lice, borers, weevils, and worms. A demonstration that the common click beetle, or elater, and the wire worm are the same thing at different ages. That was the sort of thing she liked with her coffee. Or this paragraph, summarizing a lecture on Goethe:

"Goethe, who died just a century before March 22, 1932, was the author of *Iphigenia on Tauris* and of *Faust*, his greatest poem.

While living he was the associate and close friend of Karl August, Grand Duke of Saxe-Weimar, at whose court he did a large part of his best work."

She smiled, thinking of the student mind, desperately grasping at tangible facts, unable to order the facts or to find value and significance in them. She liked also to think of the lecturer, reading this report of his lecture, in which presumably he had presented and argued to a brilliant conclusion some thesis on the life, work, and meaning of Goethe.

Thus breakfast passed pleasantly. Gilda folded the paper and rose. But as she was turning away, her eye caught a large box on the first page. It was an appeal to the students and faculty. Every person who had left the Library between ten and ten thirty p.m. Thursday was asked to report to the Librarian's office immediately.

This was the police, clearly. Lieutenant Kennedy or one of his men would be in the Librarian's office, examining the students, trying to find out when Hyett had entered the Library, and whether any of the logical suspects had been seen going in or coming out.

Well, good luck to the investigators. In the meantime she had a call to make.

She took a bus to a section of town, on the fringe of the University, that had gradually slipped down from residential to rooming. Student supply stores, candy stores, restaurants, groceries, and barber shops stood eagerly by the sidewalks. Daintily withdrawn were the homes of the nineties, their lines strangely altered with bulges, tumors, and excrescences, which showed where a bathroom had been added or an attic enlarged to make two rooms and a kitchenette.

Gilda turned in at one of these houses, crossed a strip of gray lawn, and climbed a creaking veranda. She looked at the name-plates above the bells. Yes; one of them bore the name of Mlle Lucie Coindreau. Lucie had economized on lodgings in order to spend, in better times, her summers in France, departing on the first French liner sailing after June exams, and returning on the last one docking before registration.

Gilda rang the bell of the ground-floor apartment: Mr. and Mrs. Herbert G. Burns.

A tall, gaunt, elderly woman with an early-American face opened the door. Gilda recognized her. She had been Martha Edgcumbe, one of the Edgcumbes who had first settled the city. She had married, against her family's opposition, Herbert Burns, a handsome clerk in her father's dry-goods store, an intoxicating dancer. At her father's death she had put her husband in charge of the store. By easy stages the couple had lost everything except the family mansion, which they had transformed into a set of apartments.

"Mrs. Burns!" said Gilda brightly. "I'm Gilda Gorham, from the University Library. I've heard about you. You gave a talk to the D.A.R. about the early history of the city, didn't you?"

Mrs. Burns's suspicious face relaxed. "Yes, Miss Gorham. I've heard about you, too. You're in the paper this morning."

"I wanted to know if I could see Miss Coindreau's apartment."

"What for?"

"Why, she had some Library books out that are wanted urgently. And I wanted to see if by chance she had them here."

"Come in, Miss Gorham."

The two entered the ground-floor apartment. A fat, bris-

tle-chinned man in shirt-sleeves, reading a newspaper and rocking in a rocking-chair, rose without a word and went into the
kitchen.

"What I want to know, Miss Gorham, is who is going to pay
for Miss Coindreau's apartment? Here it is the beginning of
school with everybody established for the year, and who is going to rent an apartment now? Miss Coindreau hadn't paid me a
cent, but I have her lease all signed. That's legal, and I expect to
get my money!"

"I'll ask the University's legal expert about it, Mrs. Burns, if
you will just let me look around a little."

"Will you? That's very kind."

Mrs. Burns took a key from an ancient desk and led the way
to Mademoiselle Coindreau's apartment.

"I don't know if I really should let you in here. The police told
me not to let anyone in. But I don't know how I'm ever going to
rent the apartment if I can't show it."

"The police? Did they take anything?"

"Took all her letters and papers."

"Oh." This was too bad. Gilda had hoped to do a little prying,
which she would justify as "investigation."

"You didn't happen to see around a French toy I have a sort
of sentimental interest in? Just a little silvered ball on a string?"

"No. I don't know what I'm going to do with all Miss Coindreau's stuff. It ought to come to me in place of rent. But it don't
amount to much. Mostly books. French books. I don't know
who'd buy a lot of French books."

Gilda was swiftly appraising the book-shelves. A section devoted to French classics. A long row of poets, mostly the Ro-
mantics, Musset, Lamartine, Vigny. And a large collection of

modern novels, paper-backed, well worn. The great men of the last generation: Barrès, Loti, Anatole France, Bourget. And the contemporaries: Gide, Montherlant, Lacretelle, Chardonne, and the rest. Reference books, and volumes obviously presented by her colleagues, and certainly containing inscriptions expressing the respectful homage of the authors.

Not a remarkable library in any way. But Gilda was satisfied. She had found out what she wanted to know.

"I'm sorry," she said. "I didn't find the library books I was looking for. Thank you for letting me in."

"If you know anybody that wants a nice apartment. . ." said Mrs. Burns. Accompanying Gilda to the door, she praised the bathroom, the outlook, and the lavish warmth supplied to her tenants.

As Gilda took her leave, at the door of Mrs. Burns's apartment, she saw the fat man enter cautiously with his newspaper and prepare to settle down in the rocking-chair.

She arrived at the Library half an hour late. As she entered she surprised some shrieks and giggles at the circular desk. Probably Miss Loring was pinching again. The girls were getting badly out of control. And her proper work was not getting done. Well, let it go. She had other things to do before her proper work.

When the emotional atmosphere of the catalogue room had been dissipated, Gilda descended to the French Seminary. She unlocked the door. She started with surprise.

In Lucie Coindreau's favorite chair, before her drawer in the long table, Professor Casti was seated. He slouched deep in the chair. No book lay open before him. A dark scowl was on his face.

"Why, good morning, Mr. Casti! What are you doing here at this time in the morning?"

"I—oh—I just came in to look something up. An etymology. In Wartburg. What are you doing here, Miss Gorham?"

"I'm looking something up, too."

She passed along the shelves. The reference works; the dictionaries and the big Larousse; the imposing files of *Romania*, the *Zeitschrift für Romanische Philologie*, the *Revue d'Histoire Littéraire*, the *Romanic Review*, and the rest; the publications of the Société d'Anciens Textes and other sets; the shelves filled with books reserved for the use of the seminaries. The portraits of dead professors of the romance languages, masterly studies in boredom by a bored Professor of Fine Arts, watched her, bored.

"Did you find it?" said Professor Casti.

"Find what?"

"The manuscript. I had the same idea. I thought the thief might have shoved it in some such place as this till the hue and cry was over. But it isn't here."

"You seem worried."

"Worried! Of course I'm worried! I was planning to use a phonetic technique on that manuscript, a technique I've developed myself. It would have caused a tremendous sensation. It would have made my reputation forever!"

"Well, there are other things you can use your technique on."

"Yes, but there are other things I'm worried about."

"What?"

"Haven't you read the papers? Don't you know that every paper in the country is running headlines: Greek Prof Strangled in Library Treasure-Room—Priceless Manuscript Missing? And then a description of the manuscript, and a statement that it was being studied by Belknap, Parry, and I—me, I mean. Right away we're under suspicion. It's all right for Belknap and Parry, because they're full professors, and have tenure, but I don't. Everybody in the M.L.A. will remember this, and when my name is mentioned they'll say: 'Casti? He's done some good work, but wasn't he mixed up in a theft and murder case once?' *Accidente!*"

Casti craned his neck sideways, and Gilda had the feeling that he barely restrained himself from spitting on the floor.

Strike while the iron is hot, thought Gilda. Or strike while the assistant professor is hot. When they are hot they throw off sparks.

"Who do you think did it?" she said.

"I'll tell you who I think did it. I'll tell the world. I ain't scared!"

"Who?"

"Belknap!"

Gilda was silent.

"Belknap! That scrawny old windbag, who goes around here like he was the guy who invented scholarship!"

"But why should Belknap—"

"I'll tell you something. Night before last, when I was taking a walk around about ten o'clock or so, I saw someone looked like Belknap standing outside the Library. Tall and scrawny like Belknap. I'm pretty sure it was him—he."

"You aren't quite sure, then?"

"Well, I wouldn't absolutely swear to it. I didn't see his face, and I wasn't paying much attention anyhow, because I was thinking about something else."

"I thought you told the Lieutenant you didn't see anybody on your walk."

"When I told him that I didn't remember. It was only afterwards, when I got to thinking about it, that I seemed to recall seeing someone who looked like Belknap."

Professor Casti's anger had passed. He sat grumpily in his chair.

"Maybe you ought to tell this to Lieutenant Kennedy. Someone from the police was to be in Dr. Sandys's office this morning."

"I have told him. I was just up there."

"What did he say?"

"Well, he acted as if he didn't believe me. Said if I wasn't willing to swear it was Belknap it wouldn't do him any good. He seemed to think I was making it all up."

A face peered through the glass door of the seminary. It was Professor Belknap.

A key turned in the lock, and the professor entered.

"Good morning, Miss Gorham. Good morning, Casti. I was looking for you."

"Well, you found me."

Professor Belknap stood, cavernous and compelling, fingering his Phi Beta Kappa key.

"I hear you told Lieutenant Kennedy that you saw me outside the Library on Thursday night."

"Well, what if I did?"

"You're perfectly sure that you recognized me?"

"Of course. I wouldn't have mentioned it otherwise."

"But I was in my room at the time, as I had previously told Lieutenant Kennedy. You were therefore mistaken. What clothes was this person wearing whom you mistook for me?"

"I didn't pay any attention to the clothes."

"Was this person wearing a hat?"

"I—didn't notice."

"In short, you were deceived by some fancied resemblance. Unless your imagination has created the incident out of whole cloth."

"Are you calling me a liar?"

"I am suggesting that you were mistaken." Professor Belknap smiled. "I thought it my duty to tell Lieutenant Kennedy of your curious eagerness to get the *Filius Getronis* into your own hands, in violation of all the University rules, and, in fact, of all common sense. Lieutenant Kennedy seemed much impressed."

Professor Belknap walked with measured steps toward Professor Casti. Casti pushed back his chair and sprang to his feet. His face was twisted with rage.

"Are you threatening me?" he cried.

He pulled from his pocket a knife of the Boy Scout type, flashed it open, and stood in an attitude of defense, the knife held low with the blade's cutting edge up.

Professor Belknap continued to smile.

"I'm not threatening you. But I am warning you against making unjustified and unjustifiable accusations. The training of a scholar should have taught you, above all things, caution."

He bowed slightly to Gilda, turned, and walked, unhurried, from the room. Casti still stood with his knife at the guard.

(Strike while the iron is hot.)

"Mr. Casti," said Gilda, "is that the knife you used to pry open Lucie Coindreau's drawer?"

The knife fell clattering to the floor.

"What—I—you mean—what?"

"On the night that Lucie Coindreau died, you were seen prying at her drawer in that seminary table. What were you looking for?"

Casti sank into the chair.

"Have you told the police?"

"Not yet. The matter didn't come up at the inquest on Lucie, and the question of her death has not been reopened."

"What are you telling me this for?"

"I thought you had better know that you were observed. Knowing that, you might think it wise to tell me the whole story."

Casti reflected for a moment.

"I will tell you the truth, Miss Gorham. The fact is, I bought a car a month ago. A remarkable bargain. A Pierce-Arrow!"

"You've bought a car! But what on earth—"

"I won't deny that Mademoiselle Coindreau and I had been— very good friends. But when I got my beginner's driving permit, of course I had to drive with people who had operators' licenses, and Mademoiselle Coindreau didn't know how to drive. We had a terrible quarrel about it, and for a couple of weeks we didn't speak to each other. I thought that was very awkward, our being in the same department, of course, so I tried to patch things up. It was Monday, the day she died. You remember, I tried to find her in the Library that day?"

"Yes."

"I didn't find her then, but I met her at the President's reception. I apologized, and then she asked me to lend her my beginner's driving permit, so she could learn to drive, too! I told her she was crazy; she could get one of her own easily enough, and they aren't transferable. If she should get picked up driving with my license, we would both get into trouble. But poor Lucie, she would never believe that you could do things simply, in the regular way. She always thought there was some better, roundabout system. 'Le système D,' we say in French. Well, I refused. And then she left me, and I got to thinking that after all we had been very good friends, and there was no reason why I shouldn't do her a little favor, because if she should have an accident I could always say that I didn't know she was actually going to use my beginner's permit. So I looked around for her at the reception, but I didn't see her. Then I went out the front door and I thought I saw her skipping across the campus to the Library. So I went to the Library. I thought she'd be in here in the seminary, but she wasn't. So I thought about it for a while, and then I just slipped the permit in the top of her drawer. That way I could always swear that I hadn't actually given her the permit. Then I came out just before closing-time, and I saw Parry going up to the Wilmerding, and all the lights were on there. And then you went up there, looking very sick, and I thought all of a sudden that something might have happened to Lucie. And when I found out, I got scared for fear they would find my permit in her drawer, and people might suspect there was something up between us. You've got to be careful in this business. So I came back here and pried with my knife and got the permit out. It hadn't slipped down to the bottom of the drawer. And that's all there is to it."

A strange story, thought Gilda. But not too strange to be true. It fitted with everything she already knew: Casti's search for Lucie at the President's reception, his actions before and after her death, his revelation, on seeing her body, that he had known or suspected that she was in the Library. It all fitted. But that did not prove it true.

"Have you got the permit on you?" she said.

Casti looked in his pocket-book.

"Yes, I think so. No, it isn't here. I must have left it at home, with my car-keys and things."

He looked at Gilda curiously. "I suppose you wanted to see if there are any knife-marks on it."

Gilda nodded. Well, she had spoiled that. If there weren't any knife-marks on it now, there would be soon.

A key turned in the lock of the seminary door. A grim, spectacled graduate student entered, with a bulging brief-case. He nodded to Gilda and Professor Casti, and drew a couple of books from his brief-case. From the shelves he took the etymological dictionaries of Wartburg, Meyer-Luebke, and Koerting, a volume of Godefroy, and one of Ducange's *Glossarium Mediæ et Infimæ Latinitatis.* He arranged them in an orderly rampart before him on the desk.

"How was the concert last night, Miss Gorham?" said Casti.

"Interesting. I found it interesting."

The graduate student tapped sternly on the table with his pencil.

"Well, I must be going," said Gilda. She left the room, followed by Professor Casti.

The graduate student drew from his brief-case a copy of the *Saturday Evening Post,* and settled down happily to a story about young love.

Gilda decided that she would stop in at Dr. Sandys's office, to see if there was any news.

She found there Lieutenant Kennedy, Dr. Sandys, the Sergeant, and the young man from the District Attorney's office.

"How are you getting along?" she said brightly from the doorway.

"Fine. We're doing fine," said the Lieutenant, tucking his gum in his cheek.

"Did you get any news about people who were in the Library night before last?"

"Nothing important. Prof Noble says he was talking to Doc Sandys in the entrance at ten twenty-five. And that Prof Casti was in, to say that he saw someone who looked like Prof Belknap outside the Library."

"Do you think that's a fact?"

"Naw. Imagination. Or else he wants to put the rap on Belknap. Maybe Casti's sore at him for some reason."

"Well, I'll be going."

"No. Come in here a minute, Miss Gorham. Something I want to show you."

Gilda advanced uncertainly.

"Over here. On the desk."

Lieutenant Kennedy reached out, and flipped away a newspaper, revealing a small blue morocco-bound volume.

"Djever see that before?"

"Why—why, it's the *Filius Getronis*!" Gilda opened the book at random. "Yes, it's the *Filius Getronis*. Where did you get it?"

"Came in by mail. Ordinary parcel post, addressed to the Library."

"Was there any indication where it came from?"

"Mailed last night. Right here in town. Fake sender's name and address. Here, look at the label."

Kennedy showed her the wrapping, with a typed label pasted on.

"Do you know what typewriter that was written on?"

"Why—" gasped Gilda, "why, it looks like mine!"

Kennedy nodded solemnly.

"Yes," he said. "That's what we figured."

Chapter XVIII

"Sɪᴛ ᴅᴏᴡɴ here, Miss Gorham," said Lieutenant Kennedy. "I got a few little questions to ask you. Just—"

"Routine questions, no doubt," said Gilda, taking the unofficial witness chair. Lieutenant Kennedy glared.

"How come you have that manuscript in your possession?"

"But I didn't, Lieutenant!"

"Ho, you didn't, hey?" He turned to the Sergeant. "Write down she denies that the manuscript was in her possession. Now, Miss Gorham, if you didn't have that manuscript in your possession, how come you send it back?"

"I didn't send it back."

"Then how you happen to write out this label on your typewriter?"

"I didn't."

"Then who did?"

"I don't know."

"Anyone else have access to your typewriter?"

"Certainly. It's on a movable typewriter stand beside my desk. Anyone could get at it. But I don't remember anyone using it in my presence during the last few days. The members of the catalogue room staff wouldn't be likely to use it, because there are other typewriters available for them. And if some outsider, say a professor, should come in and use my typewriter, it would be unusual enough so that the girls would probably notice it and remark about it."

"How about after hours? Is the catalogue room locked?"

"The hall door is. But the door into the stacks is ordinarily left unlocked, so that anyone with a stack permit—that is, the faculty and graduate students—can consult the bibliographi-cal works. So almost anyone could have gone in there after five o'clock, or between eight and nine in the morning."

"Are the lights kept on there at night?"

"Not in theory. But the people who use the room are as likely as not to leave them on when they go."

"Can your desk be seen from the doors?"

"No."

"So almost anyone could have gone in there and sat down and typed off this here label without no one observing them?"

"That's right."

"Huh."

"How about fingerprints?" said Gilda timidly.

"Aw, fingerprints my left foot!"

The Sergeant looked up inquiringly.

"Cut out 'my left foot.'"

"Leave 'fingerprints'?"

"Naw, cut out 'fingerprints,' too."

The Sergeant obediently crossed out a line in his notebook.

Lieutenant Kennedy took a strip of chewing gum from his pocket and added it to his cud.

"Let me point out," said Gilda, "that if I wanted to send back the manuscript anonymously, I wouldn't address it on my own typewriter. It would therefore appear that whoever used my typewriter did so to divert suspicion from himself."

"That's psychology, is it?"

"Yes, I think so."

"Well, it's my experience that murderers don't act according to psychology. Psychology!"

"And you suspect me of being the murderer?"

"Hell, no, I don't suspect you. You can go if you want to."

But he did suspect her, thought Gilda, as she made her way to the catalogue room. She had no alibi for the time of Mr. Hyett's death. The Lieutenant might suppose that in her library work she had somehow obtained a duplicate key to the locked press, and had learned the combination of the safe. That she was interrupted in her theft by Mr. Hyett, and had strangled him in an access of desperate strength. That she had stolen the precious manuscript, and had returned it out of fear. And how about the death of Lucie? Why, that was still an accident, in the official view. Gilda would be tried for one murder, not for two. Lucie's death would be left conveniently in the shadow. Or a prosecutor might make dark hints to the jury, suggesting a drama of jealousy, Gilda jealous of Lucie. Gilda had no alibi for the time of Lucie's death, either.

This was very bad. It was high time she did something. She knew who had murdered Lucie and Mr. Hyett, and she knew, approximately, how and why. Should she go to Lieutenant Kennedy and tell what she knew?

The trouble was that her proof, while entirely satisfactory to her, was not legal proof. It would not satisfy a jury. Nor Lieutenant Kennedy. He would laugh at her. There was too much psychology in her argument.

Clearly, she must get legal proof.

How?

For some time she sat meditating, chin on hand.

"How's the detective work going, Miss Gorham?"

It was Cameron, appearing suddenly and silently from the rear, as was his annoying habit.

"What? Oh, all right."

"You couldn't manage to pin the crime on Lieutenant Kennedy?"

"Look here, Cameron, there's something I wanted to ask you."

"Okay."

"Let's—ah—go down to the crypt, where we won't be disturbed."

"Okay. I have to check in at the delivery desk. I'll be there in a couple of minutes."

Cameron, a monster of tact, probably wished to arrange, for appearances' sake, that the two would not be seen entering the crypt together.

A minute later Gilda was descending the circular stairs to the crypt. This was the Library's grave, she thought. Here the dead books were buried. As long as one person opened a book and read a line, he communicated to it life. But these books no one ever opened; they were dead, and buried in this tomb, in the quiet and the cool. A gruesome fancy.

"Yes, Miss Gorham?"

Gilda had not heard Cameron descending the stairs.

"Cameron," she said, "we were talking about that door to the ventilating apparatus."

"Why, so we were, Miss Gorham."

"And you said you were sure that no one had gone out that way on Thursday night."

"That's right. The screen was screwed in place when I looked at it early Friday morning."

"I notice, however, that the screws are abraded on both sides of the groove. They have been screwed in and out apparently several times. Would that observation stimulate your recollection at all?"

"Miss Gorham, you've got the real detective eye. You're wasted in that catalogue room. How about you and me setting up a detective agency?"

"You haven't answered my question."

"Just what is your question, now?"

"Was that grille unscrewed on Thursday, the night of the murder?"

There was a long silence.

"Miss Gorham, I don't really know whether to tell you the truth or to stall you. I don't want to get into trouble, and either way I may get into trouble. But I think I'll tell you the truth, on condition that you don't go and tell the Loot. I don't think the truth would help him to find the murderer. If I do think it will help him, I'll tell him myself. Do you agree to that?"

"Well—well, all right, I agree."

"Okay. All right then. That grille was not unscrewed on Thursday night."

"Oh."

"But it was unscrewed on Monday night, when Miss Coindreau died."

"But who unscrewed it?"

"Mr. Hyett!"

"Mr. Hyett? But why—"

"It isn't perhaps a very pretty story to tell a nice girl like you. But you might as well find out about the facts of life sooner or later. Well, anyhow, you know that Mr. Hyett took care of his cousin, Dr. Pickard, last year. And somehow or other he got a chance to make a copy of the key to the locked press. And what's more—I don't know this really, but I'm willing to guess—Mr. Hyett found out the combination of the safe. Maybe the old Doc was delirious."

"But do you mean to say that Mr. Hyett had serious designs on the Library's treasures?"

"No. What he was after was the erotica."

"What? He would go to all that trouble—and danger—just to look at some dirty books! He could have ordered them at the delivery desk, in the usual way. That is the faculty's right."

"Yes. But he would have let people know that he was taking a reading-course in the rough stuff of all ages. People talk, you know. He wouldn't have liked that. What he liked was to sneak into the Library before closing-time and hide somewhere—usually, I guess, right in the locked press, if the Wilmerding was empty. And then he would turn on the reading-light, which you can't see from outside, and stay there an hour or two, just gloating. And then come down and unscrew the grille to the ventilating machines. He carried a big knife with a screwdriver on it. And he'd walk out the door, which has an ordinary latch that opens from the inside. And in the mornings when I made my rounds I would take a look to see if the screen was unscrewed. He would usually come around early and screw it up himself, but sometimes I got ahead of him."

"Why, that old devil! I still don't quite see why he went to all that trouble."

"You know, I've seen a lot of funny business in my time. You wouldn't believe some of the things that people do. But in some ways this campus is the funniest place of all. Because here people don't usually do anything; they just think. And that probably isn't very healthy. Now you take this old Hyett. He'd probably never done anything much in his life. But what he knew! Some of the things he knew even surprised me. Well, the way I figured it out, he'd exercised his imagination so long that facts didn't have any grip on him, you might say. I mean—if you'll excuse me, Miss Gorham—"

"Go ahead."

"He'd get a big thrill out of a picture of a naked woman, but a real naked woman would make him sick. And it was no good for him to practice dirty tricks, or even to see them. It was no good for him unless he could read about them. You might say even his sins were literary sins. It's a kind of fetishism, like the psychology books say. I could give you some examples—"

"You make it perfectly clear, Cameron; you needn't labor the point. You seem to have got pretty chummy with him."

"We used to talk a lot. And he showed me some of the funny pictures sometimes. But they don't mean anything to me. I've seen quite a lot in my time."

"There is one thing I don't understand, Cameron," said Gilda, slowly. "You should have reported this invasion of the locked press to the Librarian. You were not doing your duty to the Library. If this business of the ventilating screen were known, you would be discharged immediately. Why did you permit it to go on, then?"

"Mr. Hyett used to tip me. Very nicely."

"You don't deserve to keep your job."

"Oh, Miss Gorham! Remember that I knew Mr. Hyett well enough to know he wouldn't take anything out of the Library. He was too well trained for that."

"Nevertheless—"

"Look here, Miss Gorham. I can only hold this job for a few years more. I'll get rheumatism, or I'll break a leg or something, or I'll just get too tired to do the work. And I'll be retired on Workmen's Compensation of about fifty cents a day. And I may live for twenty-five years. I don't get any pension like you people on the faculty and in the administration. There's no children to take care of me. I've got to take care of myself, and I plan to do it. It's hard for a low-paid man like me to put money away, so I've had to take some chances. But I can assure you that I have always watched out for the interests of the Library."

"You ought to tell Dr. Sandys. And I think he would be justified in discharging you."

"I hope Dr. Sandys don't discharge me. I'd hate to be obliged to spread the news about his debt to the Excelsior Personal Loan."

"But this is a threat!"

"All right. It's a threat."

Gilda pondered.

"After all," she said, "there's nothing shameful about borrowing money. Look at the United States Government!"

"That's right. It all depends on what you're borrowing it for."

"You're suggesting—"

"I'm not suggesting. I'm saying."

"You're suggesting that Dr. Sandys has some reason, probably shameful, for needing money. So he borrows it, probably at exorbitant interest, from the Excelsior Loan, in return for secrecy."

Cameron grinned. "You're the one who's doing the suggesting. Don't blame me."

"But what reason could he have?"

"Maybe he plays the ponies. Or the stock market. Or maybe he keeps an expensive jane somewhere."

"That doesn't seem to be in character."

"Or maybe he's got a wife who drinks two bottles of benedictine a day, and he has to pay her high to make her stay out of town. Or maybe he's a werewolf and he runs around at night biting babies, and every now and then he gets caught and has to pay up. I could think of lots of things."

"Could you think of the real reason?"

"Yes."

"What is it?"

"That's one thing, Miss Gorham, I'm not going to tell you. It cost me something to find out, and it may be worth a good deal to me."

"So, you are planning a little blackmail. Aren't you pretty indiscreet in telling me all this?"

"I guess I am. I really shouldn't have done it. I guess I just like to show off. But I don't think you'll go and squeal. If I lose my job, Dr. Sandys is pretty likely to lose his. And what's more, I wouldn't be surprised if Miss Gilda Gorham would leave the library business and take up stenography in some big city."

"What do you mean?"

"Don't forget, Miss Gorham, that I really like you very much, and I don't want to hurt you, but I have to look out for myself. And I might begin passing it around, for instance, that you and

Mr. Hyett used to meet in the locked press after closing-hours, to read those funny books together. And, after all, you haven't any alibi—"

"Good-by, Cameron."

Gilda turned away with an effort at dignity. Cameron slapped her in mid-section.

"Now don't forget, Miss Gorham! Don't forget!"

Gilda ran for the stairs, to the sound of Cameron's laughter.

She ran through Biology and Physiology, and only paused when she saw a professor reading in an aisle of Anthropology. She found a quiet alcove, within hailing distance of the professor, and sat down.

That Cameron! Blackmailer, usurer, conscious, shameless liar, conniver in the misuse of library books! A thorough immoralist! It would be a pleasure to bring him to his just deserts.

What had he suggested about Dr. Sandys? Was that a bluff, or did he have a blackmailer's knowledge of Dr. Sandys's past? It would hardly be sufficient, for effective blackmail, to possess the mere fact that William Sandys had been a messenger at the Hopkinson Library at the time of the 1916 book-theft. Perhaps Cameron had learned, by some underworld connection, that Dr. Sandys was the actual culprit in the case. Or perhaps he had some other reason to believe that Dr. Sandys was a book-stealer, a victim of bibliokleptomania, you might say. But if Dr. Sandys stole for gain, he should be rich, and the puzzling thing was that he was so poor. Perhaps he was already in the hands of a blackmailer, and Cameron would blackmail him because he was being blackmailed. A superfetation of blackmail.

What was Dr. Sandys's secret?

Gilda had already had some success in finding things out by

simply asking the people concerned when they were off their guard. A primitive form of sleuthing, no doubt, but it seemed to work.

She would ask Dr. Sandys what he was so carefully concealing. If she caught him just right, he might even tell her.

She stopped at the catalogue room for her bag, went to the women's rest room, and worked on her face and hair. Then she went to Dr. Sandys's office. He was alone. She entered the room and closed the door.

When she emerged, a few minutes later, her face bore a somewhat puzzled look.

She went to the pay telephone booth, shut the door carefully, and used up several nickels.

Chapter XIX

ON SATURDAY afternoon the catalogue room was very quiet. Most of the girls observed the half-holiday strictly, though two or three of the more conscientious had returned after lunch. Gilda was at her desk, trying to get caught up on some of her neglected work.

In this task she was considerably balked by Miss Cornwell, whose life was made a hell by Pseudonyms. The Library rule was that books should be entered in detail under the author's real name, with only an added listing under his pseudonym. But in certain cases the rule was violated. Thus Voltaire's works were entered in full under Voltaire, with an added listing under Arouet, François Marie. After years of bitter argument, the works of Mark Twain and the scholia upon him had been transferred from Clemens, Samuel Langhorne, to Twain, Mark. Gilda had recently decreed that listings for Farigoule, Louis, should be re-entered under Romains, Jules, on the ground that M. Romains had now created for himself a sufficient reputation under his pen-name. Miss Cornwell, a rigorous formalist, held to the strict letter of the rule. She spent half an hour of Gilda's time arguing against any concession to popular ignorance. The discussion was to Gilda irritating, but at the same time a refreshing return to the normal concerns of her normal days.

Miss Cornwell retreated, vanquished but unconvinced. She put on her hat and left, with another lingering worker. Gilda was alone in the catalogue room. From time to time she glanced at her watch.

It was four o'clock when Professor Belknap entered the room. He came to Gilda's desk.

"Good afternoon, Miss Gorham. I received your message."

"Oh yes, Mr. Belknap. A small matter really. I just wanted to ask you about that Hodgkin book, before Monday—"

"I am glad that we can return to our everyday occupations, in these trying moments. And let me seize this occasion to apologize for the scene you witnessed in the French Seminary this morning."

"Not at all. I thought you were entirely justified. Mr. Casti's accusations seemed to me at the least irresponsible."

("Funny how I get to talking like the person I am talking to," thought Gilda.)

"I fear he is an intemperate and headstrong young man." Professor Belknap sighed.

"But you were wonderful, the way you put him in his place. That knife of his! I was frightened to death of that knife!"

Professor Belknap smiled his difficult smile.

"There are times when one must fear a knife. But not when it is held in the hands of a weakling."

Gilda gazed at him, her eyes large and wide.

"But you were going to speak of Hodgkin's *Italy and Her Invaders*?" said the professor.

"Oh yes. You wanted two sets put on reserve for your students in History 101, and you specify the latest edition. We have only one set of that edition, but we have a good set of the old edition in the duplicates. I wonder if that wouldn't do. It's a pretty expensive book, in eight volumes, and we hate to order another one."

"I don't object in principle. But I'm afraid I don't recall exactly how far this new edition differs from the old. I should want to make sure about that."

"I'll have it sent up. Or no, it's Saturday afternoon, and the boys at the desk now don't know their way among the duplicates. Maybe if you would come down with me to the crypt?"

"Why, certainly, Miss Gorham."

Gilda led the way to the crypt's entrance, snapping on the light at the head of the spiral stair.

"This is interesting. I have not been in the crypt for years. It is rather an eerie place," said Professor Belknap.

"I like it. It makes a nice solitary retreat for me, when I want to get away from all the to-do in the catalogue room. There is hardly ever anyone here, especially out of office hours. I even like the smell, so cool and musty. The smell of dead books, I sometimes think. What is it that poor Lucie Coindreau used to call it—the *odeur du renfermé,* the shut-up smell."

Professor Belknap was silent.

Gilda, leading right, left, and right among the high, solemn aisles, reached up occasionally to turn on a hanging, open lightbulb.

"I always expect a bat to fly out," she said. "Ah, here we are."

She took down a volume of Hodgkin's *Italy and Her Invad-*

ers, and handed it to Professor Belknap. As he turned the pages Gilda stood close beside him and looked respectfully over his shoulder.

"Yes, this will do, I think," he said. "The additions in the later edition are not essential, for beginning students. The pagination is different, but I can easily arrange for that in my assignments. Yes, that will do." He handed the book back to Gilda. She replaced it on the shelves.

She stood for a moment, unmoving.

"Well, if that is all—" said Professor Belknap, with mild surprise.

"It isn't really all. There is something else I wanted to show you."

She drew from her pocket a small silvered leaden ball, dangling from a string about eighteen inches long.

"Did you ever see this before?"

Professor Belknap looked at it coldly.

"It appears to be a child's toy. Or no, I believe it is one of those divining instruments which had a considerable vogue in France recently. Mademoiselle Coindreau once demonstrated the thing to me."

"Did she demonstrate it to you on the night she died?"

"Really, Miss Gorham!"

"Because it was found beside her body on the floor of the Wilmerding."

"Really, Miss Gorham! I don't know if you realize what you are saying, but it amounts to an accusation—"

"Call it a reconstruction. Would you like to hear my reconstruction?"

"I think I might find it curious, though probably not convincing."

"I think that last Monday at the President's reception Lucie Coindreau persuaded you to meet her in the Library just before closing-time. She probably took advantage of your interest in medieval grimoires, and promised to show you something remarkable she had turned up in the Occulta. Maybe some medieval justification of her radiesthésie. She said she would meet you in the Occulta in a few minutes; she didn't want to put you to the embarrassment of walking over with her. She slipped out of the President's house by the back way, to get away from Casti. Anyway, she liked to do things in a mysterious, roundabout way. I suppose she just liked intrigue.

"The two of you met in the Occulta, and Lucie showed you some book, perhaps the Nostradamus. And she showed you this radiesthésie ball. She dangled it in front of your eyes. And you were seized by a fit of unreasoning rage, and gave her a push, and she fell over the rail. You realized in a flash that it must look like an accident, so you shoved the pair of steps over to the rail under the electric light, and turned off the light. And then you dodged probably into the Philosophy Seminary. And you watched the main entrance of the Library until you saw the coast was clear, and then you simply walked home and went to bed."

Belknap laughed, his rare, harsh laugh, betokening contempt, not amusement.

"But, my dear Miss Gorham, you must realize that this is the veriest nonsense. What earthly reason would I have for pushing poor Mademoiselle Coindreau to her death? 'In a fit of unreasoning rage,' you say. Perhaps because she showed me the wrong reference, or something? I must be very subject to fits of rage. Have you ever seen me angry?"

"No."

"I am not even angry now, in the face of your fantastic suppositions. Do you blame me also for the death of poor Hyett, and for the theft of the *Filius Getronis*?"

"Yes. I think that when you and Lucie went up to the Occulta, Hyett was already hidden in the locked press. He had the lights off, of course. He saw everything, but was afraid to do anything about it. Afterwards he was unwilling to go to the police, because he would have had to reveal that he was in the locked press. So he adopted the melodramatic method, typical of him, of frightening you into a confession, by patching 'Thou shalt do no murder' into his microfilm, which he was going to substitute for yours. Probably he was planning to keep on tormenting you, by putting 'Thou shalt do no murder' in your classbook, and in anonymous letters to you, and by pinning it on your pillow or something. He thought he would break your nerve and send you jittering to the police."

Professor Belknap laughed again. "He wouldn't break my nerve by such methods. But that almost sounds like one of his ideas. Poor old Hyett! I find your story fascinating. And how did I murder Hyett?"

"Of course, you heard about the mysterious warning in the microfilm, and you put two and two together and realized that the warning must come from Hyett. So on Thursday night you followed him to the Library, just a few minutes before closing-time. It probably was you whom Casti saw. You saw Hyett unlock the locked press and go in. He was being careful and working in the dark. You could probably gather from the sound of his movements that he was opening the safe. I suppose that he was going to slip that warning card, you know, the thesis slip with 'Thou shalt do no murder' on it, into the original manuscript of the *Filius Getronis*. He knew you would consult it sooner or later. The card, you remember, was found in his pocket. Before he had time to put it in place, you had followed him into the locked press and strangled him. And then you reached into the safe, in the dark, and took the *Filius Getronis*. You knew just where it was kept, and you recognized it by the feel. Then you shut the safe door and spun the combination, and apparently had the wits to wipe it clean of fingerprints. You set Mr. Hyett's body on the chair, shut the door of the locked press, took the key out of the lock, put it in your pocket, and walked out the main door just before it was locked for the night. I suppose the whole thing didn't take more than five minutes."

"This is really very absorbing. Why did I take the *Filius Getronis*?"

"Perhaps on impulse. An old secret longing for the book. Or else as a blind, to make people think that robbery was the motive. But it soon appeared that it was too dangerous for you to keep the manuscript, and you couldn't bring yourself to destroy it. Anyway you were anxious, above all things, to publish it. So you sent it back to the Library, typing the address on my typewriter."

"That was unkind of me."

"You thought it was a good false scent, and you knew that I could not be convicted of the crime."

"Miss Gorham, I urge you to go to Lieutenant Kennedy and to tell him your thrilling tale. You recognize that there is not an atom of proof in all this. As a historian, accustomed to the weighing of evidence, I should throw it out relentlessly. It is a pure hypothesis. You may remember Pascal's words, reported in Bishop's masterly biography: 'To make an hypothesis an evident truth, it is not enough that all the phenomena should follow.' The law follows the same principle. If you can make up a story which includes all the known facts, the story is not proved true. I have no doubt that I could invent a romantic tale which would indicate equally well the guilt of Casti, or Parry, or Sandys—or yourself. Have you told your story to Lieutenant Kennedy, by the way?"

"No."

"That is really sensible of you."

"But my reason is not that I am afraid of being laughed at."

"What is it, then?"

Gilda was silent for some time.

"Mr. Belknap, I shall have to make a confession to you. This is the first time in my life I have been involved in a problem of this sort; a problem, let me say, in which I have to make some serious moral judgments. I have had to decide whether I would accept without question the code of society, and report you to the police, and let society take over the obligations of morality, according to its own code. Or whether I would venture to establish my own code of morality, and act according to it.

"Well, I am afraid I have discovered that I am fundamentally immoral. I don't want you to be tried and convicted for murder. Perhaps death doesn't seem so dreadful to any of us now as it did a year or two ago. Death seems a small matter. And I am sorry to discover that I am not particularly grieved by the death of Lucie

Coindreau and Mr. Hyett. I don't think that because they have died, you should die."

"You shock me, Miss Gorham."

Gilda spoke rapidly, feverishly, as if entranced.

"You are strong and they were weak. I don't think the strong should die because the weak are weak. There is a kind of power about you which I can't help feeling. You may be a murderer; I don't care. Maybe it's because you are a murderer that I feel something—well—a sort of admiration for you."

"You are out of your head, Miss Gorham; I don't know what's the matter with you!"

"I feel weak in the presence of your strength! You have put some sort of spell on me. I would do anything you ordered me. Oh, my dear, I love you! I love you!"

Gilda, with a hysterical laughing cry, flung her arms about Belknap's neck and clasped him tight. Her head fell on his breast.

Belknap tore at her arms, in an effort to loosen them. His face lost all its lines of grim control and put on a mask of rage. His eyes dilated; his mouth fell open, and saliva oozed forth from the corners and dribbled down his chin. Still Gilda clung to him with a frenzied grip.

Belknap's hands crept to her throat; his thumbs found her windpipe and pressed, cutting off her breath, and in a moment cutting off the world.

The pressure lessened.

"I just wanted to tell you something before you die," said Belknap. "You might like to know while you're dying—and after. It's all true. I killed them, just as you said. But that's not why you're dying!"

The pressure was resumed on Gilda's throat, and her mind darkened. Belknap was laughing, a horrible giggling laugh. Gilda's last coherent thought was that she had never heard him laugh so before. As if he were really amused.

She was drowning in deep water. All struggle was over, and all pain. Yielding, she had a dim awareness that she was passing over gently to death. Death. Come, lovely and soothing death, undulate round the world, serenely arriving, arriving. . . .

But if you were dead, would you be aware of it? And would you quote poetry from the little old world? Well, possibly. But would it be quite so noisy in the after life? People being banged around so?

She opened her eyes. She was lying on the metal floor of the aisle. A few steps from her face was the face of Belknap. He too was lying on his back, motionless. Dr. Sandys knelt on his chest and with each hand held one of Belknap's arms pinned to the floor. Blood was dripping from Dr. Sandys's cheek and flowing down into the red quagmire of his beard.

Francis Parry danced beside them. "Shall I kick him?" he cried, in a high, unnatural voice. "Or sit on his feet?"

"No, I've got him all right. He's knocked out. You tend to Gilda."

"All right." Francis leaped to her side and began uncertainly patting her face.

Gilda sat up. "Don't bother. I'm all right."

Down the aisle came Lieutenant Kennedy, limping.

"Fell over a damn stool in the dark. Brought down a stack of books on my head. I don't know what they was, but they felt like dictionaries."

Gilda groaned.

"Gilda! Are you all right?" said Parry.

"Yes. I was just thinking that the Lieutenant must have brought down the Siamese classics, and we'll never get them back in the right order."

She started to rise, painfully. Parry helped her to her feet.

The Lieutenant blew his whistle. There was a clattering from the stairway, and in a moment the Sergeant appeared.

"We'll take this fellow off to the station and charge him," said the Lieutenant.

"You have the confession all right?" said Gilda.

"Sure. Prof Casti's little machine worked fine. But we had to set it up way off at the other end of the crypt, so Belknap wouldn't hear the machine. That's why we were a little slow getting here."

"Dr. Sandys seemed to be right on the job."

"He was certainly quick on his feet. I could hardly make him wait for the pay-off. I would have put a mark in the next aisle, only you said there wasn't any danger."

"I didn't want you interfering too soon. I had an idea Mr. Belknap would say something incriminating, and I thought it might come toward the end."

"Gilda!" said Parry and Sandys, reproachfully.

Professor Belknap, supine, opened his eyes. The Lieutenant and the Sergeant dragged him to his feet and snapped on the handcuffs. He gazed about, bewildered.

"Why," he said, "what does all this mean? I'm afraid I don't understand."

The Lieutenant replied in a tone of great satisfaction. "It means, buddy, or prof, rather, that you are charged with the murder of Miss Coindreau and Prof Hyett!"

Professor Belknap sneered. "On what grounds?"

"On your own confession, took down by a kind of dictograph machine set up by Prof Casti. Is there anything you want to add?"

Belknap looked around at the group facing him.

"No. I will say nothing except in the presence of my lawyer."

"It'd better be a damn good lawyer," said Kennedy, cheerfully. He urged Belknap toward the stairs.

Belknap halted.

"Yes, there is something. Parry, will you see my assistant, young Wanley, and tell him to meet my classes Monday? Tell him to give out the reading-lists and make the assignments. And announce that the classes will meet as usual. If I am not released, the department, in consultation with President Temple, will arrange for a substitute lecturer."

"Certainly, Belknap. Anything else?"

"Yes. Say that on the reading-list the corresponding chapters in the first edition of Hodgkin's *Italy and Her Invaders* may be substituted for the chapters in the latest edition. That is all, I think. Good-by."

As he turned, he paused before Gilda and spat full in her face.

Parry pulled out the handkerchief which always peeped, neatly folded, from the breast pocket of his coat.

"There's one thing I'm glad to learn!" said Gilda, with a hysterical little laugh. "It's real!"

"What's real?"

"The handkerchief. I always thought it was a dummy, sewed in your coat."

"No. I was saving it for just such an emergency."

"Dr. Sandys, do you, too—"

Dr. Sandys held out his handkerchief. It was red and sticky with blood.

"Oh, my poor William! We were forgetting all about you! You must tend to that immediately!"

"Oh no, it's all right. Just a scratch. The blood has stopped flowing already."

"Really? Yes, it doesn't look so bad. You know, you were wonderful!"

Dr. Sandys shifted, and blushed under the dried blood above his beard.

"Oh, it wasn't much. I just caught him a rabbit punch behind the ear, while he was throttling you, and then he turned and I gave him a one-two and he went down. He only landed once on me, and then it was a kind of scrape."

"Who ever would have thought you were such a fighter!"

"Well—as a matter of fact, I used to box a little when I was in the army. Indeed, I was light-heavyweight champ of my regiment."

"Why didn't you ever tell us? The girls will be so thrilled!"

Dr. Sandys stood uneasily on one foot and then the other. "Well, it all worked out nicely, didn't it? Casti's part was very well done. Belknap clearly had no suspicion of a microphone among the duplicates."

"By the way," said Parry, "where is Casti?"

"That's true," said Gilda. "I hope nothing has happened to him."

The three went rapidly to the storeroom. Beside the recording machine lay Casti, at full length on the floor.

"Not another crime!" cried Gilda.

Dr. Sandys was shaking him by the shoulder. Casti opened his eyes.

"Just fainted," said Sandys. "He'll be all right."

"How about the record?" said Gilda.

"It seems to be all right. Lieutenant Kennedy will probably be sending for it in a minute."

"You know," said Parry suddenly, "there are a number of things about this whole affair that I don't understand."

"Let's go up to my office," said Sandys. "Miss Gorham—Gilda and I need to wash our faces. And Casti would feel better for a cold sponge."

"What I need is a smoke," said Gilda. "In spite of a nasty sore throat I seem to have picked up somewhere." She felt her neck ruefully.

Dr. Sandys looked around cautiously and lowered his voice.

"It's late Saturday afternoon. I think, in the circumstances, we would be justified in smoking in my office. If we are very careful, and never tell anyone."

He lowered his voice still farther.

"I also have some brandy, which I keep there in case someone in the Library should need first aid."

"My God, I need first aid!" said Parry.

Casti rose suddenly to his feet, and the four climbed the stairs to the Librarian's office.

Chapter XX

Gilda, with the three men, entered the Librarian's office. Dr. Sandys closed the door carefully, pulled down the shades, and turned on the ventilating fan. He found some reproductions of Roman lamps to serve as ashtrays. Each of the men drew a package of cigarettes from his pocket and gave Gilda her choice.

Dr. Sandys unlocked the bottom drawer of his desk and felt in the back of the drawer. He brought out a bottle of brandy wrapped in a towel.

"You see, it's never been opened," he said. "In mint condition."

Professor Parry looked at it doubtfully.

"Have you got a corkscrew?"

"No."

"Then how are we going to get it open?"

"We could break off the neck," suggested Professor Casti.

"Where were you during Prohibition?" said Dr. Sandys, scornfully.

"I carried a pocket corkscrew," said Parry.

Dr. Sandys carefully wrapped the base of the bottle in the towel.

"This wall would be safe," he said. "Only my lavatory on the other side."

He pounded the base of the bottle against the wall, with strong and careful taps. The cork began to protrude tinily from the bottle-neck.

"Casti, get the glass out of my lavatory, will you?"

"There's one in the women's rest room, too," said Gilda. "I'll get it and be right back."

In the rest room, she gave her face a good treatment. She returned, with the drinking-glass concealed, as far as possible, under folded arms. Though she met no one, her heart was in her mouth. For the first time she had a sense of guilt.

When she reached the Librarian's office, the men looked cleaned and refreshed. A policeman, they told her, had called for the record of Professor Belknap's confession. Dr. Sandys had borrowed two Bohemian glass goblets from the display in the Wilmerding. He poured the brandy.

"Gentlemen," said Parry, "I propose a toast to Miss Gilda Gorham, who has saved all of our reputations—and perhaps more!"

The three men solemnly drank.

"I did it only for the Library's reputation," said Gilda.

"I propose a toast to the Library!"

All drank the toast. They settled themselves in the chairs where they had so lately sat as suspected witnesses.

"One thing I want to know," said Parry. "Gilda, where did you get that radiesthésie ball? I thought it was confiscated by the police with the rest of Lucie's things."

"It was. I went to Lucie's room and looked for one, in the hope of startling the murderer with it. I couldn't find one, so

Casti turned me out a very good substitute in his laboratory."

"What I want to know is how you were so sure the murderer was Belknap," said Sandys.

"It all came clear at the Giulia Thalmann concert."

"It didn't come clear to me," said Parry.

"There was one thing that had puzzled me. I didn't tell any of you, because on principle I suspected all of you equally. Cameron told me that on Monday morning he heard Lucie talking to a man in the Occulta. And she called him 'Papoose.' Well, that doesn't make any sense, in either French or English. But I thought it might be a clue, and I wondered about it quite a lot.

"Then at the concert Giulia Thalmann sang that thing from *Thaïs*: 'Qui te fait si sévère.' Thaïs sings it to Athanaël, in reproach for his coldness. And I got to thinking that Athanaël is a fine sonorous singable name, but I didn't remember him in Anatole France's *Thaïs*. Maybe Massenet changed the name because the original was too hard for a singer. The corresponding character in Anatole France, I seemed to remember, was Paphnuce.

"And Paphnuce was Papoose! At least, it is what Cameron might have supposed, because he probably doesn't know any French. To check up, I looked over Lucie's books. She had in her room quite a row of Anatole France. Her *Thaïs* was falling to pieces. I have determined by exhaustive tests that if you read a French novel three times it falls to pieces. Lucie probably fancied herself as Thaïs."

"I still don't see——" said Casti.

"Remember the story. Thaïs, the irresistibly seductive courtesan of Alexandria, tries all her blandishments on Paphnuce, the grim ascetic from the desert, and in vain. And then——"

"Oh yes. I remember the rest of it now."

"So I guessed that Lucie had tried out some of her little cajoleries on Belknap in the Occulta, and he had remained impervious."

"Wouldn't he have recognized the implications of 'Paphnuce'?" said Sandys.

"Probably he didn't. That wasn't his field. Or else he didn't care. At any rate, Lucie lured him back to the Occulta that evening."

"She was awfully persistent," said Casti.

"Wouldn't take no for an answer," murmured Parry.

"What troubles me about the whole affair," said Sandys, "is the essential question Why. I don't see why Belknap should have pushed Lucie over the rail. The motivation seems to me insufficient, as the boys say."

Gilda took another cigarette and lighted it slowly.

"I think I know why. But it is pretty hard to tell, and impossible to prove."

She was silent, knitting her brows at the curling smoke.

"Try it anyhow, my dear," said Parry.

"You started it, Francis, by reflecting on the virginity of some of our male faculty members. That thought has returned to me a good deal. And I have an idea that a middle-aged female can really understand a middle-aged male virgin better than his own men friends can."

"Why Gilda, what a revelation!" said Parry.

"About my age?"

"No."

A slow, furious blush mounted to Gilda's face. Parry laughed, and the others joined in uncertainly.

"Well, if you're going to make a joke of it—" she said.

"No, no! Go ahead! I'll be quiet."

As Gilda continued, Parry's lips moved imperceptibly.

"Anyway," she said stubbornly, "I think I understand Belknap pretty thoroughly. He's always been awkward and shy, but he's not weak. He is strongly attracted by women, but he regards his impulses as weakness, and he hates weakness, so he has suppressed them violently. Women are aware of that contained strength, and feel it and are drawn by it. And that is his secret pride.

"I imagine that he had a bad adolescence. To cover his shyness, he posed as a woman-hater, and he has never been able, or willing, to get rid of the pose. Usually young women-haters have their pose broken down for them when they are young men, by some determined girl. Or else they enter the Church, or become explorers or something. But Belknap went to one of the small monastic New England colleges in the mountains, and when he was a graduate student he buried himself in the library, and in time his habits, or his character, became so fixed that he was nearly secure against feminine wiles. By way of compensation he has consecrated himself to scholarship. As he stalks up and down the campus, he enjoys seeing the girls whisper to one another in awe. When he is attracted by some woman in particular, all he can do, when it comes to the point, is to humiliate her. Thus he humiliates the whole female sex for its lewd and sexy behavior. And he conceals the fact that he doesn't know what else to do. If he should try to make love he would reveal that he is ignorant, awkward, and pitiable. But in his chastity he is magnificent."

"Remy de Gourmont classes chastity as a sexual perversion," said Casti. "I suppose your idea is that as a sexual perversion it can lead to crime. Like the funny fellows who—"

"Here, Casti," broke in Parry. "Keep this on a high plane, will you?"

"I think you are right, Gilda," said Sandys. "But I don't see how it would be in Belknap's character to go as far as murder."

"I think he had come to some sort of crisis in his development. You remember that recently someone attacked with a stick a boy and girl sitting on a bench in the moonlight? I suspect it was Belknap, suddenly overcome by his hatred of sex, of youthful wooing. And, anyway, I don't think he had any intention of murdering Lucie.

"But this is the most difficult part of what I am trying to say. I think he was very strongly attracted by Lucie, or he wouldn't have met her in the stacks on Monday night. If she had been a little more astute, a little gentler, she might have broken down all his barriers and converted him into a great lover. But she was too impetuous; she went too fast. She put her hands on him, and her touch roused in him all his accumulated horror of sex. It was a virgin's horror. I think men have it, just like women. I don't think men are very different from women. Except that they are stronger, and they strike, when a woman screams and runs away."

"I understand thoroughly. It seems to me very reasonable," said Sandys. "The history of the Church is full of such examples. Many of the early saints were terrible woman-haters, and were obviously men of great power and strength. Saint Martin boasted that he had only once been touched by a woman, and that was a queen, who flung herself at his feet. Took him off his guard. I remember a story Saint Jerome tells of a young Christian who was tempted by his friends to sin. He was wrapped in a net of silk among lilies and roses, and was cajoled by a most beautiful— ah—courtesan. And the young man bit off his tongue and spat it in her face. As the phrase went, 'so by the smart of his wound he extinguished the rebellion of the flesh.' He probably had the virginal horror you speak of."

"Applesauce," murmured Casti. "Or, I beg your pardon. I mean, I don't entirely accept your analysis."

"I think I proved it in the stacks," said Gilda, primly. "When I touched Belknap he went crazy. He tried to murder me. But I still think he just gave Lucie a frenzied sort of push, and she went over the gallery rail. He murdered Hyett deliberately, to protect himself. And he did it without remorse, because he thought Hyett a wicked, lewd old man. And he tried to murder me, in part because he wanted to eliminate someone who knew too much, but in part also because he had found the right treatment for nasty, seducing women. He had established a kind of reflex action. He had found that murder is easy. And probably he had found it kind of enjoyable. It's the ever-widening stain."

There was a silence.

"I think," said Sandys, "maybe we had better have another little drink."

All had another little drink.

"You know," mused Gilda, "all this fits with some reflections of mine about motives for murder. I tried out the seven deadly sins. The first and deadliest of the seven deadlies is Pride. I struck out Pride because I didn't understand how it could be a cause for murder. But Belknap committed murder as a result of the sin of Pride, by refusing to accept the rules laid down by Nature, or God if you like, for the conduct of human affairs. Dante was right, after all."

Parry came out of a long trance. He was smiling happily. "A cad with designs on a virgin—" he announced.

"What?"

> *"A cad with designs on a virgin*
> *Made her swallow champagne by his urgin';*
> > *But he went much too far*
> > *When he bought caviar,*
> *For it made her reflect on the sturgeon."*

The laughter was a trifle forced.

"You know," said Sandys, "I thought all the time it was Cameron."

Gilda's lips set grimly.

"You will have to do something about that Cameron, William. He knew that Hyett was entering the locked press, and he took money to keep silent. He let Hyett go out at night by the ventilating grille. And he is threatening you with blackmail."

"On what grounds?"

"He wouldn't tell me. But I think perhaps I know."

Dr. Sandys looked long at Gilda. His manner was sad rather than defiant.

"What do you think is the reason?"

"Do you really want me to say?"

"Yes."

Gilda took a long breath.

"I think you were the messenger who was questioned about the theft of the Paris Donatus from the Hopkinson Library in 1916."

"And you think I stole the book?"

Gilda made a helpless gesture. "I don't know. You were just a kid then, and you didn't understand those things—"

"You think I did. Well, I must tell you the truth. I can't pledge you all to secrecy; I haven't the right. But I will ask you not to repeat what I am going to say, unless by doing so you will serve the cause of justice. Do you agree?"

All agreed.

"Well, I didn't steal the Paris Donatus. But my father did."

"Oh!"

"My father was a great booklover. And I am afraid that great lovers, even of books, are not always moral. Every now and then he would be overwhelmed by a lust for a book which was too strong for him to resist. I first discovered it when I was messenger in the Hopkinson Library. Father came to visit me, and I showed him some of the treasures I happened to have access to. He carried out the Donatus wrapped up in his raincoat. He wasn't suspected. Several days afterwards I found the book in his bureau drawer, when I was borrowing one of his shirts. I sent it back anonymously, and as soon as it looked right I gave up my job.

"Well then, after the war I went back into library work. And every once in a while Father would have one of his seizures. He would take a valuable book from a library or bookstore. Usually I would be able to find it and send it back. But Father wasn't really normal during those spells, and sometimes he didn't know himself what he had done with the book. So I had to replace it, or pay its value, and to do so took all the money I could raise or borrow. And once some private investigators caught him, and held him up for blackmail. And that has kept me penniless ever since. It would have broken his heart to be carried off to jail. He wasn't really responsible."

"You speak of him in the past tense," said Gilda.

"Yes. He died this summer. In July. Just after I had paid my last shake-down. I had to borrow the money from a cheap money-lending outfit here. Poor Father! No one could have been a better man, if it weren't for that disease, for in fact it was a disease."

Gilda reached over and patted Dr. Sandys's hand. He remained sunk heavily in his chair.

"It's late," said Gilda. "My, how late it is. I must go."

"I'll take you home," said Parry.

"I'll be going back to the Club," said Casti.

Dr. Sandys said nothing.

"Well, good night, Dr. Sandys," said Casti.

"Good night, Sandys," said Parry.

"Good night, William," said Gilda.

Dr. Sandys smiled and bade them farewell. He sat down again before his desk.

In the lobby Francis and Gilda met Cameron.

"Good evening," said the janitor. "Been having a nice talk?"

"In a way," said Gilda.

"Talk about me?"

"Yes."

"And the idea is that I'm to be fired?"

"Exactly."

Cameron showed no sign of emotion.

"Well, I couldn't stay on much longer anyhow. And I'm tired of the long hours. You know, my ambition is to start a little café and restaurant downtown. I used to be a cook, and I know how restaurants are run. My idea is to start a place with really good food, and some good wines, and I hope good conversation."

"That's a most noble aim, Cameron," said Parry, heartily.

"I can put up half the capital. But I need a little more. My idea is to make it a company and sell shares to a few of my friends on the faculty. I may say that this is strictly on the up-and-up. A chance to make a nice piece of jack."

Gilda and Francis looked at each other.

"I think," said Gilda, "that if it's all as you say, you will find several of us who will be glad to come in. But it will have to be a good restaurant. Good night, Cameron."

Smiling, Cameron bade them good-night.

Francis showed Gilda into his convertible.

"Speaking of restaurants," he said, "will you have dinner with me?"

"No, Francis. I don't feel like it tonight."

There was silence for three blocks. Stopped by a red light, Francis turned to Gilda.

"Gilda, will you marry me?"

"No, Francis."

"Why not?"

"I am very fond of you, Francis. We have a beautiful time to-gether. I like you better than almost anyone, but—"

"But not better than anyone. Whom do you like better?"

"I like William Sandys better."

"Sandys! You prefer big, burly Sandys, with his beard?"

"Maybe he'll shave it off for me."

"Does he know about this?"

"Not yet. But maybe he suspects. There was a strange mo-ment in the locked press yesterday. I thought he was yielding to an attack of homicidal mania, but I'm inclined to think now that it was the first shy stirring of love."

"Very natural mistake. Of course."

"He will learn all the truth soon. I've made one proposal to-

day, and I don't find it so hard. To be sure, I nearly got murdered—"

The wild honking of automobile horns reminded Francis
that the lights had already changed to green. He drove forward
just as the red lights came on again. The car behind him stopped
short, rocking with fury.

Francis drove the rest of the way in silence. At Gilda's door
she give him a comforting little consoling pat.

"Gilda," he said, "did you ever live in Bermuda?"

"No. Why?"

"It's too bad. But anyhow:

> *There was a young miss of Bermuda*
> *Who said of her fiancé: 'Who'd a*
> > *Thought he would look*
> > *Like a god in a book!'*
> *She must have been thinking of Buddha.*"

Gilda laughed and said good-night.

In the Librarian's office Dr. Sandys sat somberly at his
desk. He took from a drawer a photograph of his father, a
distinguished, benignant gentleman. He looked at it for a long
time, and then replaced it. He found a pocket mirror in the
drawer; for some minutes he gazed critically at his goatee.
Picking up a pencil, he traced on a pad before him, hesitating-
ly, the word "Gilda." He paused a long minute, and added the
word "Sandys." He then tore off the sheet, ribboned it small,
and dropped the pieces in the waste-basket. He hid the brandy bottle and replaced three of the glasses. The fourth he left
on his desk. He wrote on his engagement pad for Monday:

"9 a.m. Have G. G. return glass to W. R. R." He then threw up the windows and fanned away the last of the cigarette smoke. He emptied the butts and ashes into a Library envelope, which he sealed and put in his pocket. He then set off for the O. K. Diner, for a late and solitary supper.

THE END

DISCUSSION QUESTIONS

- Were you able to predict any part of the solution to the case?

- Aside from the solution, did anything about the book surprise you? If so, what?

- Did any aspects of the plot date the story? If so, which ones?

- Would the story be different if it were set in the present day? If so, how?

- What role did the setting play in the narrative?

- If you were one of the main characters, would you have acted differently at any point in the story?

- Did you identify with any of the characters? If so, who?

- Did this novel remind you of anything else you've read? If so, what?

- Which of the limericks was your favorite?

AMERICAN MYSTERY CLASSICS *from*

*Available now
in hardcover and paperback:*

AMERICAN MYSTERY CLASSICS

from

*Available now
in hardcover and paperback:*

And More to Come!

Visit penzlerpublishers.com, email info@penzlerpublishers.com for
more information, or find us on social media at @penzlerpub

Charlotte Armstrong
The Unsuspected

Introduction by Otto Penzler

*To catch a murderous theater impresario, a young
woman takes a deadly new role ...*

The note discovered beside Rosaleen Wright's hanged body is full of rea-
sons justifying her suicide—but it lacks her trademark vitality and wit,
and, most importantly, her signature. So the note alone is far from enough
to convince her best friend Jane that Rosaleen was her own murderer, even
if the police quickly accept the possibility as fact. Instead, Jane suspects
Rosaleen's boss, Luther Grandison. To the world at large, he's a powerful
and charismatic figure, directing for stage and screen, but Rosaleen's letters
to Jane described a duplicitous, greedy man who would no doubt kill to
protect his secrets. Jane and her friend Francis set out to infiltrate Grandy's
world and collect evidence, employing manipulation, impersonation, and
even gaslighting to break into his inner circle. But will they recognize what
dangers lie therein before it's too late?

CHARLOTTE ARMSTRONG (1905-1969) was an American author of mystery
short stories and novels. Having started her writing career as a poet and
dramatist, she wrote a few novels before *The Unsuspected*, which was her
first to achieve outstanding success, going on to be adapted for film by
Michael Curtiz.

> "Psychologically rich, intricately plotted and full of
> dark surprises, Charlotte Armstrong's suspense tales feel
> as vivid and fresh today as a half century ago."
> —Megan Abbott

Paperback, $15.95 / ISBN 978-1-61316-123-4
Hardcover, $25.95 / ISBN 978-1-61316-122-7

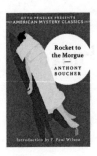

Anthony Boucher
Rocket to the Morgue

Introduction by F. Paul Wilson

A Golden Age mystery set in the world of science fiction in its early days

Legendary science fiction author Fowler Faulkes may be dead, but his creation, the iconic Dr. Derringer, lives on in popular culture. Or at least, the character would live on, if not for Faulkes's protective and greedy heir Hilary, who, during his time as the inflexible guardian of the estate, has created countless enemies in the relatively small community of writers of the genre. Fully aware of his unpopularity, Hilary fears for his life after two near misses with potentially mortal "accidents" and calls the police for help. Detective Terry Marshall and his assistant, the inquisitive nun, Sister Ursula, will have to work overtime to keep him safe—a task that requires a deep dive into the strange, idiosyncratic world of science fiction in its early days.

ANTHONY BOUCHER (1911-1968) was an American author, editor, and critic, perhaps best known today as the namesake of the annual Bouchercon convention, an international meeting of mystery writers, fans, critics, and publishers. Born William Anthony Parker White, he wrote under various pseudonyms and published fiction in a number of genres outside of mystery, including fantasy and science fiction.

"Stellar."—*Publishers Weekly* (Starred Review)

Paperback, $15.95 / ISBN 978-1-61316-136-4
Hardcover, $25.95 / ISBN 978-1-61316-135-7

John Dickson Carr
The Crooked Hinge

Introduction by Charles Todd

An inheritance hangs in the balance in a case of stolen identities, imposters, and murder

Banished from the idyllic English countryside he once called home, Sir John Farnleigh, black sheep of the wealthy Farnleigh clan, nearly perished in the sinking of the Titanic. Though he survived the catastrophe, his ties with his family did not, and he never returned to England until now, nearly 25 years later, when he comes to claim his inheritance. But another "Sir John" soon follows, an unexpected man who insists he has absolute proof of his identity and of his claim to the estate. Before the case can be settled, however, one of the two men is murdered, and Dr. Gideon Fell finds himself facing one of the most challenging cases of his career. He'll soon confront a series of bizarre and chilling phenomena, diving deep into the realm of the occult to solve a seemingly impossible crime.

JOHN DICKSON CARR (1906-1977) was one of the greatest writers of the American Golden Age mystery, and the only American author to be included in England's legendary Detection Club during his lifetime. Under his own name and various pseudonyms, he wrote more than seventy novels and numerous short stories, and is best known today for his locked-room mysteries.

> "An all-time classic by an author scrupulous about playing fair with his readers"
> —*Publishers Weekly* (Starred Review)

Paperback, $15.95 / ISBN 978-1-61316-130-2
Hardcover, $25.95 / ISBN 978-1-61316-129-6

Erle Stanley Gardner
The Case of the Careless Kitten

Introduction by Otto Penzler

Perry Mason seeks the link between a poisoned kitten, a murdered man, and a mysterious voice from the past

Helen Kendal's woes begin when she receives a phone call from her vanished uncle Franklin, long presumed dead, who urges her to make contact with criminal defense attorney Perry Mason; soon after, she finds herself the main suspect in the murder of an unfamiliar man. Her kitten has just survived a poisoning attempt, as has her aunt Matilda, the woman who always maintained that Franklin was alive in spite of his disappearance. It's clear that all the occurrences are connected, and that their connection will prove her innocence, but the links in the case are too obscure to be recognized even by the attorney's brilliantly deductive mind. To solve the puzzle, he'll need the help of his secretary Della Street, his private eye Paul Drake, and the unlikely but invaluable aid of a careless but very clever kitten.

ERLE STANLEY GARDNER (1889-1970) was the best-selling American author of the 20th century, mainly due to the enormous success of his Perry Mason series, which numbered more than 80 novels and inspired a half-dozen motion pictures, radio programs, and a long-running television series that starred Raymond Burr.

> "One of the best of the Perry Mason tales."
> —*New York Times*

Paperback, $15.95 / ISBN 978-1-61316-116-6
Hardcover, $25.95 / ISBN 978-1-61316-115-9

OTTO PENZLER PRESENTS
═══ AMERICAN MYSTERY CLASSICS ═══

Frances Noyes Hart
The Bellamy Trial

Introduction by
Hank Phillippi Ryan

*A murder trial scandalizes the upper echelons of Long
Island society, and the reader is on the jury...*

The trial of Stephen Bellamy and Susan Ives, accused of murdering Bellamy's wife Madeleine, lasts eight days. That's eight days of witnesses (some
reliable, some not), eight days of examination and cross-examination,
and eight days of sensational courtroom theatrics lively enough to rouse
the judge into frenzied calls for order. Ex-fiancés, houseworkers, and as-
sorted family members are brought to the stand—a cross-section of this
wealthy Long Island town—and each one only adds to the mystery of the
case in all its sordid detail. A trial that seems straightforward at its outset
grows increasingly confounding as it proceeds, and surprises abound;
by the time the closing arguments are made, however, the reader, like
the jury, is provided with all the evidence needed to pass judgement on
the two defendants. Still, only the most astute among them will not be
shocked by the verdict announced at the end.

FRANCES NOYES HART (1890-1943) was an American writer whose stories
were published in *Scribner's*, *The Saturday Evening Post*, where *The Bellamy
Trial* was first serialized, and *The Ladies' Home Journal*.

"An enthralling story."—*New York Times*

Paperback, $15.95 / ISBN 978-1-61316-144-9
Hardcover, $25.95 / ISBN 978-1-61316-143-2

Dorothy B. Hughes
Dread Journey

Introduction by
Sarah Weinman

A movie star fears for her life on a train journey from Los Angeles to New York...

Hollywood big-shot Vivien Spender has waited ages to produce the work that will be his masterpiece: a film adaptation of Thomas Mann's *The Magic Mountain*. He's spent years grooming young starlets for the lead role, only to discard each one when a newer, fresher face enters his view. Afterwards, these rejected women all immediately fall from grace; excised from the world of pictures, they end up in rehab, or jail, or worse. But Kitten Agnew, the most recent to encounter this impending doom, won't be gotten rid of so easily—her contract simply doesn't allow for it. Accompanied by Mr. Spender on a train journey from Los Angeles to Chicago, she begins to fear that the producer might be considering a deadly alternative. Either way, it's clear that something is going to happen before they reach their destination, and as the train barrels through America's heartland, the tension accelerates towards an inescapable finale.

DOROTHY B. HUGHES (1904–1993) was a mystery author and literary critic famous for her taut thrillers, many of which were made into films. While best known for the noir classic *In a Lonely Place*, Hughes' writing successfully spanned a range of styles including espionage and domestic suspense.

"The perfect in-flight read. The only thing that's dated is the long-distance train."—*Kirkus*

Paperback, $15.95 / ISBN 978-1-61316-146-3
Hardcover, $25.95 / ISBN 978-1-61316-145-6

Craig Rice
Home Sweet Homicide

Introduction by Otto Penzler

The children of a mystery writer play amateur sleuths and matchmakers

Unoccupied and unsupervised while mother is working, the children of widowed crime writer Marion Carstairs find diversion wherever they can. So when the kids hear gunshots at the house next door, they jump at the chance to launch their own amateur investigation—and after all, why shouldn't they? They know everything the cops do about crime scenes, having read about them in mother's novels. They know what her literary detectives would do in such a situation, how they would interpret the clues and handle witnesses. Plus, if the children solve the puzzle before the cops, it will do wonders for the sales of mother's novels. But this crime scene isn't a game at all; the murder is real and, when its details prove more twisted than anything in mother's fiction, they'll eventually have to enlist Marion's help to sort out the clues. Or is that just part of their plan to hook her up with the lead detective on the case?

CRAIG RICE (1908–1957), born Georgiana Ann Randolph Craig, was an American author of mystery novels, short stories, and screenplays. Rice's writing style was unique in its ability to mix gritty, hard-boiled writing with the entertainment of a screwball comedy.

"A genuine midcentury classic."—*Booklist*

Paperback, $15.95 / ISBN 978-1-61316-103-6

Hardcover, $25.95 / ISBN 978-1-61316-112-8

Mary Roberts Rinehart
Miss Pinkerton

Introduction by Carolyn Hart

*After a suspicious death at a mansion, a brave nurse
joins the household to see behind closed doors*

Miss Adams is a nurse, not a detective—at least, not technically speaking. But while working as a nurse, one does have the opportunity to see things police can't see and an observant set of eyes can be quite an asset when crimes happen behind closed doors. Sometimes Detective Inspector Patton rings Miss Adams when he needs an agent on the inside. And when he does, he calls her "Miss Pinkerton" after the famous detective agency.

Everyone involved seems to agree that mild-mannered Herbert Wynne wasn't the type to commit suicide but, after he is found shot dead, with the only other possible killer being his ailing, bedridden aunt, no other explanation makes sense. Now the elderly woman is left without a caretaker and Patton sees the perfect opportunity to employ Miss Pinkerton's abilities. But when she arrives at the isolated country mansion to ply her trade, she soon finds more intrigue than anyone outside could have imagined and—when she realizes a killer is on the loose—more terror as well.

MARY ROBERTS RINEHART (1876-1958) was the most beloved and best-selling mystery writer in America in the first half of the twentieth century.

"An entertaining puzzle mystery that stands the test of time."—*Publishers Weekly*

Paperback, $15.95 / ISBN 978-1-61316-269-9

Hardcover, $25.95 / ISBN 978-1-61316-138-8